OLD LIES
CAST
LONG SHADOWS

by

Keith Pearson

Grosvenor House
Publishing Limited

The right of Keith Pearson to be identified as the author of this
work has been asserted in accordance with Section 78
of the Copyright, Designs and Patents Act 1988

The book cover picture is copyright to Inmagine Corp LLC

This book is published by
Grosvenor House Publishing Ltd
Link House
140 The Broadway, Tolworth, Surrey, KT6 7HT.
www.grosvenorhousepublishing.co.uk

A CIP record for this book
is available from the British Library

ISBN 978-1-78623-030-0

COMPANION TITLE

CHILDREN IN HER SHADOW

ISBN-10: 1908105429
ISBN-13: 978-1908105424

Published by Grosvenor House Publishing Limited

About the Author

Sir Keith Pearson has spent more than thirty five years working in the health sector in England, Ireland, Mainland Europe and the Far East. Keith received a Knighthood in Her Majesty the Queen's Birthday Honours List in June 2010 for services to healthcare, a sector in which he continues to work.

Despite being very busy working across a portfolio of roles that span many sectors, Keith has been able to realise a lifelong ambition to pen a novel. His first novel, *Children In Her Shadow* was published in 2011 and was well received for its vivid dialogue and a writing style that was able to draw in the reader. This novel, *Old Lies Cast Long Shadows* forms a companion to *Children In Her Shadow*.

Two further but quite different novels are well advanced and should be in print soon.

Dedication

I dedicate this, my second novel to my granddaughters, Megan, and Reece. You are inspiring young people to be with and for every day spent with you, God gives me back two. Papa.

Prologue

It was nearing noon in the Welsh market town of Bridgend on the morning of Wednesday, April fifth, nineteen ninety-four.

The family's vigil at the bedside of their mother Ruth was now at an end, and a chilling silence fell upon the dimly lit bedroom. The angels of death had done their work; Ruth was now finally at peace.

Mary Morgan, the elderly and frail stranger who had entered the house only moments earlier, gently released Ruth's lifeless body from her embrace, placing her head on the soft white pillow.

With tear filled eyes, she kissed Ruth on the forehead and in a barely audible whisper she falteringly said her goodbye to a lifelong friend.

"I love you Ruth and have done so from the moment we first met over fifty years ago."

Lowering her voice, even more, she continued. "Although our lives have taken us on very different journeys, and despite having not seen you for many years, you have meant more to me than anyone, other than my darling Clarissa."

As the tears flowed from the very depths of her soul, she sobbed, and what little composure she had displayed to this point, slipped away as she gently ran her fingers over Ruth's cheek.

"Now we are to be parted again, but I know that as my own life is rapidly coming to an end, I will join you soon," she falteringly whispered.

Mary was utterly oblivious to the movements at the door to the bedroom where Ruth's family stood watching this complete stranger say her emotional goodbyes to their mother.

But the uncontrollable sobbing coming from Daianne, who was Ruth's youngest child, and the posthumous daughter of Dai Evans, who had died many years earlier, soon broke the penetrating silence.

Daianne, a vivacious, spirited thirty year old rushed towards Mary and in a gesture of overwhelming humanity, she took the distraught Mary into her arms to comfort her. As she did so, she looked towards the lifeless body of her mother, now visibly at peace and devoid of the pain that had wracked her body for months.

Daianne's other siblings quietly moved from the doorway into the bedroom, each sitting on the edge of the bed or kneeling on the floor alongside their mother.... all visibly moved by the tragedy and sorrow of the occasion.

Although the three week long bedside vigil was over, and their mother was now thankfully at peace, their grief was palpable.

It was Huw, the eldest of Ruth's children who broke the melancholy, suggesting with some authority that they all now go downstairs while he called the family doctor. But, before leaving the room, he moved to the head of the bed, rested a hand on his mother's and quietly whispered, "I love you Mam; you fought hard, but you are now at peace and with Dai."

Huw immediately brought to mind one of Ruth's favourite Welsh poets, the great Dylan Thomas.

Ruth had told Huw of a dear friend from her past and how she had bravely read Dylan Thomas' challenge to the perceived wisdom of a quiet passage to the gates of heaven at her funeral. The poem was the powerful; *Do Not Go Gentle Into That Good Night*.

Huw knew the poem well, and as he left the room, his mind scanned the opening verse:

Do not go gentle into that good night,
Old age should burn and rage at close of day;
Rage, rage against the dying of the light.
Though wise men at their end know, dark is right,
Because their words had forked no lightning ...they
Do not go gentle into that good night.

One by one Ruth's other children, David, Joan, Deborah and Mary also quietly, personally and emotionally said goodbye to their mother. The last to leave the room was Daianne, who having kissed her mother whispered in the Welsh language, *"Hwyl fawr am nawr;"* 'goodbye for now.'

Daianne then took the arm of the frail and desperately ill Mary Morgan and gently guided her down the stairs.

~

But there were three of Ruth's children who were missing from the passing of their mother; Charlotte, Maria, and Robert, the *children in her shadow*. These were the abandoned children Ruth had so skilfully managed to prevent this second family from discovering.

The deception that was so prophetically foretold by a gypsy fortune teller whom Ruth and Mary had visited in Blackpool in nineteen forty-two had haunted Ruth throughout her life.

The gypsy had said: *'In your life, you will have the blessing of many children, but you will endure lifelong sadness. I can see the life you have yet to live, and I warn you now that you will go through life seeing children in your shadow.'*

In life, Ruth was able to use subterfuge and her authority as a mother to these six children to conceal her past. A past in which she had deserted a husband and abandoned three small children. But it was inevitable that at some time in the future, curiosity would drive these children or her abandoned children to understand more about Ruth and her much guarded, secretive and shocking past.

CHAPTER ONE

Daianne (a carefully crafted forename name to reflect her father's name) cautiously guided the frail, unsteady Mary Morgan down the stairs and into the sitting room at the front of the house. As she passed through the narrow dimly lit hallway, she could hear Huw already speaking on the telephone to the doctor reporting Ruth's death.

In the background, there was that familiar sound of teacups being gathered together, and the whistle of the kettle, as the family aimlessly busied themselves in the kitchen preparing tea.

As Daianne settled Mary Morgan into a chair, she remembered the other lady who had brought Mary to the house earlier. She was now visible through the sitting room window, nervously pacing up and down in the street, occasionally leaning against the car in which they had arrived only a few minutes earlier.

"Can I invite your friend to join us for a cup of tea?" Daianne asked, barely waiting for the response.

With a nod from Mary, Daianne went to the front window and in keeping with local custom she slowly closed the heavy blackout curtains. This was as much a mark of respect as it was a gesture to signify to visitors that there had been a recent death in the house.

Daianne switched on the standard light at the side of the fireplace and left the room.

She slipped out of the house and into the quiet street with its endless row of identical terraced houses.

As she approached the car, the elegant, very smartly dressed elderly lady stepped swiftly towards her.

Noticing both the look on Daianne's face and the drawn curtains, she knew instantly that the news from within the house was bad.

Anticipating the lady's anxious question, Daianne explained; "I'm Daianne Evans, Ruth's daughter. I'm sorry to have to tell you that my mother has just died. Your friend Mary was with her, and unsurprisingly, she like the rest of us is very distressed."

Once again, the gentle, compassionate side of Daianne reached out to the visibly shocked lady. Taking her arm, she asked: "We were wondering if you would like to come into the house and have a cup of tea with our family before you and Mary leave?"

Looking startled, the stranger cautiously asked, "Was Mary able to speak with your mother before she slipped away?"

Daianne was initially puzzled by the question but was able to reassure her that Mary had spent just a few minutes alone with Ruth before she died.

As Daianne walked towards the house, the lady introduced herself.

"I'm Clarissa Hawes, Mary's partner," she explained, with barely a thought to how this might be received.

Daianne was taken aback, but inwardly she smiled thinking to herself, 'Now I bet these two have an interesting story to tell!'

When they entered the house, Daianne introduced Clarissa to the rest of the family as they settled down to a cup of tea and Welsh cakes in the dimly lit front room.

Clarissa sat protectively at Mary's side watching her every move, consumed by her concern for the impact the death of Ruth would have on Mary's fragile health.

Hardly registering the presence of Mary and Clarissa, Huw explained that the doctor would come to the house within the hour and issue the death certificate, enabling funeral arrangements to be made in due course.

Suddenly, with mention of a funeral only minutes after their mother's death, the family was confronted by the stark reality that their mother was gone, and the practicalities of needing to inform family and friends and arrange a funeral were upon them.

Joan and Deborah, who were sitting on the floor near the fireplace, could be heard quietly sobbing. They were bathed in the light from the standard light above them which served only to draw attention to the unguarded, open expression of their feelings, something this family rarely did, having been brought up to believe that any visible signs of emotion could be seen as a sign of weakness.

This was not an affectionate, embracing, close, or emotional family; this was a family that existed on the boundaries of emotion only coming towards each other for support and succour when they needed to.

Ruth had been a deeply loving mother but sparing with contact, and was utterly self-sufficient, shunning any attempt at closeness with anyone including the family.

Though this was outwardly a close-knit family, emotion played little part in their upbringing as each child was encouraged to be emotionally self-sufficient.

Their mother was protective in the extreme, and this, coupled with her obsessively secretive nature, led the family to be very private and guarded, some would say secretive and even evasive.

As small children, when arguments led to siblings not talking to each other, the silence could last for weeks. All lived separate lives within the walls of the family home, where rooms separated and enclosed each family member within their personal bubble.

As adults, these behaviours remained, with lengthy periods when one or other of the children was not in communication with the other, often for petty, long forgotten reasons.

They were each in their way, a mirror image of their mother, something that would challenge them all as they went through life also guarding themselves as their mother did from too much probing into their past.

As tea was poured the mood lifted from their painful loss to a surreal light, practical discourse. They chatted about who would need to be informed, who was to contact the funeral director, who would speak to the family lawyer and what other arrangements would need to be made. There was a frenzy of uncoordinated unfocussed discussion; more a release of tension and emotion than any real structured planning.

Until this point, no one had spoken directly with Mary; that is until Deborah broke the mood by curtly, perhaps even bluntly asking; "How long have you known our mother?"

There was an awkward, but expectant silence as the family turned to face Mary awaiting an immediate and revealing answer.

But it was Clarissa who spoke to say that Mary was clearly in shock and needing some time before she would be able to meet their questions.

"We're staying at the Angel Hotel in Cardiff," she announced emphasising authority and purpose, "and perhaps it would be better if we were to leave now and come back on another occasion, once you have had time to recover from the shock of your mother's death."

But Deborah was not to be content with such a loose arrangement and equally bluntly suggested that Mary and Clarissa should come back to her mother's house on the following day.

There was some nodding of approval as the family began to stir, uncomfortably responding to the new tension in the room.

Mary rose from her chair, supported by Clarissa and walked slowly towards the door to leave, but purposefully stopped and turned back to speak to this expectant family.

"I don't want to build your expectations too much," she said, "but I will fill-in whatever gaps there are, without compromising the confidences your mother and I shared."

This only served to heighten expectations, as Deborah was firmly stopped from further probing by Daianne, who could see that now was not the time for such questions.

Mary left the house on Clarissa's arm agreeing that they would return at two o'clock the following day.

As they walked to their car, a small group of neighbours along the street quickly broke up their obvious gossip about what was happening at Mrs. Evan's house, each anxious to appear to be going about their daily routines.

But the drawn curtains at Ruth's house had immediately started a chain of reactions from inquisitive neighbours. Speculation fueled gossip in the street and telephone calls would ensure Ruth's presumed death was already being discussed throughout the town of Bridgend where she had lived for many years. Her death was also the subject of gossip in the valley village of Senghenydd where she had been born in nineteen twenty three.

News, good or bad would move swiftly in these close-knit communities along with colourful, vivid speculation. Such gossip filled the gaps between reality, imagination and informed truth.

~

On arrival at Ruth's house on the following day, Mary and Clarissa were met by a family that by now had fully absorbed the devastating reality of their mother's death.

The initial shock was replaced by a preoccupation with questions about their mother's much guarded past, and they were consumed by a need to delve deeply into her hidden and secretive life.

But the most pressing matter for the family to deal with was why upon being told of Ruth's death in the arms of Mary Morgan the family solicitor had immediately insisted upon an urgent and private meeting with her.

The family solicitor was insistent that Mary should call at her office in Bridgend for a meeting at two thirty that afternoon. This urgent and intriguing message was conveyed to an equally bemused Mary and Clarissa upon their arrival at the house at a little before two o'clock.

Following the telephone call to the house from the solicitor at nine thirty that morning, the family had explored every variant of speculation as to why she needed to see Mary Morgan a complete stranger to the family, and why she was asked to come alone.

To say the air was frosty when Mary tried to greet the family would be an understatement as she was unceremoniously redirected to the solicitor's office before she could step a foot out of the car. However, there was a stern reminder from Deborah that Mary should return to the house immediately following the meeting.

Once again, this secretive family became consumed by thoughts that one or other of them knew what was going on and wasn't sharing that knowledge.

Distrust and jealousy between family members meant that at a time when most families would draw themselves together, these siblings sought comfort either in their thoughts or with their partners and their immediate family.

The solicitor's office was a ten minute drive from the house. But that short distance provided ample time for Mary and Clarissa to speculate as to why, after years of there being no contact between Ruth and Mary, she should be summoned with such urgency to see Ruth's family solicitor.

On arrival at the solicitors' office, a detached former Victorian town house set back on the High Street of Bridgend Clarissa helped Mary into the small, beautifully furnished waiting room.

The oppulence underscored that this was clearly a successful and long established law firm evidenced by the gallery of photographs of former and current partners dominating the dark, oak clad walls.

Barely two minutes had passed, before the smartly dressed young secretary, who had met them on their arrival, took Mary's arm and slowly walked her towards the door. She purposefully reinforced again that only Mary would be welcome at the meeting, leaving Clarissa only to imagine why there was such a veil of secrecy hanging over Ruth.

On entering the room, Mary was surprised to be introduced not only to Ruth's solicitor but also to the manager of the local bank.

The tall, smartly dressed young solicitor, Rhiannon Jones, immediately put Mary at ease as she helped her towards a comfortable, high backed chair alongside her desk. The secretary, with some deference and equal concern, brought in tea and biscuits before slipping unnoticed from the room.

The manager of the local bank, Marcus Thomas, an elderly almost reassuringly portly man of some considerable distinction, gently placed a hand on Mary's shoulder.

"I share with you the loss of a dear friend," he said, explaining that he had known Ruth personally and professionally for more than thirty years.

He went on to explain that Ruth's *Last Will and Testament* would be shared with Ruth's family later in the week. But he also explained in a now more formal tone that there was one matter that needed to be dealt with "before" he and Rhiannon could meet with the family.

As Rhiannon and Marcus busied themselves pouring tea, gathering papers and rearranging chairs, Mary scanned the office. She was immediately transported back to the War years and a time when she had worked as a secretary in the Central Post Office, in Cardiff.

The solicitor's office itself had many similarities to that of her wartime employer's, with its commanding roll top desk and the array of chairs, each strategically placed a sufficient distance from the desk to ensure that clients would never feel entirely at ease.

Knowledge oozed from the yards of legal tomes lining the shelves behind the desk, and the dozens of legal documents that were strewn across the groaning table that stood against the wall. Each sheaf of documents was secured with a treasury tag in the left hand corner, and colourful binding ribbons bound them together.

Rhiannon moved one of the carefully placed chairs closer to Mary as Marcus, rather pompously strode around the office describing the circumstances leading up to this meeting.

"Many years ago," he explained, his hands gripping the lapels of his suit jacket as he theatrically strode around the room, "your friend Ruth Evans passed into my personal trust a small suitcase, in which she told me was her *box of memories.*"

Marcus extracted every bit of drama as he continued his monologue. "I was asked as a friend, to give the suitcase, and its entire contents to you personally and to no one else if your whereabouts were ever to become known to me after Ruth's demise. I know nothing of its contents," he explained, adding a touch more to the intrigue that now surrounded Ruth.

"In order to satisfy the requirements of Probate," he continued, "Rhiannon will need to be sure that the contents can reasonably be regarded as having no intrinsic value to Ruth's Estate and that they are entirely personal in their nature."

Mary looked puzzled, musing what Ruth might have placed in the suitcase and why she should have been singled out to be given its contents.

Marcus moved to the back of the room and picked up a very ordinary old small brown suitcase. It was unremarkable; distinguished only by the leather corner protectors, and the sheen of many years of careful polishing, but otherwise, it was an old, rather drab and dated suitcase.

He brought the case to the desk and gave Mary a set of keys.

"You will be the first person to have seen inside the case since Ruth last opened it some two or three years ago," he explained adding further drama to an already intriguing story.

He continued the monologue in his still rather pompous way.

"We do not seek to read any documents we might find in the case that are merely personal papers or letters, and nor will there be any record made of what is in the case unless there are items of value," he concluded, moving to take a seat next to Mary.

Mary was overcome as she stared at the suitcase with tears welling up in her eyes.

She was once again transported back in her memories, this time to a bright Sunday afternoon in Cardiff in the September of nineteen forty. She was twenty years of age again; beautiful, happy, young and carefree.

She remembered as though it were only yesterday the vision of an eighteen-year-old Ruth stepping off the bus from the Welsh village of Senghenydd. She recalled how Ruth clumsly tried to brush away tears as she embarked upon her first day away from her family, and her home back in the Valleys.

And there, at Ruth's side was the very same small brown suitcase she saw before her now.

She remembered her excitement that Ruth would be coming to live with her and her mother, the redoubtable 'Mrs. Morgan' at their home in Splott on the edge of the City. And she was also thrilled that her new friend would be working alongside her at the Central Post Office.

Mary also remembered the reassuring hand on Ruth's shoulder placed there by her less than maternal mother, as she uncharacteristically acknowledged that she knew something of the sadness Ruth was feeling in being so far away from her family for the first time.

Mary's pained body, for a brief moment, was that of a young woman skipping along the pavement busily chatting to Ruth, establishing a bond of love and friendship that all these years later had brought her to Ruth's bedside only twenty four hours earlier.

Mary was jolted back to the present when Marcus stepped to her side to ask if she would like him to unlock the suitcase.

Mary paused, overwhelmed by the enormity of what might unfold in the coming minutes; concerned, even afraid of what this small suitcase might hold. Nonetheless, she gestured to Marcus that it should be unlocked.

The sense of expectation was palpable, as Marcus opened first the left lock and then the right. Then, with one final glance towards Mary for reassurance, he slid aside the small brass locks releasing with a loud crack the retaining catches.

Rhiannon stepped forward, deciding that she should end the theatre that Marcus was so enjoying creating and that she should take control. She swiftly and unceremoniously lifted the lid of the case.

There was order and tidiness in the way the contents were arranged even after all these years; to the left of the suitcase was a colourful shoebox, enclosed with a lid. To the right of the case were a bundle of what appeared to be letters bound carefully with a pink ribbon, and next to these were some large brown envelopes, each appearing to be carefully labelled.

The three of them were silent as they stared for a moment into the small, unremarkable case and its contents before Rhiannon quietly broke the silence.

"Mary," she said, placing a reassuring hand once again on her shoulder, "I will need to open everything in the case in your presence...is that all right?" Mary nodded, but in an instance, her hand went out to the bundle of envelopes.

Rhiannon took them from the case and could immediately see that they were unopened letters. On more careful examination, it was evident that the letters were all addressed to Mary Morgan at an address in London.

Mary looked at the envelopes, each in Ruth's neat handwriting, and all addressed to Mary.

With tears streaming down her cheeks, she quietly explained their significance to the spellbound company.

"I was not to know that Ruth had returned to live in Wales, and she must not have received my letter explaining that Clarissa and I had moved to live together in nineteen forty eight. My darling, Ruth must have thought I had abandoned her when her letters were returned. What must she have thought?" she questioned, weeping uncontrollably.

Another reassuring touch by Rhiannon on Mary's arm seemed only to increase the pain of realising that she and Ruth had both been writing to each other at addresses where they no longer lived.

Rhiannon and Marcus looked to each other with some concern, which Mary, though still deeply upset, picked up on and immediately composed herself.

"I'm an emotional old lady, who is realising for the first time that I should have looked harder to find Ruth all those years ago. Instead, I was consumed by my own happiness and overlooked my dear, dear Ruth...."

But Mary noticed a letter in the case marked; 'To *be given to Mary Morgan,*' and she ceased upon it.

"Can I open this?" she asked, hardly waiting to be told that she could.

She took the letter from its envelope and rested back in her chair to read the short, hand written note.

'*My dear Mary: For some reason, we have lost touch with each other over the years, but I know that like me, you will have tried to get in touch. As you are now reading this note, you will be aware that I have died having been ill for some time. But I could not leave you without saying how much I have cared for you in all these years. I have missed you and have longed that we could meet again.*

It will not be long before you find out that my life has been one of terrible sadness, much of it brought about by my foolish pride; old lies cast long shadows. Please don't think too badly of me and please try to remember me as the carefree person I once was.

I have left you with an awful task to undertake for me, but I wouldn't ask if I thought you would not help me.

Marcus, who will have given you this note and my small box of memories, will explain everything. Please forgive me.'

The letter was signed: *'Your loving friend. Ruth'*

Mary was deeply upset by the letter, but she hardly had the time to absorb it before Marcus came to her side.

"I have another letter to give you," he announced, returning once again to his pompous authoritarian style. "The letter is not for you, but I will explain its relevance in a moment," he explained, leaving Mary ever more confused.

Rhiannon moved back to the suitcase and setting aside the bundle of letters, reassuringly advised, "I have no interest in these which are entirely your property, and they need not be opened."

With that, she picked up what turned out to be several large envelopes. The first simply said, 'Certificates.'

Rhiannon turned to Mary and explained; "I will need to open this envelope to establish if there are documents that are essential to me in managing the Estate and affairs of Ruth."

Marcus at this point intervened. With his hands clasped once more to the lapels of his jacket, he looked directly into Mary's swollen blue eyes.

"There are secrets in Ruth's life that I know, even in death she would be anxious to shield her children from," he protectively explained. "And might I say as a friend, I am anxious to preserve her reputation as much as might be possible, so I urge you to be very circumspect in your decisions about how you handle these sensitivities."

His message was aimed primarily at Rhiannon but was equally a message to Mary as he sought to safeguard Ruth's reputation.

Rhiannon was by now having nothing to do with all this sentimentality and with little ceremony removed the contents of the envelope and placed them on her desk. She expertly examined each document and after some careful thought, turned to Mary and Marcus as she replaced the documents into the case.

"There are no documents here that are of interest to me, and they can be taken away by you today," she said exerting her authority in this matter.

This rather surprised Marcus as even he could see that one document was an original birth certificate, and the others appeared to be copies of other birth certificates. He also noticed that there seemed to be a copy of a marriage certificate.

Marcus turned to Rhiannon. "It would appear you have overlooked a marriage certificate which surely will be important in settling the estate?" he questioned feeling sure she would concur.

Rhiannon hesitated before responding. "In this room, we should all acknowledge that Ruth was never married to Dai Evans with whom she lived and had a family here in Bridgend. I settled his estate upon his demise, and I'm satisfied that there are no documents here that I need, to deal with Ruth's estate."

She went on, "The original birth certificate while being a public document is of no concern to me. Ruth was perfectly entitled to regard all of them as personal papers and was, therefore, at liberty to give them to Mary."

Mary, though confused simply said nothing.

She knew nothing of Dai Evans but was rapidly realising that the family she met in Ruth's house only yesterday were the children of that relationship. She considered for a moment whether she should mention to Rhiannon that she knew Ruth had been married previously. She was alert to the line in Ruth's letter, 'old lies cast long shadows'. On swift reflection, she said nothing as the second very large envelope was about to be opened.

This envelope contained what looked like a lengthy essay or manuscript, carefully typed and bound on the left by large bulldog clips to hold the pages together. The cover of the document read simply; 'the children in my shadow.'

Mary knew in an instant the reference to the children in her shadow. She had remembered as though it were yesterday the chilling warning from a fairground gypsy they had both visited in Blackpool at the height of the War years.

Slowly, Mary began to see that the warning to be careful with Ruth's memory and the document, possibly an autobiography were inextricably linked and might be Ruth's attempt to explain her evidently complex life.

Despite the intriguing cover, Rhiannon replaced the document into the frayed envelope and moved to the remaining three envelope, and these proved to be far more interesting to the lawyer in Rhiannon.

Each sealed envelope was carefully addressed to, *Charlotte Carmichael, Maria Carmichael*, and *Michael Carmichael*. Looking puzzled, Rhiannon turned to Mary and asked if she knew who these people were.

Mary knew that Ruth had married Edward Carmichael back in nineteen forty-three, as she and her mother had attended the wedding, but she had no idea whom the three named people on the envelopes were.

Once again, it was Marcus who sought to bring clarity.

"I have been less than candid with you both," he explained rather gallantly. "Ruth confided in me about ten years ago that she had previously married and in that relationship, she had four children. Three of those children remained with their father, Edward Carmichael, with the fourth, Huw, coming with her to Wales. Ruth would only say that she was tormented by the events that led up to her leaving the three children with their father but would entertain no further questioning on the matter. I have, therefore, retained that confidence until today...a confidence I urge you to respect," he asked, turning firstly to Mary and then Rhiannon.

Mary looked intently at the envelopes and asked; "What would Ruth have wanted me to do with these? I don't know the people, and if these are her children, it places a tremendous responsibility upon me to ensure they get them."

Marcus went on: "I know that Ruth spent many years trying to track down the whereabouts of her three other children. But I sensed she was cautious, nay fearful that her endeavours should not be known to her ex-husband," he explained without further explanation. "For whatever reason, Edward Carmichael held some control over Ruth, a control that brought fear to her even in her later years," he reasoned, turning to Rhiannon.

Once again, Rhiannon asserted that the suitcase so far contained only personal papers and in that regard, she urged, for Mary's sake, that they complete the examination of the contents of the case by opening the final item, the small shoebox itself.

There was some unease in the room as Rhiannon, who for the first time seemed ill at ease, removed the lid from the box.

Mary inquisitively leaned forward to look into the box.

Neatly folded inside the box were some small baby clothes. There was a pair of baby shoes and tucked into an envelope were some old discoloured photographs.

On careful examination, Mary saw that two of the photographs were of herself and Ruth taken on the Blackpool promenade and that another was of Ruth with Edward Carmichael. The final few photographs appeared to be of Ruth's parents and family, some of which she had seen before.

Rhiannon swiftly replaced the lid on the shoebox and hurriedly pulled the lid down on the suitcase. There was an eerie chill in the room; a sense that for a very brief moment they had all looked into the very soul of Ruth and what they had seen was disturbing.

For a moment, each looked at the other until Rhiannon sat at Mary's side again and carefully explained.

"I too have been less than candid with you both. Ruth also confided in me and, as Marcus has already mentioned she was clear in her instructions that the case and its contents were to go to you alone. She was equally clear that her children were not to hear anything of her marriage to Edward Carmichael and her past while she was alive, in the hope that she would at least die without having to explain herself to them."

Mary slumped in her chair as she realised that in her selfish bid to meet Ruth once more before she died; she had walked into a complex family whose very existence was built upon less than honest foundations.

Mary could now see why Ruth's daughter Deborah had reacted with such suspicion the previous day. She could now see that any suggestion, even a hint that there was a bigger story to their mother than she had divulged in life, would be like putting a match to a powder keg.

CHAPTER TWO

With further clarification that she was to do whatever she wished with the contents of the suitcase, Mary stood to leave the office. But as she did, Marcus took an envelope from his jacket pocket.

"I received this letter from Ruth only three weeks ago with instructions to place it in your hands," he explained. "You will see that the envelope is addressed simply 'To the Carmichael children' and Ruth has asked that you place it in their hands, unopened if you can locate them."

Bewildered, Mary left the solicitor's office with Clarissa now carrying the unexplained suitcase to the car. They sat in their car outside the office for what must have been half an hour as Mary related what had transpired in the office.

Clarissa, always the level headed part of their relationship, listened with intense interest and compassion, as Mary related what was in the suitcase and its links in part, to a time when she and Ruth had been such close friends.

Eventually, with Mary emotionally drained, Clarissa suggested that they go back to Ruth's house to say goodbye to the family and return to their hotel where Mary could rest.

Mary could see that although this might be the least painful way of disengaging with Ruth's family, she also acknowledged that they would wish to hear something of Ruth's earlier life at least.

While she was very ill herself, Mary was adamant that if her health held up, she would like to stay and pay her final respects to Ruth at her funeral before returning to Brighton and the Hospice that awaited her.

Agreeing that they would speak nothing of the suitcase and its contents to the family, Clarissa and Mary drove to the house with some apprehension, particularly following the icy reception they had received earlier that afternoon. They agreed only to say that there had been some personal letters from Ruth to Mary and, at Clarissa's suggestion that they would also confirm that Mary did not expect to be mentioned in the Will.

On arrival at Ruth's house, the earlier lukewarm reception was replaced by a heightened sense of anticipation that Mary would bring into a family that was riven with uncertainty, mistrust, and grief....some information and insight into their limited understanding of their mother's past and her evident secrets.

There was to be no such enlightenment, but at least upon entering the house, there was the encouraging news that a funeral had been arranged hastily for four days hence in the hope that Mary might be able to stay and attend.

The underlying reason was perhaps more that these siblings, who rarely saw each other and were in themselves secretive and private people were eager to return to their lives. They were clearly anxious to leave a house that was previously their home, but which now was a place of questions and reflections.

Mary and Clarissa agreed that they would stay on at the Angel Hotel in Cardiff and would attend the funeral hoping that, with this agreed, they would be able to get on their way back to Cardiff. However, Mary felt that they should not leave Ruth's home until she had spoken to the children and attempted to fill in some of the gaps, in their mother's life.

Mary was taken once again into the darkened sitting room and seated in the armchair nearest the window from where she was able to see the whole family gathered before her. They sat on the sofa, the remaining chairs and the floor with cups of tea in hand as Mary began.

She explained that she had only known their mother for a very short time from nineteen forty through to about nineteen forty six or forty seven when they lost touch. She explained that while she was at the lawyer's office, she had been given a bundle of letters; letters that their mother had written to her but had been returned unopened.

With tears welling up in her eyes, Mary explained that clearly, their mother had no idea she had moved to Brighton, and each of the letters sent by their mother to her London address had been returned.

"But where are the letters now and what do they say?" spluttered Deborah, who, like the others seemed to have lost any sense of propriety in her quest to know more about their secretive mother.

"They're in my car and will come with me to Brighton, where I will look at them when I'm good and ready," asserted Mary in an attempt to establish some boundaries to this conversation.

With a reflective smile, Mary's memory returned her to the happy days when she and Ruth worked together at the Central Post Office in Cardiff. She also recalled how they would giggle and laugh at the events of the day as they returned to her mother's home.

When Mary mentioned the post office, there was a collective gasp as Daianne explained: "Mam used to say that she worked in a post office, but she never said where and she never said when - now we know it is true."

Mary thought that an odd thing for her to say, inferring once again that there were too many secrets and an underlying mistrust in this family.

Moving on, Mary began vividly to describe the night of January second, nineteen forty-one, when she and Ruth had been caught up in the terrible bombings in and around Cardiff.

To an awe struck family, she spoke of the horrors of that night. Her voice faltered as she described how she and Ruth, had sheltered until the bombings were over. They had then set off into the acrid smoke of the night to tend the sick and dying in the nearby suburb of Adamsdown.

She vividly described the aftermath of the bombings; the homes torn apart by the blasts, and the resulting devastating fires. Her eyes welled up as she recalled the solitary figure of Ruth, fearlessly tending to the injured, and she spoke of her abiding memory of Ruth cradling a dying man in her arms.

Mary described the courageous and heroic interventions of Ruth, who had tended many poor souls whose lives were torn apart on that terrible night. "Some of the people who she nursed had awful disfiguring burns. And there were some, whose last earthly memories as they died in your mother's arms, would be of her youthful kindness on that bloodiest of nights," she explained to her silent audience.

Looking up from the well of her memories, which even now she saw with a clarity that belied the many years, Mary could see that this story had never before been told to Ruth's family.

How could it be, she pondered that this of all stories, a story that could serve as a role model to any child could not have been told?

But Mary realised that she and Ruth, like so many who had experienced the horrors of war had never told the story of *their* war....not even to Clarissa, who was as awestruck as were the rest of them.

Mary's intense description of the bond that built between Ruth and herself was not lost on Clarissa. She had never probed; never questioned, but had always thought that for Mary at least, her relationship with Ruth was deep and loving.

The journey into her past was painful for Mary, who was by now visibly tiring. But she went on to describe how Ruth had left her family home in Senghenydd after the bombings to live with an aunt in Blackpool and related how she went on to work in an aircraft assembly factory.

With a wry smile on her face, she also described how she and her mother had visited Ruth in Blackpool for a couple of days. She recalled how they danced at the Tower Ballroom and how they soaked up the atmosphere of this small Lancashire seaside resort that seemed completely immune from the impact of the ongoing war.

In her enthusiasm, Mary unwittingly revealed the trip she and Ruth had made to the gypsy in Blackpool, something she wished she had avoided.

"What did the gypsy say to Mam about her future and was she right?" quizzed Deborah.

"My darlings," she began, looking at each of Ruth's children intently. "Your mother and I were foolish young girls grabbing a moment of fun in the middle of a horrid war. The gypsy probably said we would live long and happy lives," she explained, turning to Clarissa and smiling.

But Mary was astute enough to say no more on this subject.

Carefully navigating around the fact that she had seen Ruth again at her wedding to Edward Carmichael in nineteen forty-three, Mary described the regular letters updating each other on the trivia of life; how friends and acquaintances they both knew had been killed in the war. How people were stoically getting on with their lives despite the food and clothing rationing, and the enforced night time blackouts and the constant fear of bombing and possible Nazi invasion.

When Mary's story was told, there was a stunned silence in the room as Ruth's children absorbed the full impact of this new window on their mother's life. Surprisingly, given the questioning and ingenuity of children when growing up, only the tiniest hints of Ruth's past had ever been revealed by her.

But there was also a code of conduct that the children seemed to live by when they were young. A code that no one dare breach for fear that an unwelcome truth might break the fragility of the relationship between mother and children.

Inevitably, today's insight into Ruth's past and the resulting questions meant that the previous reticence to ask questions could now be abandoned for the first time. Each of Ruth's children had different angles to pursue: What did she know about why their mother returned to Wales? Where had she lived besides Blackpool? Did she have any previous addresses?

The questions were relentless after so many years of silence and secrecy, as the family forensically pursued any avenue that might reveal more than had already been said.

Mary was careful to guard the memory of Ruth, though, at times she felt distinctly uncomfortable. But even Mary was beginning to realise that she too had more questions than answers. And this was puzzling, given that she and Ruth at one time knew everything about each other and nothing was ever a secret.

But, on reflection, Mary acknowledged that Ruth was already beginning to become secretive and withdrawn from her when they last met. Mary hoped that the letters and the apparent manuscript would provide at least some of the answers she was now looking for.

The one person who remained silent throughout was Huw, the eldest of Ruth's children here in Wales. Mary noticed a remoteness in Huw, but also an intensely silent interest that suggested he may know more about his mother than the others.

But Mary, with her newly found information, now knew that Huw was Ruth's son from her marriage to Edward Carmichael. This helped her to begin at least to understand why he might be less questioning and why he was perhaps, more guarded. Mary mused that he too might be a *guardian* of Ruth's secrets; perhaps he was also charged with preserving her legacy as a good and loving mother.

After more than two hours, Mary signalled that she needed to go back to her hotel and rest. She rose painfully from her chair, breaking the spell she temporarily held over Ruth's family here in the rural town of Bridgend.

But Mary noticed that as the family rose from their seats, there was no conversation between them. Each seemed to slip back into a private individual and personal space.

As Mary and Clarissa left the house, Huw took Mary to one side.

Outside the earshot of the rest of the family, he whispered; "My Mam was a good woman, and I was delighted to hear some of her past. But it would not do for the family to be further upset, at least until after the funeral so it may be best if I ring your hotel with the funeral details rather than you coming here again."

Mary was in no doubt about the underlying message but was content that Huw was right. Even she could see that this emotionally charged family would gain nothing more from further probing their mother's past.

CHAPTER THREE

Mary and Clarissa left a somewhat pensive family to return the short distance to their hotel in Cardiff. On their journey, Mary was consumed by what the document in the suitcase might tell her; a document that was simply entitled: *The children in my shadow*, and she was eager to settle into the hotel to read it.

Despite the protestations of Clarissa, Ruth's suitcase and its contents were carefully taken into the hotel bedroom and after a short rest, Mary began to read its contents.

The document had clearly been written over many years possibly drawn together in this neatly typed final format from jottings, diaries and scraps of paper, some of which were still to be found in the bottom of the envelope.

Even from reading the opening few paragraphs that described Ruth's childhood, it was clear that this document started its life as a diary and had evolved into a deeply reflective and revealing autobiography.

As the evening drew on, Mary became lost in the writings. She was taken on the familiar journey that saw Ruth's move to Cardiff, and she was reminded of the time Ruth spent, living with her and her mother.

The vivid memories captured both the youthful disregard for the severity of the War years and the horrors of the bombings that she and Ruth were so caught up in.

Mary went on the roller coaster ride that was Ruth's life, and she wept at the thought of the many challenges Ruth faced.

But Mary was still left in disbelief that Ruth would abandon three children.

It was three o'clock in the morning when Clarissa gently woke Mary from a deep sleep slumped in the high backed armchair in their room.

The autobiography was closed, and besides it were the many tissues Mary had used to wipe her now swollen eys. She experienced Ruth's journey through life from innocent child, through youthful adolescence to becoming an elderly woman consumed with remorse, guilt, and pain.

As Clarissa helped Mary to her bed, all that Mary would say was; "She abandoned three children. She walked away from three innocent souls whose only fault in life was to be the children of Edward and Ruth Carmichael. She attempts to justify this terrible act, and I can see much of her reasoning....but to abandon children, just babies oh, what pain she must have endured."

On the following morning, it was clear to Clarissa that this was neither the time nor the place for her to ask questions, despite it being clear in the face of Mary that her few hours of restless sleep had given her no comfort.

Clarissa knew that when Mary was good and ready, she would open up and share what she had read.

~

The deeply loving relationship between Mary and Clarissa, built in the rather less tolerant times of the late nineteen forties and early nineteen fifties, had endured the prejudices and societal intolerance of a less enlightened era.

For Mary, leaving Cardiff for a life in London at the end of the nineteen forties to share a life with Clarissa was a brave and exceedingly modern move, and one that on reflection they both recognise as carrying many risks.

While London was more tolerant, even here, gay relationships remained for a large part, unspoken and underground. It was in the night-time clubs and some city pubs where slowly, both men and women emerged to give witness to their sexuality and even more slowly, where society changed, and a tolerance was slowly built.

When Mary arrived to live in London, Clarissa was already forging a successful career as one of a small number of women in stock broking. While women were still fighting for their position alongside men in the general workplace; upper class parents saw stock broking as a *suitable* career for their daughters. It was also a career where entry was, for the most part, achieved through connections, and Clarissa's family were not short of those!

Her father, an exceedingly wealthy landowner with a family home in the Chilterns, had left the City stockbroking firm he founded once he had *placed* Clarissa there. While he was acknowledged to be retired, her father retained a large controlling interest in the business. He was content that Clarissa, and, as he put it, 'her strange ways' was becoming established in the City…and she was indeed established.

Clarissa was bequeathed an apartment in Eaton Place, Belgravia, a highly fashionable area of London by her grandmother not long after her eighteenth birthday and only weeks after taking up the appointment at her father's firm. The apartment was large with four bedrooms and three spacious reception rooms.

For a young single woman embarking on a stock broking career, Clarissa had the pedigree, the London home, and the stock broking lineage that the firm's wealthy clients expected. But Clarissa took nothing for granted, and when Mary first met her, the twenty six year old Clarissa was by then established, successful and entirely independent of her family.

For Mary, her career path was to take a rather less affluent route.

She at first chose not to accept the invitation from Clarissa to live in the Belgravia flat with her. Instead, at the end of the War, she rented a room in a house in Balham, South West London having taken up a job as a shop assistant in the food hall at one of London's premier department stores. It amused Mary that one of her many well-heeled clients was Clarissa!

Mary resisted Clarissa's ongoing offers to live in the apartment with her as she was anxious to ensure that theirs was a relationship that would last. She had seen other young women, seduced by the potential trappings of a high society relationship, later cast off when boredom or social differences managed to get in the way. For all the unorthodox nature of the burgeoning relationship with Clarissa, Mary wanted courtship and certainty, and saw their slowly, slowly approach to their romance as the right way forward.

Within two years of working in the department store, Mary had become a supervisor in the prestigious food hall moving swiftly to establish herself as a formidable organiser with a keen eye to high standards and even higher quality stock.

Even Clarissa was aware of the changes Mary had made in the store. She was impressed that for someone who had no experience of the demands and expectations of the store's wealthy and fiercely fickle clientele, Mary was able to both meet and exceed their insatiable appetite for an ever wider range of exotic foods and drink.

Throughout their *courtship* Mary and Clarissa became inseparable, spending any spare time they could in each other's company until it became obvious that the time was right for them to be together.

But Mary was still unsure about moving into the opulent London flat and, moreover, she was increasingly keen to establish herself in business, running a high-class food store of her own.

The idea had been planted in her mind by one of her suppliers. He had mentioned that the owner of a small delicatessen in Brighton with a very good reputation but poor business acumen was looking to retire and sell the business.

Clarissa was immediately supportive of Mary's ambitions and with no further ado they arranged to go down to Brighton to view the business.

When they arrived at the front of the shop in the narrow Lanes area of Brighton, Mary could see immediately why the food shop was so popular. The produce was wide-ranging and fresh, and the clientele were clearly prosperous.

Clarissa was rather more interested in the haberdashery shop next door that looked tired and run-down and not at all in keeping with the other upmarket businesses in the area. While Mary ventured into the food shop to speak with the owner, Clarissa, unbeknown to Mary went next door to do the same thing.

After some time, Mary emerged from the delicatessen rather less excited than when she had ventured in there an hour and forty five minutes earlier. Clarissa chose not to probe but instead suggested that they walk to the sea front and sit and talk over a cup of tea.

They stopped at a small teashop and settled behind a windbreak. They ordered tea and cake and sank back in their seats watching the comings and goings of Brighton's residents and visitors - neither saying anything.

It was Mary who finally broke the long silence by saying that the owner of the food shop was very keen to sell and already had some interest. However, Mary's greater concern was that the sale of the business would have to include purchasing the shop premises as well, something that Mary considered to be entirely outside her ability to finance.

But Clarissa probed. "In your view, is the business sound? Could you see it growing and is there potential for a real livelihood to be had?"

Mary went into the finances of the business that clearly were healthy, but she saw the overarching problem being how she could raise the money to buy the business and the premises.

Clarissa listened to the animated but somewhat dejected Mary and then went on to explain how she had occupied her time.

She explained that she had spoken with the owner of the business next to the delicatessen who confirmed that the shop was always busy. He also mentioned to her that the owner wanted to sell the premises and the business together. Finally, Clarissa was told by the haberdashery shop owner that he too was also keen to sell his business and retire.

It was at that point when Mary and Clarissa's personal and business futures were sealed.

Clarissa, with an eye to both their futures and to what appeared to be a good business opportunity, saw the potential in buying both of the premises and expanding the delicatessen business.

They spent several hours, at the small teashop discussing the overarching implications of what this business opportunity might mean for their long-term personal relationship.

They ultimately agreed that Clarissa would purchase the two premises and the delicatessen business leaving it to Mary to begin the task of converting the premises into one much larger business.

Within months, the purchase of both premises and the businesses was complete. Initially, Mary lived above the converted business with Clarissa coming down to Brighton at weekends to be with her. But it was only a matter of time before Clarissa abandoned her stockbroking life in London and purchased a house in Brighton.

Mary moved into the Brighton house with Clarissa and, over the course of the next forty years, they expanded their business to encompass a chain of eight similar food stores, mostly located along the south coast of England. But to the delight of them both, they also opened one branch in London's fashionable Knightsbridge.

As their businesses grew, they moved into a larger residential property which became their home. To the outside world, it was the business that defined these two, increasingly eccentric elderly ladies, who took holidays together in either Malta and Bavaria, simply to be alone.

At times, they were like a bickering pair of spinster sisters, but for the most part, their very small circle of friends met their deeply loving relationship with fondness and without question. They were soul mates, lovers, and business partners but above all else they were inseparable.

But the news that Mary had been diagnosed with aggressive and terminal cancer was devastating. They cried; they talked, and they examined what Mary wanted to do in her last few months of her life. To Clarissa's surprise and concern, Mary insisted that she must find Ruth.

Clarissa had never probed the friendship between Mary and Ruth because she saw it as one that, for whatever reason seemed to have come to an abrupt halt in the nineteen forties. Clarissa never brought up the subject and remained ambivalent when Ruth's name was mentioned in passing. But she also knew that the renewed, urgent drive for Mary to say goodbye to Ruth was as strong as anything she had seen over the many years they had been together.

And now, in the aftermath of Ruth's death, Clarissa knew the toll that delaying a return to Brighton would have on Mary's life. In short, she knew that Ruth had stolen weeks away from her and deep down this hurt the caring but silent Clarissa.

CHAPTER FOUR

The day of Ruth's funeral arrived, and Mary and Clarissa packed their suitcases, planning to leave their hotel for Brighton immediately after the eleven o'clock service. The funeral arrangements conveyed to them by Huw indicated that there would be a church service followed by the interment, both to be held in Bridgend.

The day could not have been worse for the ailing Mary. It was a cold, windswept April morning that met the couple as they drove the short distance from Cardiff to Bridgend. The driving rain slowed their uncharacteristically silent journey. Each was deep in thought concerned about what the day ahead held in store for them. For Clarissa, her greatest concern was for the impact this day might have on Mary's health in the few, precious weeks that lay ahead.

They arrived at Ruth's home at about ten thirty and joined the family as they gathered in the sitting room. Sombre attire was the order of the day with the men wearing dark suits and the obligatory black tie. Many were wearing heavy winter overcoats against the unseasonably cold weather, and others were carrying black trilby hats and rolled umbrellas.

For their part, the women who were present also dressed in sombre black though several of the younger ones were wearing what might generously be called cocktail dresses, which in Mary's view managed to bring a touch of unwelcomed glamour to the occasion.

Some of the rather older ladies relied upon dresses that might not have been out of place at Queen Victoria's funeral, with their high collars and black lace neckline and straight, calf length skirts.

The Undertaker had returned Ruth's body to the house the previous day and as long established tradition would have it here in the Welsh Valleys, a slow but continuous stream of people came to pay their respects beside the open casket, before going on to the church and then the cemetery.

How Mary disliked the old Welsh tradition where women would be expected to remain behind after the church service with a funeral party of men only, going on to the burial. She made clear her plans to attend both the church service and the burial.

There were some murmurings from both the men and women, but this would not deter Mary, who also detected an unwelcoming atmosphere in the room as she and Clarissa sat isolated from the family and neighbours.

She was aware of censuring mutterings from behind the hands of several of the men present whose eyes darted disapprovingly from her to Clarissa. One woman who entered the room, ostensibly to say goodbye to Ruth was clearly here to condemn the relationship between Mary and Clarissa....a relationship that had quite obviously been the subject of gossip and had overtaken any concern for Ruth's family.

The woman approached Clarissa and dramatically and clearly for effect threw her head back as she turned away in apparent disgust, muttering loudly enough for all to hear; "Disgusting I say.....and they shouldn't be allowed to be here."

Mary and Clarissa had met prejudice and intolerance throughout their lives together and had learnt not to react. But Clarissa could not resist the opportunity to gently stroke Mary's hand. As she did she whisper loudly enough for all to hear; "This day is for Ruth's *friends* to mourn her passing, and you darling, well you were her closest and most dear friend."

Despite her weakness, Mary abruptly rose to her feet and approached the coffin. She looked for the last time into the face of her dear friend and keeping her thoughts to herself she placed a small wreath on the table. On the wreath was a card with a simple message: *Departed, but never forgotten. Mary Morgan*

The funeral directors arrived and with care to ensure that the last of the mourners had viewed the body, they carefully replaced and secured the lid.

Having respectfully manoeuvred the coffin out of the house, they placed Ruth's body in the hearse. The family members slipped into the three funeral cars, and the cortege slowly pulled away from the house.

Clarissa guided Mary to their car and helped her into the front seat. But as they were drawing away from the kerb, Mary cried, "Stop Clarissa, please, stop!"

Fearing that Mary was unwell, she stopped immediately. The colour had drained completely from Mary's already pale face as she stared towards a lonely figure on the pavement opposite.

"What is it?" cried Clarissa as she placed her hand on Mary's.

"It's him," she said, pointing to the man on the pavement opposite. "I recognise him but can't place him," she said as the man purposefully stepped into a car and appeared to follow the funeral party on its journey to the church.

On arrival at the church, Mary was about to step out of the car when she tugged on Clarissa's arm.

"I know who it is....his is a face and his is a demeanour you can never forget," she confided as Clarissa closed the half open car door again and listened intently.

"It's Edward Carmichael; the man Ruth married back in nineteen forty three. I disliked the man then, and as I look at him now, I see the same person; older, greyer and without the swagger of the young man he was then, but he still has that unmistakable, penetrating look in his eye that makes you feel uncomfortable."

As Mary moved to open the car door, she saw Edward Carmichael stepping from his car. He purposefully paused and looked towards Mary, very clearly recognising who she was.

Mary shivered as she felt his penetrating eyes menacingly challenging her to respond. And, for a fleeting moment he grinned at her with a familiar air of self-confidence, but then in a moment, he was gone.

The grin and the self-satisfied smirk sent a shiver down the spine of both Mary and Clarissa.

"My God, I now can see what you mean about the man....he gives you the creeps," Clarissa whispered as they stepped from the car and slowly followed others into the church.

As they entered the small stone church, Mary pulled Clarissa towards the row of pews at the very rear of the church. She indicated to Clarissa that they should sit at the end of the row, forceing others to choose another seat or to ask them to stand to let them pass which none did.

Sitting at the rear of the church was a deliberate ploy on Mary's part. She didn't want to become part of the family mourners group and neither did she want to be amongst the *others*; the friends; distant relatives and business associates. She wanted to pay her last respects to Ruth from a distance.

But the overarching reason for sitting at the rear of the church was that she could see the comings and goings of the mourners and in particular, she could see where Edward Carmichael would sit.

To her disappointment, Edward didn't enter the church and nor did anyone else from outside the family or from Ruth's past that she might recognise.

The service was, as all funerals are, a juxtaposition of those who feel uncomfortable with the intense emotion of the occasion and hide their feelings, and the uncontrollable outpouring of emotions from those who feel the pain of loss the most.

Mary scorned the modern indulgence of those left behind, in which they try to encapsulate a life in a eulogy of platitudes; perceptions, and what she saw as crass ill placed humour. Still more, she loathed the now inevitable music track from a recording that was *supposedly* the song to say all the things the mourners were incapable or unwilling to say themselves.

Mary wanted to shout out: "She was beautiful, mischievous and fragile. She was my friend, and I loved her." She wanted to scream: "Ruth was a heroin in the War, and she built Wellington Bombers that helped end that horrid war. She danced and flirted with airmen, many of whom will have been shot down with the scent of her perfume still on their collar and she was my friend, and I miss her."

Clarissa, with the knowledge of intimacy, knew Mary's thoughts as she slipped her a small silk handkerchief to dab away the tears. She didn't seek to probe Mary's thoughts she was simply there to pick up the pieces.

The moment arrived when the vicar moved to the centre of the isle, and the funeral bearers took up position raising Ruth's coffin to their shoulders.

Mary felt a sudden urge to sweep out of the church now and to abandon her plans to attend the interment. But with great composure, she sat as the coffin and the family moved slowly passed her and on into the graveyard.

As the last of the funeral party left the church, Daianne reappeared and took Mary's arm.

"Please stand with me Mary, and give me the strength to see this through?" she asked, and with that Mary walked slowly to the plot with Clarissa supporting one arm and Dianne the other.

The large funeral party, made up mainly of men surrounded the burial plot, a last resting place Ruth would share with Dai Evans, her partner of many years.

As Mary, Clarissa and Daianne arrived at the graveside a small gap opened next to Huw where he invited them to stand.

The vicar completed the final religious act at the graveside with a prayer while Ruth's coffin was slowly lowered into the ground. He took a handful of earth and cast it onto the coffin inviting the family to one by one do the same.

As Daianne moved forward she carefully brought Mary with her and together they completed the final symbolic act of goodbye; ashes to ashes, dust to dust.

As the last of the mourners cast their handful of earth onto the coffin below, slowly but increasingly perceptibly, the small gathering began to hear the sounds of a choir.

The funeral party turned to see, appearing from the grey, damp distance, the full-throated voice of *Cor Meibion Penybont*, the Bridgend Male Voice Choir.

Their song was the ballad that stirs the soul of every Welsh man and woman....*Myfanwy*. As the choir drew closer and their rich voices filled the cool air, so the strongest of men took a handkerchief from their pocket to wipe away a tear.

Myfanwy, rendered in the Welsh language was the song that drew Ruth back to the Valleys of Wales; the song that crossed the generations, and the only song that could reduce the strong, resilient Ruth to tears. It brought back for every mourner present, a personal memory that would always be rooted here in Wales.

As Mary returned to Clarissa, unsteady on the uneven ground, her eyes again alighted upon the distant face of Edward Carmichael. He sheltered under a large black umbrella and was wearing that same unnerving arrogant smirk on his face.

Daianne caught the same glance and quietly asked Mary; "Do you know that man?" Mary shook her head, but Daianne again asked. "We saw him outside the house as we were leaving, and it seemed to upset Huw who was anxious that we didn't speak to him. Who is he Mary?" she asked, and once again, Mary replied that she didn't know.

But with a second glance in the same direction she saw Edward Carmichael stride away with a jaunty spring in his step, pausing only to turn and doff his hat, smiling as he did, and with that, he was gone.

It would puzzle Mary how, after all, these years Edward Carmichael was so well informed that he should know Ruth had died and when the funeral would be held. What she didn't know was that Edward received a copy of the Glamorgan Gazette each week something he had done for years and had read the obituary notice.

Most of the family and friends dispersed back to the house leaving Huw and Mary alone for a brief moment as Clarissa explained to Daianne that they would be leaving for Brighton from the cemetery.

In that moment alone, Huw turned to Mary and asked; "You knew that man, the one who stood by the tree, under the umbrella didn't you?" Without hesitation, she said she did.

Huw took Mary's arm and began to walk her towards Clarissa.

"He is my father," he said in an utterly detached and unemotional way. And with that he moved towards the last of the funeral cars and with nothing further said, he stepped into the car and left.

Against her better judgement and the advice of Clarissa, they did return to Ruth's house.

The sombre mood of the church and graveside gave way to that jocular, familiar post funeral elation; that sense of overwhelming relief that the emotions of the funeral were now over.

The family was genuinely pleased to see Clarissa and Mary despite the insistence from Clarissa that they could only stay a few minutes for a cup of tea and to use the toilet; itself a very popular place on this cold April morning.

Huw came to Mary's side once again and as though the brief conversation in the cemetery had never taken place, he chatted with her about the weather and how the rain had held off at least for the burial itself.

Mary found this whole post funeral experience surreal. She felt an overwhelming urge to shout, 'There are three people out there who should be here; three of Ruth's children that you don't know exist, two sisters and a brother that your mother chose not to tell you about'.

She looked on at this complex family catching up with the time that had passed since they last met, and she knew it was not for her to tell them what their mother had chosen to keep from them.

Mary caught the occasional glance from Huw whose whole demeanour and presence now as the head of the family seemed to be challenging her to say something or leave, and she chose the latter.

To the surprise of everyone including Clarissa, Mary moved purposefully towards the door, announcing as she did; "Clarissa and I are leaving now to make our way back to Brighton."

The family members shuffled past the other guests and the small family group and found themselves uncomfortably waiting to say goodbye to these two intriguing strangers, strangers who brought a tantalising insight and a knowledge of their mother they had never been party to before.

Instinctively they all knew there was yet to be found a key to unlock their mother's past fully, but each seemed unwilling to reach out to find it. Perhaps it was Huw who summed up the mood of the group as Clarissa helped Mary into the car.

As though he were signing off on behalf of the family he simply, but warmly said; "Goodbye and thank you for talking to us about Mam. Have a good journey home."

Apart from the now obligatory hug or handshake, that short goodbye brought to a close the connection the family would have with Mary Morgan, Ruth's dear friend and most important link so far to her so jealously guarded past.

As Clarissa and Mary slipped out of the street and out of the lives of these people, Mary closed her eyes. She reflected once more upon the family who were not here; Charlotte, Maria, and Michael, Ruth's abandoned children.

These three were the missing link in Ruth's life and Mary knew that their story also needed to be told.

CHAPTER FIVE

Mary slept for most of the journey back to Brighton, unaware of the tiresome traffic that made what should have been a three and a half hour journey almost five.

On arrival at their home, Clarissa found Mary so weakened by the journey and the events of the preceding days that she was unable to help Mary from the car. Mary's health had clearly deteriorated to such an extent that Clarissa immediately drove to the hospice where arrangements for Mary to be admitted had been made some weeks earlier.

On arrival, experienced, caring palliative nurses gently helped Mary into a wheelchair and swept her into a private room. The nurse who had been supporting Mary at home before their trip to Wales saw her quickly.

Clarissa was finally called into the room and was shocked by what she saw.

She did not need to hear the prognosis from the clinicians to work out for herself that Mary was now in the end stage of life. She looked weak, drawn and exceedingly frail.

Clarissa had felt that in a small way she had already lost Mary the moment that she had become embroiled with Ruth and her family in Wales. She had watched Mary become melancholic and deeply reflective. She saw that the ordering of her life in preparation for her death was now complete, and apart from the final goodbyes, Mary was now ready to meet her end.

The following seven days saw Mary slip in and out of consciousness. The pain management ensured that there were the occasional few lucid moments for Clarissa to reminisce with Mary and those moments were precious.

A dominant theme of Mary's weakening conversation was the constantly repeated request to Clarissa to find Ruth's three other children.

"Find those children Clarissa; promise me you will do all you can to find them and give them the envelopes and the letter Ruth entrusted to me" begged Mary.

Clarissa was initially uncomfortable to do more than simply nod an acceptance of the dying wishes of Mary. But the degree of importance placed upon this dying request was finally acknowledged, and Clarissa agreed.

"I will find them Mary; I will ensure that your obligation to Ruth is discharged, and I will personally place the letters in their hands," she assured the much relieved Mary.

Mary passed away peacefully in the arms of Clarissa, her friend, confidant, lover and her rock.

~

It was to be many months before Clarissa felt able even to consider the task of trying to find the illusive three children abandoned by Ruth in nineteen forty six. Clarissa was overwhelmed by the task and the importance of this final act for Mary, on behalf of Ruth.

She pondered where she should start in her search for these three people and struggled with the responsibility. Every time she began to think through her options, she was engulfed by her sadness at the loss of Mary. The task was simply overwhelming for a woman who had only recently buried her partner and her lifelong friend.

The first poorly constructed plan saw Clarissa driving to Blackpool, following in the footsteps of Ruth, who had made this journey with the same ambition on several occasions. Like Ruth, Clarissa centred her search on examining public records at the town library. However, she met the same outcome; no death or marriage records and a search of newspaper archives similarly uncovered nothing for the Carmichael children or family.

Disheartened and depressed, Clarissa returned to Brighton and set aside any further thought of the Carmichael children. That is until some years later.

In the August of the millennium year of two thousand, Clarissa read an article in a Sunday newspaper centred on the continued use of the personal columns of national newspapers to track down lost friends and families. She was intrigued, particularly by the spectre of people in our society who avidly read the personal columns not necessarily to find people they may have known, but more likely to have a window into the private lives of others.

Being an avid *Times* reader, she decided immediately to place an advert in the personal column. She knew it should be short and to the point.

'*Would anyone knowing the whereabouts of Charlotte, Maria, and Michael Carmichael please make contact with PO Box 2410 Brighton.*'

The advert was placed for five days and Clarissa waited.

A week passed before Clarissa went to check the post office box. She was pleasantly surprised to see at least a dozen envelopes in the box and with a spring in her step, she went to a nearby seafront café eager to read the letters.

Once her coffee had arrived, Clarissa opened the first envelope with some trepidation. What had she let herself in for she thought as she removed a type written letter from the envelope?

She was only one sentence or so into the letter before she realised that the writer was from a firm of heir hunters; soliciting for business. Clarissa shoved the letter angrily back into its envelope and wearily opened the second, and the third and the fourth, only to find almost identical letters offering the 'expert' services, of their 'successful and professional' heir hunters.

As she was about to abandon the remaining unopened letters, Clarissa's eye was drawn to a hand written envelope. This couldn't be an heir hunter she thought and quickly tore open the envelope and began to read the hand written letter.

'I am Robert Carmichael, though I am aware that I was given the name Michael at birth, by my mother. This name was later changed to Robert by my step-mother. My sisters, Charlotte and Maria know that I am responding to your letter in the Times in the hope that in some way it relates to the whereabouts of mother, Ruth who went out of our lives sometime in the mid to late nineteen forties'.

The letter invited the recipient to write or telephone as soon as possible, and Robert Carmichael provided a mailing address and a telephone number at his Cardiff flat.

Clarissa set the letter to one side and quickly opened the others letters, speedily satisfying herself that none of the other letters were in any way meaningful. There were two asking for money in return for immediately providing the contact details of the Carmichael family, and the rest were from solicitors offering search services.

Having gathered the letters together and paid her bill, Clarissa slowly walked back to her car. As she did so, she decided that there was sufficient in the brief letter to give her hope that these were indeed the children she was searching for, and she determined that she would telephone Robert Carmichael that very evening.

Clarissa was nervous as she dialled the phone number, and her heart missed a beat when the phone was swiftly answered by the confident, self-assured voice from the other end of the phone.

"Good evening...Robert Carmichael."

Clarissa was taken aback but mustered up an apprehensive courage and explained.

"I'm Clarissa from Brighton. I received your letter this morning and wanted to get back to you as quickly as possible."

She went on to outline the broad circumstances leading up to her placing the advert. She explained that her recently deceased partner, Mary Morgan had been a close friend of his mother Ruth Carmichael during the war years.

Clarissa explained that Mary's dying wish was that she should try to locate Ruth's three children on her behalf. But Clarissa was careful to be brief so that she could engage Robert sufficiently to ensure that he knew enough about Ruth Carmichael for her to proceed further.

Robert could hardly hold back his excitement and quickly explained that he and his sisters had been trying to find their mother for most of their adult lives without success. He immediately acknowledged that from his personal research it appeared that his mother had abandoned the three children. But protectively, he explained that he felt sure that there must have been a good reason for her doing this.

Robert's knowledge of his mother was very limited, but he was able to place her in Blackpool at the right time, and he knew her date of birth. He also knew that his father had divorced Ruth in nineteen fifty; something Clarissa was unaware of from her research.

Clarissa was satisfied and began to relax into the rather one-sided conversation. But, the inevitable question came rather sooner than she was expecting.

"Do you know where my mother lives?" he asked, clearly unaware that his mother, had died.

Clarissa broke the news of Ruth's death to a deeply shocked and saddened Robert Carmichael. Like his sisters, he had held out the hope that they might yet see her even, as he put it if that was to be "from afar."

Robert explained that he had prepared a letter on behalf of the three of them that they would have sent to their mother if they had found her.

"We were prepared for the fact that she might have a new life, and the letter explained that we would understand if she didn't want to see us, but we hoped that she would." The sadness in Robert's voice was palpable.

Their twenty-minute rambling conversation concluded with an agreement that Robert and his sisters would make contact again with a view to meeting Clarissa in Brighton. But as Clarissa was about to draw the conversation to a close, the one question she had not prepared for struck like a bolt of lightning.

"Did my mother have any other children, and if so, do they know about us?"

There was a lengthy pause before Clarissa skilfully closed down the conversation for the time being.

"I think those things are best explored when we meet, when we can pace ourselves a little and when we can put Ruth's life into some context. I owe Mary Morgan and Ruth Carmichael that much, but I will say only this, you do have other siblings and, no they don't know about you or your sisters. The circumstances and the details can wait," she said, drawing to a close any further conversation until they met.

She did however indicated to Robert that she would be able to give him the address of the cemetery in Bridgend where Ruth was buried sensing that visiting her grave might provide some closure for the Carmichael children.

CHAPTER SIX

Several weeks passed before arrangements could be finalised for the three Carmichael children, now very much adults, to visit Brighton. Clarissa helpfully suggested that as they might want to talk in private, they should come to her home and have lunch.

During the following week, Clarissa took Ruth's small suitcase from the attic room and for the very first time, she sat and looked at its contents. She never had so much as opened the case, let alone examined its contents while Mary was alive and certainly had never thought to do so since she had died.

Clarissa could smell the mustiness of age as she opened the small suitcase and as she did, was immediately drawn to a large envelope on the top of the other contents. She knew immediately that this was the envelope containing what Mary had referred to as an *autobiography*.

The document was half inside a very large brown envelope. As she opened it, she could see what looked like a lengthy manuscript, carefully typed and bound and held together on the left by large bulldog clips.

Reading the cover of the document sent a shiver down Clarissa's spine. It read simply, *the children in my shadow*.

As Clarissa sat in her chair and looked again at the cover page, the tears were already flowing down her face as she recalled the impact this document had on Mary, when she read it.

The following hours, stretching from early morning until the late afternoon saw Clarissa being drawn into Ruth's life story. She read Ruth's defence of her decision to leave her three children, and she read of Ruth's life of regret for having done so.

Clarissa had never read anything that was so sad and so poignant. She felt Ruth's pain, and she also felt Mary's anguish, but she also felt anger; anger that Ruth had given up so easily, no matter what the circumstances.

Clarissa's opinion of men was hardly enhanced by Ruth's account of Edward Carmichael's dalliances, but she also felt anger at what she saw as the feeble attempts by Ruth to fight to keep her children. While recognising the different times these events were unfolding in, she simply could not forgive Ruth for her actions.

But Ruth's autobiography, which might have begun as a way of putting on record her version of events, also had borne the hallmarks of a cathartic journey as she carefully and meticulously wrote down her past. Perhaps she sought to recall and to understand her own emotions at that time. However, it was evident that Ruth's mood had swung from self-forgiveness to abject shame and revulsion at what she had done.

The manuscript's recollection of Ruth's many journeys back to Blackpool, ostensibly to find her children was far from convincing to Clarissa. She saw it as an attempt to salve her conscience, rather than a genuine attempt on Ruth's part to find and to meet her children.

Ruth's shame and her fear that her family and friends might discover she had abandoned three children were the overwhelming messages that Clarissa took from the latter part of the document…. and still she was outraged by Ruth's willingness to walk away from her children.

Clarissa's hope that she might discover why Ruth and Mary had such a bond of friendship in the war years, perhaps even love was not to be found in this manuscript. While Mary was mentioned on many occasions in the early years of the manuscript, Clarissa was struck by the distance that Ruth placed between anyone who knew of her past and the existence of these three children.

The overwhelming message was that Ruth would do anything to prevent her past from coming into contact with those people who now occupied her new life in Wales.

Clarissa once again felt a tear slip down her cheek as she reflected that Mary might also have reached the same conclusion. A conclusion that even the deepest of friendships should be sacrificed so that Ruth could protect the fragile image she had created for herself in Wales.

Clarissa set aside the manuscript and glanced once more into the suitcase.

She saw the box that Mary had previously mentioned; a box that contained mementoes of Ruth's children and without hesitation resisted the temptation to open it.

Notwithstanding her lack of maternal feelings, Clarissa couldn't dismiss the disingenuous nature of Ruth's relationship with her version of the past and the stark reality that however you dress it up; she abandoned three children. Clarissa also viewed the suitcase and the *box of memories* as gruesome reminders of Ruth's unforgivable past.

Clarissa saw the individual envelopes that Mary had so insisted must be placed into the hands of the Carmichael children which brought her rather closer to these people's lives than she normally felt comfortable doing.

But this reminded her that she also had another letter that she had been instructed to give to the Carmichael children which she took from her bureau and placed alongside the case.

Clarissa also found the bundle of letters, sent by Mary, but returned unopened having been posted to an address Ruth had long moved away from.

There was no temptation on Clarissa's part to open and read these letters; she regarded them as personal, so personal that to open them would betray the lifetime of love she had for Mary and the trust they had in each other.

But she also felt that as personal letters, they had no place in the lives of Ruth's three abandoned children and with no further consideration, she decided that she should immediately destroy them.

She took the bundle of letters to the wood burner in the sitting room and without a further thought for her actions, she put a light to them and sat in an armchair and watched them burn to ash.

~

Friday arrived, the day when Clarissa was to meet the Carmichael children. It had been their plan that they would stay in a hotel in Brighton and on either the Saturday or Sunday, they would drive to Bridgend to visit their mother's grave.

Clarissa had arranged that her housekeeper, Brenda, would prepare a cold buffet lunch, which she was scurrying around laying out under covers on the breakfast room table.

Clarissa had chosen to use the breakfast room for their meeting because it was large and afforded the space for people to relax, either around the large dining table or to sit in the array of comfortable chairs that were haphazardly placed around the roaring log fire. The whole setting made the room pleasantly warm on an otherwise chilly early October day.

At precisely noon, Clarissa saw a large car sweep into the driveway. The occupants, quite clearly the Carmichael family, stepped warily from the car, pausing to take in the breath-taking views to the south, which looked out over the English Channel and towards France.

"Hello, my darlings," called Clarissa, who had rushed out to greet them wrapped in a long fur coat as a shield against the chilled air. "Views like this are best on picture post cards on days like this," she observed, ushering the group into the splendid hallway of her Georgian house.

As they entered the house, Robert introduced himself and his sisters to Clarissa, who by now was hurriedly guiding the group into the sitting room.

Brenda was introduced to the family as she dithered and fussed over each person's request for tea or coffee.

"Now go on Brenda, push off," Clarissa quipped as her hand briefly brushed Brenda's arm; "go and meet up with your young friends and thank you for your help today." With that, the sound of the front door could be heard closing, and they were alone.

Clarissa broke the uncomfortable silence as she moved to her favourite chair in the bay window.

"It's lovely to meet you Robert and also to meet your sisters, and I know that you have travelled some distance to be here. I also know from the expectant look on all your faces that your anticipation and hopes are very high."

She rose from her chair and stood by the fire.

"You should know that I never met your mother but my darling Mary, who died a few years ago, knew your mother very well when they were young. My part in this sad saga is to discharge Mary's dying wish. That was that I pass on to you, the contents of a small suitcase that belonged to your mother, the contents of which I know will answer many, many questions for you."

Clarissa explained the events that led up to her and Mary visiting Wales and to the evident distress of the Ruth's children, Clarissa explained that Mary had held their mother as she died in her arms.

Clarissa went on to describe the meetings with Ruth's family in Wales, and she also explained how their mother's lawyer had entrusted to Mary, Ruth's small suitcase.

Finally, before the inevitable barrage of questions began, Clarissa explained that she had letters for each of them from their mother.

The questions began to come thick and fast and carried on as the group eventually moved through to the breakfast room where they had lunch.

As they settled into the comfortable armchairs after lunch with the whole group feeling far more relaxed, Clarissa explained that before they left to return to their hotel, she would pass on Ruth's small suitcase, which now lay tantalisingly on a table close to the doorway.

But she asked that before they left the house Robert, Charlotte and Maria should tell her their story.

Charlotte, the eldest of the Carmichael children, rose from her chair and walked to the French windows overlooking the garden and the sea beyond, pausing as though she needed some inspiration to begin.

She returned to her chair, and staring deep into the blazing fire where its flames danced and flickered their mesmeric light onto the faces of Ruth's abandoned children; she began to tell their story to an expectant Clarissa.

CHAPTER SEVEN

For Clarissa to understand the story of Ruth's abandoned children, it was necessary for Charlotte to return to the summer of nineteen forty-six. She was two and a half years of age and Maria was not yet a year old.

By post war living standards, the Carmichael family enjoyed an idyllic life on a small farm, immune for the most part from the on-going effects of post war food rationing. But, the family's personal circumstances were less than ideal or orthodox.

Their mother Ruth had recently decided to leave Eastbrook Farm the home she had previously shared with her husband Edward Carmichael, their two children, Charlotte and Maria and Edward's parents, Ellen and Sam Carmichael.

Her relationship with Edward was broken, not helped by the pressure from his family who had never approved of Ruth and who were intent upon bringing to an end what they saw as nothing more than a marriage of convenience.

Ruth had fallen pregnant on an unguarded night of passion with Edward in nineteen forty-three, and his parents had never forgiven her for what they saw as something she should have prevented. Edward and Ruth were hastily married, and though a semblance of normality occasionally fell on Ruth's relationship with Edward, her marriage was doomed from the moment it began.

But, in a last ditch attempt to alter the course of history, Ruth had invited Edward to come for supper at the nearby Bowland Moss Farm.

Ruth had been living there for a short while, originally with Edward but without the children in what had been seen by her as part of a reconciliation process. But unbeknown to Ruth, Edward, and his entire family were determined to break up their relationship, and it was not long before Edward had moved out of Bowland Moss Farm and back to Eastbrook Farm with his parents.

He had returned, to live with his parents, and to pursue his *friendship* with his first love Sarah. This was a relationship encouraged even now by his parents who held the view that in marrying Ruth, Edward, had married beneath himself.

To them, the enforced marriage of Edward to Ruth, brought about by her pregnancy out of wedlock was always seen as something doomed to fail, and they worked tirelessly to see this prediction come to fruition.

The candlelit supper at Bowland Moss Farm so carefully thought through by Ruth with the genuine hope of a new start to her relationship with Edward, though pleasant enough, resulted in her and Edward sleeping together.

Having spent the night with Ruth, callously and without the hint of feeling, Edward ordered her to leave the house, the following morning, which she did. He persuaded Ruth that this was the right thing for her and the children but in truth, the only person this was right for was Edward himself.

Edward skilfully suggested that Ruth was already becoming a stranger to her children who increasingly looked to their grandmother for support and care. He convinced her that as she rarely saw the children, it was better in the long run that she step completely out of their lives and go and build a new life for herself.

Ruth left leaving her children in the care of their grandmother, but she left.... effectively abandoning her two children, a decision that would haunt her through the rest of her life.

Ruth would later tell herself that her decision to leave her husband and children was in part because of pressure to do so from the family, and partly because she felt, for whatever reason, that this was the right course of action for her and her children.

Though still very young, Charlotte was aware of her mother's absence, but she was now scolded if she so much as mentioned her mother's name. Ruth was seen as being out of the lives of the family, and Edward and his parents were now more focussed upon how and when they could formally bring Sarah back into Edward's life.

But that night with Edward at Bowland Moss Farm was to have profound consequences. Ruth would later discover that she was again pregnant, this time with Edward's third child, which she gave birth to in April nineteen forty-seven.

Ruth's exit from the lives of her two children had little impact on them, in part because of their age and partly because of the bond they had with their grandmother Ellen, whose life seemed now to be given entirely to the care and upbringing of the children.

The children lived an indulgent and relatively happy life on a farm that was to a large extent insulated from the general hurly burly of life.

They saw their Aunts Matilda and Dorothy several times each month, and though they were formidable characters, they too indulged the children. They also saw Sarah, their father's first love and now the centre of his life since Ruth left.

The children's lives were for the most part quite ordinary, except for the absence of their mother, Ruth. But she was a person they were forbidden to speak of at any time, and also someone they were encouraged over time by the family to believe was dead; but old lies cast long shadows.

The presumption by the family was that Edward and Sarah would one day marry and that she would become the children's substitute mother. This would complete a script that Edward and the family had written many years earlier, only for it to be put on hold by Edward's dalliance with Ruth in nineteen forty-three resulting in her pregnancy and their later marriage.

But on a warm June evening in nineteen forty-seven, an evening of high drama, Charlotte though still very young, became aware that something was happening in the house that was deeply concerning to the family in the living rooms below the bedroom she shared with Maria.

There was much commotion, sparked firstly by the arrival of a nurse at the farm and then much arguing and shouting.

The three-year-old Charlotte was deeply sensitive to any such shift in the fragile balance of emotions in the family, and she knew that something very serious was happening.

The arrival of Sarah, who took more of their father's time than did the children and who was now a regular visitor to the farm, only seemed to heighten the tension in the house.

But it was the raised voice of their grandfather that shook Charlotte and Maria. Though the master of the house in every sense of the word, he was rarely seen to be angry and so the ever-sensitive children knew that something was seriously amiss.

But it was later in the evening, some considerable time after the children had gone to sleep when they were awoken by the sound of a baby crying and a commotion down stairs.

Maria crept out of her bed and into Charlotte's, confused, frightened and fearful. They spent the night huddled together and the following morning they awoke to an eerily quiet house.

Creeping down the stairs in search of the baby they felt certain they had heard the previous night; they were startled when they opened the kitchen door. There they saw their grandmother in the large wooden rocking chair by the fireside, quietly nursing a baby.

As they were about to ask loudly a string of questions their father entered the room.

He gestured to the children to be quiet and in a matter of fact way he pronounced; "This is your brother who was brought to the house late last night. He will live here with you, and you will need to help Grandma to look after him."

So that's it, thought Charlotte, if you need a brother you simply order one!

But she was wiser than that.

"Is this Mummy's baby?" she asked. And even as the words had left her innocent young lips, she realised that she had broken one of the cardinal rules of the house, not ever to mention 'Mummy.'

She knew before the raised voice of her father condemned her that she was in serious trouble.

"How dare you mention your Mother? We have told you before that we are not to speak of her in this house. She is dead do you hear me? She is dead, and that's an end to it," he barked leaving Charlotte and Maria cowering behind their grandmother's chair.

This was the terrible lie that Ruth's children, now three of them were to grow up believing; the worst of all lies, that their mother was dead. No embellishment, no attempt to give her '*death*' any broader context, simply, *your mother is dead.*

~

Throughout the remainder of nineteen forty-seven and into the spring and early summer of nineteen forty-eight, the baby became a big part of the family. Charlotte, in particular, spent much of her time helping her grandmother to care for him, building a close bond with him as she had also done with Maria.

Already, the young Charlotte was demonstrating a deep, almost motherly and protective instinct for her siblings. These were qualities that would emerge again during their adolescent years when these children were to find that, but for Charlotte's urge to protect her brother and sister, they would be devoid of love, and that emotional necessity of life for children, a sense of belonging.

The children soon began a journey that would see them baptised into the Roman Catholic Church, one of the many milestones set by the deeply devout Sarah as prerequisites for a future marriage to Edward.

The first to *enter* the Church was the baby, originally named Michael by Ruth. But Sarah was adamant that the name *must* be changed to Robert, as much to rid the child of the name given to him by Ruth, as it was a symbolic marker of Sarah's burgeoning influence over Edward.

And Edward was also put through the necessary religious *instructions* to become a Catholic, and he too was baptised into the Faith in short order by Sarah's Parish Priest. But Sarah's involvement with the children didn't go beyond their spiritual needs, leaving this to the children's grandmother.

However, the ageing Ellen was weakened by the hard life she had endured playing her part in the day-to-day running of the farm and with the added burden of being both mother and grandmother to Edward's three children.

Over the course of just a few months in early nineteen forty-eight Ellen's health deteriorated to the point that by late June, she become bed ridden and was getting visibly weaker by the day.

Maria, who was deeply caring of her grandmother, reached the point when she could not be persuaded from her grandmother's bedroom.

And so it was that in the early hours of July fourth, nineteen forty-eight, Ellen Carmichael the grandmother to Charlotte, Maria, and Robert died peacefully in her sleep.

~

That day was now to be the turning point in the lives of these three children; children whose needs were known only to their grandmother. Their father had done little for them in their upbringing to date and knew nothing about how to care for them. They were totally dependent upon their grandmother, and so the decisions that their father and their grandfather were to take over the course of the next few hours would ultimately turn out to be life changing for them.

Charlotte woke early to the sound of a car coming into the farmyard. She ran quietly to the bedroom window, being careful as she drew the curtains to one side not to be seen by her father who was standing a forlorn figure in the driveway.

It was barely six o'clock, but the bright early morning sun made it easy for Charlotte to see that the man stepping from the car was the family doctor. He was ushered swiftly into the house by the unusually unshaven, dishevelled figure of her father.

Maria was woken by the heavy sound of shoes on the wooden stairs and the unguarded conversation between her father, grandfather and the doctor.

There was a brief moment of silence when Charlotte drew Maria close to her and said; "Something's wrong, daddy and granddad have been shouting and crying, and the doctor is here."

These two young children were consumed by the evident seriousness of the situation that was unfolding. Both knew that it was probably their Grandma that the doctor was seeing, though neither said a word.

The silence was broken by a wail from their grandfather who could repeatedly be heard crying; "No, no....what shall I do now?"

What a way for these children to become aware that their grandmother had died. To the younger Maria, death meant nothing, but the demeanour of her older sister who was now quietly sobbing told its own story.

The early hours of the morning saw a frenzy of activity. For the first hour or two the children, still in their bedroom but awake and aware of something happening, were completely overlooked by their grandfather and father. Their preoccupation was with the impact Ellen's death would have upon them.

They were in shock; one grieving the death of a wife the other grieving the death of a mother, grandmother and the central female figure in his life and that of his children. Their grief was palpable and understandable but was entirely self-focussed.

To the utter surprise of the children, the bedroom door was suddenly thrown open. Charlotte, sitting upright in her bed holding Maria close to her could see the figure of Mrs. Ormroyd, a near neighbour and someone both she, and Maria liked a great deal.

Instinctively, they both ran to her side gripping her with an intensity that left her in no doubt that the children were more aware of what was happening in the house than their distraught father gave them credit for.

The children were quickly dressed in the clothes they wore the previous day and taken down the stairs by Mrs. Ormroyd, who protectively held them close to her side as they passed their grandmother's closed bedroom door.

As they walked down the driveway, another neighbour met them. As she drew alongside, Mrs. Ormroyd was overheard by Charlotte to say; "Robert is still asleep in his cot in the children's bedroom please just take him."

Anticipating a question, Mrs. Ormroyd responded; "You won't see the Carmichael's, just take Robert, and we will cope between us until Matilda and Dorothy arrive."

A little while later, a knock at the farmhouse door signalled the arrival of the undertakers. They went with Sam upstairs, and minutes later they were seen to leave the house with Ellen's body.

Sam returned to the kitchen to sit in silence with Edward.

Their thoughts were entirely centred upon their loss and how they would face the challenge of fending for themselves. Not a word passed between them, and not a word was uttered about the children who were now in the temporary care of the neighbours.

CHAPTER EIGHT

It was sometime late into the morning before a taxi arrived at Eastbrook Farm with Edward's Aunt Matilda and Aunt Dorothy, and only minutes later, another arrived carrying Sarah.

The two Aunts moved swiftly to take charge in a house consumed by a combination of self-pity and grief.

Aunt Dorothy, always to be relied upon in a crisis, prepared a late breakfast for Edward and Sam and sought to calm them both. Sarah, on the other hand, quick to establish her personal lines in the sand before others might presume an immediate role for her, set out her stall with abundant clarity.

She had already been in full scale planning for her future marriage to Edward. But for this to take place, there needed to be a mandatory three-year period between the time when Ruth had deserted Edward, to the completion of legal divorce proceedings, and that was still some two years away.

However, the immediate concern for Sarah was that in the maternal interregnum brought about by Ellen's death she might be seen by the Carmichael family as the natural and immediate carer for the children....not to mention Edward and Sam: This was not going to happen, as Sarah was about to make clear!

"And Edward," she began with some authority, intent upon setting all parties straight on her position.

"You can put out of your mind any thought that I will become a surrogate mother or fairy godmother to those children. Once we are married, I will do it because that will be expected of me, but until then *the problem* is yours to resolve."

Sarah strutted purposefully around the kitchen satisfied that she had made her position abundantly clear.

Astonishing, as it may seem, Sarah's *position* was seen as entirely acceptable by everyone present and thought was immediately given to who else might meet the needs of the children.

The distancing from *the problem* continued as Aunt Matilda followed swiftly by Aunt Dorothy also declared that they too would be unable to offer help.

"We're far too old to be taking on small children, and ill-disciplined children at that," declared Aunt Matilda as she folded both arms beneath her ample bosoms and flicked her head in the direction of Aunt Dorothy for support.

"Absolutely, my dear," declared Aunt Dorothy, "they need care and discipline," she repeated as she moved to align herself alongside Matilda.

At no time was it ever contemplated that Edward, even with help from others outside the family might naturally, as the children's father, strive to look after them. It was as though a paralysis had descended upon the family as they sat silently contemplating what should happen to the children.

It was upon Aunt Dorothy's return into the room having been upstairs to tidy the beds that she asked the whereabouts of the children, noticing as she passed their room that their beds were empty and the curtains still closed.

Edward paused and then remembered that Mrs. Ormroyd and another neighbour had taken them earlier in the morning. It had taken more than an hour for the assembled group to ask where the children were, and still, nobody asked after their emotional welfare.

The conversation eventually brought the family group to the conclusion that *the problem* would have to be discussed with the local Council, who would need to take the children into care.

"That's what the social welfare department is there for," proffered Dorothy.

"Indeed," said Sarah; "that's what we pay our taxes for and…as this is a crisis; they need to be called in."

Edward, Sarah and Aunt Matilda left immediately in the family car to take the short journey into Preston to visit the Council, having telephoned ahead to set out their dilemma and their view of the most appropriate solution.

~

At four-thirty, that afternoon, Edward, Aunt Matilda and Sarah returned from Preston closely followed by Shirley Adams, a social worker who had rapidly been assigned to the Carmichael family case.

In the space of a few hours, the social welfare department had been persuaded that the fragmented, dysfunctional Carmichael family were incapable of caring for Charlotte, Maria, and Robert.

A suggested option of Edward keeping Charlotte and Maria, the older of the three children and Robert being temporarily taken into care had been roundly dismissed by Edward as impractical and "bloody impossible."

The suggestion that at least for the coming days the social welfare department could provide a domestic helper for Edward and Sam, who could also lend some child care support, was also roundly dismissed, this time by Sarah.

A suite of options were swept aside as the social welfare department moved to the unpalatable conclusion that at least in the short term, the children were at risk and would need to be removed from the house immediately for the sake of their own welfare.

On arrival at the house, the social welfare officer was able quickly to reassure herself that their provisional decision to remove the children, though seen initially by the officers as being driven by the family, was entirely justified on welfare grounds.

A discreet telephone call back to the Preston offices by the social worker confirmed her initial assessment, and she returned to the family now gathered in the kitchen.

She advised that she would take Charlotte and Maria immediately to a foster family in nearby Inglewhite and that with the assistance of Sarah and her contacts within the Catholic Church, Robert would be taken to a foster family in Preston.

It was at this point that Shirley Adams, the young but highly thought of social worker discovered that the whole day had passed, and no one had seen fit to visit the children, nor had anyone spoken to them about what had happened to their Grandmother.

Setting aside her evident irritation she asked Sarah to arrange for the two girls to be brought to the house.

When they arrived, Charlotte was holding the hand of Maria and neither would let go of the other. Shirley

Adams asked that everyone other than Edward should leave the room so that she and Edward could talk to the children.

Edward, who previously had very little contact or relationship with the children, not surprisingly was lost for words. With a sympathetic voice, the social worker sat the two girls next to their father and began the painful task of explaining to them that their Grandma had died.

The girls once again turned to each for comfort with Charlotte holding Maria tight as though to protect her from the shock. But despite their earlier suspicion that their Grandma had died, the shock of being told was painful to them both.

It was then the social worker's responsibility to explain to the girls that they were being taken to stay with a nearby family. She carefully described that they would stay with the family for some time until their father and the Council were able to decide what to do next.

All of the careful wording and sympathetic delivery was lost on the children who were simply overwhelmed. And asked by the social worker if they had any questions, Charlotte innocently asked; "Has Grandma gone to heaven to be with Mummy?"

The social worker, clearly shocked by the question, turned to Edward but held back her question, until the children had been sent to their bedroom to get a toy and some clothes.

It was only when the children were out of earshot that she sharply rebuked Edward.

"Why on earth would your children believe their mother is dead when you have told me only a couple of hours ago that she has deserted you, and that you don't know her whereabouts?"

Edward mumbled that it seemed easier for the family to build a picture in the minds of the children that she had died rather than to say she had abandoned them.

Shirley Adams was clearly very irritated by Edward's response and turned again to him for some clarification.

"You told me this afternoon that you have no idea of the whereabouts of Ruth Carmichael, your wife. And you also told me that the last time you saw her was in nineteen forty-six when she walked out of Bowland Moss Farm. I am asking you once again Mr. Carmichael... do you have any information that could help us trace your wife?"

She paused awaiting a response from Edward.

"We need this information so that my department can investigate if we can work with her with the hope that we might reunite these children with her."

Edward looked towards the half open door. Seeing Sarah and Aunt Matilda in the shadows, he replied; "I have told you; she left in nineteen forty-six, and I have seen nothing of her since."

Edward had conveniently omitted to mention that he had been to her flat in Preston to take Robert from her in May nineteen forty seven. And, not surprisingly he also omitted to tell her that he had later been having a relationship with Ruth, resulting in her becoming pregnant once again with their fourth child, Huw!

Charlotte and Maria returned to the room with a parcel of clothes each and their dolls tucked under their arms.

The social worker reminded Edward that the foster family in Preston, organised by the Church was expecting him to bring Robert to them that evening and that he should leave immediately, once she and the girls had left the house for Inglewhite.

With that, Charlotte turned to her father and asked; "Will you come to see us, daddy?" He nodded and with a gentle tap on their heads, Charlotte, and Maria were taken away.

There were no tears; there was no affection shown towards them by any adult present; they simply walked down the driveway into the uncertainty of their own futures.

Later, Edward and Sarah took Robert to Preston and handed him over to the waiting foster family at the door of their home. Once again, there was no emotion.

Now Ruth's three children were in the care of social welfare, and Edward and his family had dealt with it, with the cold dispassion of a commercial transaction.

And so, as that day drew to a close, a day that had started with the death of Ellen, and ended with Edward and Ruth's three children being taken into the care of the local authority, Sarah and Edward drove alone back to Eastbrook Farm.

CHAPTER NINE

Charlotte and Maria arrived outside the home of Mr. and Mrs. Oliver, the people who were to become their foster parents, still clinging to each other, resigned to do whatever was asked of them by Shirley Adams, the social worker.

The pretty cottage, on the outskirts of Inglewhite, was set behind a neatly trimmed privet hedge and was located at the end of a quiet country road.

The house was surrounded by farmland with only three families as near neighbours. To the rear of the house, but in the far distance were the lower slopes of the Pennine Hills, known fondly as the backbone of England that formed a familiar landmark to Charlotte and Maria.

As Shirley Adams opened the car door, Mr. and Mrs. Oliver were already approaching with beaming, welcoming smiles.

Mr. Oliver a small, slim man in his late forties, still dressed in his grey farming overalls, and black wellington boots warmly smiled towards the children. He had come straight from milking, and the smell of cows and farmyard manure were a welcome reminder to Charlotte and Maria of their home at Eastbrook Farm, only about twelve miles away.

Mrs. Oliver, a red faced cheery looking, rather large lady wearing a flowery kitchen apron swept towards the children and gathered both into her arms drawing them into her fulsome bosom.

"Welcome my dears...and welcome to Fellside Farm, which will be your home with Mr. Oliver and me for a little while," she breathlessly gasped, as she hurriedly guided the still silent children and the social worker into the hallway of her home.

The children were immediately taken into the kitchen where, before anything else was said, Mrs. Oliver walked them over to the sink, wiped a damp kitchen cloth over their faces and hands and sat them at the table. She then produced a plate laden with sandwiches and another containing freshly baked fruit cake and local Eccles cakes.

A jug of fresh milk from the farm was placed on the table alongside the two glasses and still nothing was said as the children politely but with enthusiasm sat and ate.

This simple routine of immediately feeding her foster children was something Mrs. Oliver had done many times before. The psychology would be lost on Mrs. Oliver; all she knew was that children always settled when they knew that their bellies would be filled and that there was plenty more where that came from.

It was only when the children were settled that she turned to the social worker.

"I always give my *foster*'s something to eat the minute they come into my home....that way they know that they are welcome; and now......what are their names and their ages?" she asked, as she continued to watch over her new charges.

Shirley Adams, who had never dealt personally with Mr. and Mrs. Oliver, knew of their reputation for homely and loving care, coupled with a no-nonsense approach to discipline, school and jobs around the house began her briefing.

She explained, out of the earshot of the children the circumstances of their removal from the Carmichael house. She cautioned that she was uncertain as to how long the children would stay with them, given the unusual circumstances. And on a more practical note, she explained that Charlotte could be enrolled at the local school for admission in the September, or she could be enrolled in the following Easter term.

It was quickly decided that school and the company of other children would be good for her and that Mrs. Oliver would set about the task the following day.

In that moment, it became evident that the placement of the children into the foster care of Mrs. and Mrs. Oliver was to be no short term assignment. It was anticipated that they would at least be there beyond the summer and probably for some months after that.

Mr. Oliver quietly explained that Inglewhite was a small place and with its proximity to Eastbrook Farm and Goosnargh, it was already known that Ellen Carmichael had died. He went on; "People hereabouts talk, and it will not be long before the Carmichael's know where their children have been placed, so we don't want any trouble."

The Shirley Adams moved Mr. and Mrs. Oliver out of the kitchen and into the hallway where she could explain the circumstances in more detail.

"There will be no trouble from the Carmichael's. Being entirely frank with you, I believe that we are going to face some difficulty in getting Mr. Carmichael to plan for the time when he takes back responsibility for these two girls. Indeed, I think our biggest task will be to get Mr. Carmichael to engage with the children from what I have seen so far, but I hope to be proven wrong."

She explained that for the immediate future, she might come to the house by prior arrangement and take the children to see their father but that ultimately, it will be for him to make arrangements with Mr. and Mrs. Oliver to visit the children and take them out.

Over the course of the next hour, papers were given to Mrs. Oliver and the social worker shared what little she knew of the children's likes and dislikes, gleaned mainly from a brief conversation with Mrs. Ormroyd.

Throughout, the children sat politely at the table eating in silence. The occasional glance from Charlotte to the nineteen-month old Maria offered both comfort and a gentle reminder of how they should conduct themselves.

Though hungry, they both knew they should not eat all the sandwiches and more than one piece of cake each. It had been drummed into the two girls by their Grandmother, reinforced with considerably less affection by Sarah, that in polite society, you should never eat the last of anything as this was rude and particularly impolite for girls.

They had each drunk a glass of the cool, creamy milk swiftly, and while there was an almost full jug of milk on the table, they sat waiting to be asked if they would like another drink.

It was Mr. Oliver who quietly observed the children and knew instinctively that despite the children being in awe of their new circumstances and very much on their best behaviour, he could see that it was going to be a challenge to engage these traumatised children.

He could see that discipline was emerging as the defining quality in these girls even in the hour or so that the children had been with them, but he wanted to see a tiny spark of youthfulness.

He questioned where the normal inquisitive and playful child was. He was used to foster children who perhaps needed to be tamed rather than children who needed to be given permission to act simply as children.

He saw how Maria was entirely dependent upon Charlotte to steer and guide her and how emotionally they were completely locked together. He worried, and with some justification that the trauma of what these two small girls were experiencing might ultimately be too much for his wife to deal with.

As Shirley Adams prepared to leave, she was asked by Mrs. Oliver what was to happen to Robert, the little boy. In a quiet whisper, she explained that he was with a foster family in Preston though only for a few nights before he would be taken into a Catholic childrens home.

There was a knowing glance from one to the other as each acknowledged that the lives of these dear children would now be defined by their current and possibly their long term placements in the care system.

Having seen the care worker out of the house, Mrs. Oliver began the slow process of engaging these impossibly shy girls who were to be her charge for the coming weeks possibly months. Experience had shown her that the first night was crucial in settling new children into the house and also into the household routine.

She knew that the place for their confused minds was the present and not the past, and so as she took the children upstairs to prepare them for bed she told them things rather than asking questions. She pointed out their bedroom in which there was a three-quarter size bed and a single bed.

"I suspect that you might want to share this bed tonight," she said with the wisdom of many such occasions behind her. "But I'm sure it will not be long before you're fighting over who gets to call it theirs in the future."

Maria looked to Charlotte and pulled on her arm as she signalled her approval.

"Now my dears, until you find your tongues, let me guess who sleeps in this pretty blue nightdress," she asked holding the smaller nightdress to Charlotte. Maria giggled and smiled.

"That's mine silly."

The ice was broken. Slowly, as they prepared for their first night in this new home, Mrs. Oliver entered their space, and contact was made.

As she walked the children from the bathroom to their beds, she felt the cool hand of Maria search out hers and almost immediately, her other hand was clasping Charlotte's. Reassurance, in Mrs. Oliver's experience, particularly at bed time was everything a child needed.

As the children clambered into the big bed together each with their favourite doll, Mrs. Oliver sat on the edge of the bed gently stroking Charlotte's hair as she was nearest.

She turned firstly to Charlotte with a knowing and reassuring smile.

"It's all very confusing my darling," she explained, still stroking her hair. "But tomorrow, the sun will climb over the Pennine Hills here at Fellside, as it did today and yesterday at Eastbrook Farm. And when you are good and ready, we can explore your new home, and we will talk if you want to, but in the meantime, care for Maria and come to me next door if you need anything in the night."

Maria climbed over her sister to squeeze herself close to Mrs. Oliver. She remained there for perhaps a couple of minutes, before the leaden weight of a child who has fallen asleep in your arms prompted Mrs. Oliver to kiss her on the forehead and lay her down to sleep.

Charlotte, fighting to hold back tears threw herself into Mrs. Oliver's arms and gave in to the full emotions of the day, weeping uncontrollably.

It was some time, perhaps half an hour or so before Mrs. Oliver was able to peel Charlotte from her grasp.

Looking deep into Charlotte's eyes she explained.

"I need you to help me to look after Maria. Remember, this will be new to me too, but understand this Charlotte, Mr. Oliver and me will love and care for you, and we will protect you."

Charlotte too fell asleep in Mrs. Oliver's arms.

~

Robert, who was a little over a year old, was to have no memory of this traumatic day. He was handed over to a foster family whose role was to care for him for a few days. They would have done this on many occasions in the War years when the bombing of the industrial towns and cities of Britain saw parents killed, and children orphaned.

Places like Preston would take these orphans, relieving the pressure on the social welfare departments of those bombed out towns and cities such as Liverpool, Manchester, Birmingham and even London. The foster families played an important transitional role as they acted as part of the conduit that would ultimately see their charges transferred to an orphanage to join other children in similar circumstances.

In the case of Robert, he was quite different; there was no national emergency just a family that couldn't or wouldn't cope.

Robert was a sick child, developing eczema at a very early age and suffering from recurrent bouts of bronchitis that would later lead to asthma. He was a small child at birth and weight gain was also slow. But in all other ways, he was a bright and generally happy little boy and so would have proved to be of little problem to his foster family. But his stay was to be remarkably short.

Only two days after arriving, Robert was taken into the care of a Catholic childrens home for boys. There he entered the world of the orphan, joining other children who were indeed *orphaned*, but his label, along with many others, was that of a child without living parents or in his case, a parent capable of caring for him.

He entered the childrens home an anonymous person, simply known as Robert, identified as Catholic and categorised as 'abandoned.' There he was encouraged to adapt quickly to the strict regime that was seen as necessary to ensure a proper, disciplined and Catholic upbringing for these vulnerable boys.

Individuality was shunned, as each child was encouraged to see their benefactor, the Catholic Church as their salvation, and they were constantly reminded to be grateful for God's gifts. At all times, they were reminded that but for the generosity of Almighty God, the Catholic Church and its disciples on earth, they would have nothing.

CHAPTER TEN

Charlotte and Maria were slow to adapt to their new surroundings finding it difficult initially to accept the genuine nature of the open, loving relationship they were invited into. But slowly over the following two weeks, the familiarity of the farming life, coupled with the glorious endless summer weather of nineteen forty eight, they settled gently into a routine.

It seemed natural that the children should call these people Mr. and Mrs. Oliver as they very quickly acknowledged them as parental figures.... but their father was never far from their minds.

The children never spoke of their father to Mr. and Mrs. Oliver but in the quiet of their bedroom or when alone in the garden they would talk in forbidden whispers.

Their conversations, given Maria's very young age, were more like games where they would act out scenes from their imaginary world in which Daddy would come and rescue them, take them back to Eastbrook Farm and there, waiting for them at the farm gate would be Grandma.

Charlotte would stand some distance away from Maria and then, with exaggerated gestures and the most adult voice she could muster, she would beckon Maria to her side.

"My beautiful Maria," she would say, attempting the inflections of her Grandmother's voice, "come here for a cuddle and tell me what you have been doing all day," she would ask, gathering Maria into her young arms.

The same game but with slightly changed settings, and scenarios would be played time and again with each of the girls in turn playing the part of their grandmother.

But days were also filled with fun at Fellside Farm, as the children were given free rein to wander as freely as they liked providing they were in the sight of either Mr or Mrs. Oliver or Tom Masters.

The children knew Tom Masters as he had once been the farm hand at Eastbrook Farm but had left that position as the herd size was reduced. In the more relaxed atmosphere here at Fellside Farm, Tom would while away his spare time playing games with the children and his reassuring presence did much to settle them.

The children were never far from each other's side. But slowly they began to understand the farm routine in which they each had daily chores of visiting the chickens, collecting eggs and bringing milk from the dairy for the family's own use.

The small farm herd was made up mainly of Jersey cows that produced milk with the richest and thickest of cream on the top that the children adored.

It was three weeks after their placement with Mr. and Mrs. Oliver that the now familiar twice weekly visits from the social worker broke with routine as the children saw their father stepping from his car.

Their immediate excitement was tempered by the sight of Sarah, who elegantly stepped from the car, being careful as to where she placed her stiletto heeled shoes on the muddy driveway.

She swiftly moved to take their father's arm as they navigated their way across the farmyard and walked to the table in the garden where the children were having lunch.

The children had a deep dislike of Sarah. As young as they were, they knew both instinctively, and through some of the things she had said to them in the past that she had little or no regard for them. She displayed no empathy with the children and made no attempt to engage them as children. She was aloof, cold and as far as the children were concerned; she was "*the witch.*"

In one of their garden games, they would pretend they could cast spells on the *witch* to make her disappear. But their favourite spell was to turn her into Gertrude, the Tamworth Sow.

They would approach the pig sty, and as they did so, Charlotte would step forward and pronounce, as sorcerer in chief; "And now horrid Sarah....you are now a pig!" Excitedly, the children would climb onto the gate and would see *Sara* transformed, because of their spell into a pig.

Ensuring that no one was looking, they would then embark on name calling.

"Piggy Sarah, you're fat and ugly," shouted Charlotte giggling as she waited for Maria's response.

"She is fat, ugly and she smells," would come Maria's response expanding her limited grasp of the English language.

They would roar with laughter. Then came the *coup de grâce,* which always sent the children into fits of laughter.

"You're off to market tomorrow piggy Sarah, and you'll be bacon by Saturday." They would run off laughing and giggling to their laurel-bush den in the garden.

The children respectfully asked Mr. Oliver if they could leave the table and ran in the direction of their father and Sarah, who were accompanied by the social worker and Mrs. Oliver.

As they came alongside their father, they stopped anticipating perhaps that their father would make a move towards them. He didn't, but simply said; "You are well are you? And are you being good girls for Mrs. Oliver?"

There was a polite "yes," from Charlotte following which Edward turned away and begin a conversation with Mrs. Oliver and the social worker.

Sarah, who had drawn herself close to Edward, looked back to the girls, and for a brief moment, they thought the *witch* might cast a spell on them. But instead, she smiled and commented to Edward, in a voice loud enough for the children to hear; "There...I told you the children would be fine; it's quite clear that they are settled and happy."

The conversation between Mrs. Oliver and the social worker lasted only about five minutes. As they turned in the direction of where the children had previously been standing, they were nowhere to be seen. But it was the keen eyed Mrs. Oliver who pointed to a laurel bush in the garden, already a favourite den for the girls.

"You will want some time with the girls," she said as she pointed to the bush and the two girls sitting there holding each other's hands.

There was a momentary reluctance on the part of Edward before he was encouraged by Sarah.

"Pop over and say goodbye to them Edward so that we can get on our way," she instructed, breaking her hold on his arm so that she didn't have to walk across the grass and get her stiletto heels dirty.

The social worker carefully observed everything, including Edward's goodbye that amounted to no more than a tap on the head of each child. She saw as Charlotte, desperate to engage her father tried to grasp his hand. And she also saw how Edward was drawn to Sarah, who was impatiently calling him to return to her side.

But he turned, not to Sarah but the girls and beckoned them to his side.

For the very briefest of moments, Edward held Charlotte and Maria in defiance of the urgings of Sarah. But that moment of closeness was to end as quickly as it began.

Edward moved away from his children and was drawn by Sarah into her arms where she promptly kissed him gently on the cheek...looking sternly at Charlotte, defying the children ever to get between their father and her again.

The car swept out of the drive and silence descended once more on this rural farm. Mrs. Oliver watched as the unusually subdued children returned to their laurel bush den.

It was not immediately evident, but Mrs. Oliver knew that the children were deeply upset and crying. She left them for a moment, knowing that they needed to continue to build their bond of trust and support that would be important as they faced other milestones in their troubled lives.

That evening, the children were quiet as they took their supper. They ate little and said even less.

They went to their beds at the usual six thirty, and Mrs. Oliver sat with them and read a story until Maria was asleep. She then took Charlotte into her arms and without a word spoken there they remained for about twenty minutes before Charlotte too fell asleep.

CHAPTER ELEVEN

On the following morning, Mr. Oliver rose at his usual four-thirty to begin the morning milking. As he left the farm house, he was alarmed to see that the bolt on the kitchen door was not in its usual locked position.

It was a ritual that each night as Mrs. Oliver made the last cup of tea, Mr. Oliver would go and check the chickens and satisfy himself that all was well around the farm before returning to the house. Mrs. Oliver would wait for his familiar call; "The bolt's across," signifying that the door was securely locked, and they would then sit together drinking their tea before going to bed.

He knew that last night had followed the same routine, and this worried him. He was about to go upstairs when he heard Mrs. Oliver rush into the room.

"The children....the children are they with you?" she cried, with a note of panic in her voice.

Mr. Oliver explained that he had not seen the children but described how he was concerned that the bolt on the door had been opened. They looked to each other and immediately ran into the farmyard calling the girls names.

Mr. Oliver ran to the gate leading to the field where the cows were waiting expectantly to be taken to be milked, as Mrs. Oliver checked the children's dens and the chicken house. The children were nowhere to be found.

Panic stricken; Mrs. Oliver ran into the house and checked every room.

Mr. Oliver, who by now was as concerned for his cattle as he was for the welfare of the children, made one final sweep of the farm buildings before letting the cows into the yard where they dutifully meandered their way into the milking parlour.

At that point, Tom Masters arrived. The distraught Mr. Oliver explained that the children were missing and asked if they had ever done anything like this before. As he answered, Mrs. Oliver joined them.

"No, they haven't," he confirmed adding; "but with the shenanigans that were going on at Eastbrook Farm it's any wonder they didn't. They are good kids," he explained in a faltering voice, " but they were never properly cared for.... and as for their mother...."

Tom was abruptly stopped by Mr. Oliver and asked to get on with the milking as Mr. and Mrs. Oliver went back into the house.

Mr. Oliver decided that he must ring the Police in the neighbouring village of Goosnargh but to do this, he would need to go to a nearby farm to use their telephone. As he was about to leave, Mrs. Oliver suggested that he also drive to Eastbrook Farm to see if the children had attempted to walk there and also to alert the children's father.

Mr. Oliver had no car, and the only transport they had on the farm was an ageing Fordson tractor. And so, now in a state of panic, Mr. Oliver began the drive to Eastbrook Farm and then on to Goosnargh.

The journey took longer than expected as he was stopped by other early risers inquisitive to know why he was out and about on the tractor, and so early in the morning. As he drove from one enquiring neighbour to another, so the word was spreading that the Carmichael children were missing.

By the time, Mr. Oliver pulled up the drive of Eastbrook Farm it was almost six o'clock. The sound of the tractor and the gossiping of local neighbours at the farm gate brought Edward and his father Sam out of the house to be greeted by the news that Edward's two girls had gone missing. Still in a state of shock, Mr. Oliver used the Carmichael's phone to call the police station in Goosnargh.

The police officer at the other end of the telephone needed little information to fill in the background as he was a local, and well aware of the placement of the Carmichael children into the care of Mr. and Mrs. Oliver.

Like the rest of the local families, he found the whole issue unpalatable, and when asked by Mr. Oliver if he wished to speak to Edward Carmichael, he curtly replied, "No."

Mr. Oliver was asked to return to his farm where Police Constable Appleby would attend as quickly as possible. As he walked towards his tractor to leave, Mr. Oliver explained to Edward, the message from the station Sergeant.

To the surprise of the small gathering of locals, Edward simply asked; "If it's alright with you, I'll wait here by the telephone. Can you ask the police to keep me informed what's going on?"

A voice from the gathering by the gate could clearly be heard calling out.

"You're a disgrace Edward Carmichael; your kids are in care, and you don't bat an eye lid. Now they've gone missing, and you don't seem concerned or bothered. Well.... me, I'm going to search for them even if you're not. Now, who's going to join me?" he defiantly asked of his neighbours.

As Edward moved to enter the house, the voices of several neighbours could be heard saying they would join the impromptu search party. They could also be heard condemning Edward and Sam Carmichael, but the focus of their anger was again turned upon Edward.

"You're a bloody disgrace Edward Carmichael, shame on you."

The police and Mr. Oliver arrived back at Fellside Farm at about the same time to find Mrs. Oliver beside herself with worry for the welfare of the children. Alongside PC Appleby was another police officer, a young woman who quickly introduced herself as WPC Mortimer.

She quickly took Mrs. Oliver into the house and asked to see the girls bedroom. As they entered the house, WPC Mortimer reassured Mrs. Oliver that in her experience the children would be fine and most probably were asleep in the warm morning summer sun following some great adventure.

A quick check of the children's bedroom and the wardrobe enabled them to establish that the children had changed into day clothes and had left their nightdresses neatly placed under their pillows.

WPC Mortimer saw this as promising and moved Mrs. Oliver quickly into the kitchen.

"Can you quickly check to see if there is food missing or a basket in which the children might have carried some provisions for the day." At the same time, she began looking around the kitchen for the children's shoes and Wellington boots.

Mrs. Oliver established that there had been half a loaf of bread left over from the previous day's bake, and there was also a bottle of freshly made lemonade missing from the larder.

Satisfied, WPC Mortimer relayed the information to her colleague and returned to the house to be with Mrs. Oliver. She then began gentle questioning of Mrs. Oliver, probing for more than an hour: "Had the children been scolded the previous day for being naughty? Had they talked about going for a picnic recently?" And then; "When had they last seen their father?"

Mrs. Oliver was about to start explaining the events of the previous day when Shirley Adams the social worker hurriedly entered the kitchen looking visibly distressed. She took over the situation explaining that she was exceedingly concerned about the meeting the children had the previous day with their father, explaining his coolness towards them. But Mrs. Oliver, a wise and experienced foster mother stopped the conversation.

"Mr. Carmichael is grieving for the loss of his mother in just the same way that the children are coming to terms with the loss of their grandmother. Yes, we would have liked to see Mr. Carmichael offer more comfort towards his children yesterday, but my impression is that he doesn't know how to. He doesn't have a relationship with his children, but then that's no different from many men around these parts. The only person in his life at the moment seems to be that woman

Sarah and like it or not, if they eventually marry, she will become the mother these children need so desperately. And, let's remember" she added, "yesterday was the first time the children had seen their father following Mrs. Carmichael's death, so it was bound to be difficult."

Mrs. Oliver described how the two girls were extremely close and that whatever this folly led to, she knew that Charlotte would take good care of Maria.

"These children are deeply sensitive, and yesterday will have confused them. In their little minds they think that they are alone and as much as we try to give them love, they cannot help but sense that they are on their own."

There was a collective acceptance that Mrs. Oliver was probably right.

Mrs. Oliver described how the children were upset when they went to bed and that she had spent some time with Charlotte in particular before she fell asleep. She explained that it was her view that their disappearance was either an attempt to find Robert, their brother or an attempt to go and see their father.

She explained that Robert's whereabouts had been a preoccupation of Charlotte's in the last few days and that Charlotte had a strange notion that for some reason, Robert had been sent away because she had not been caring for him enough and that she was being punished.

Mrs. Oliver continued. "Charlotte is very sensitive and sees herself at the tender age of four and a half as the maternal figure to both Maria and Robert and is increasingly concerned to bring Robert to join them.

Whether we like it or not, this little band of children sees their world in a quite different way to us. And while we do what we think is right for the children, what they see as right is that they should remain together as a family."

Shirley Adams was about to speak when Mrs. Oliver sprung to her own defence.

"I would have taken Robert, but having two children at one time is a very new experience for Mr. Oliver and me, and we simply could not cope and run the farm with a baby as well as the two girls."

Shirley Adams reassured her that everyone involved with the case was hugely grateful that at least the two girls were able to be kept together.

The speculation about the whereabouts of the children continued into the late afternoon with increasing levels of anxiety for their welfare. But, to the relief of all concerned a neighbour ran into the kitchen to say that the children had been found safe, hiding in the shed of a neighbour's garden barely half a mile away.

A relieved and tearful Mrs. Oliver scooped the two children into her arms as they sheepishly entered the kitchen, rather dirty, and particularly frightened about the possible consequences of their escapade. But, with some authority, Mrs. Oliver pronounced; "There will be no discussions tonight....all I want to do is to bathe these children and get them some tea."

PC Mortimer smiled.

"There will be no further questions from us either we're just delighted that they are home safe and sound." But, as he gathered his helmet from the hall stand, he could not resist a gentle chiding of the children.

"Now my dears, let's not be doing that again eh....
you had a lot of people worried, Mrs. Oliver here
especially."

The children buried themselves further into the folds
of Mrs. Oliver's dress, hiding their embarrassed faces.

Shirley Adams rose to leave the room explaining that
she also felt that the best person to bring the day and
the escapade to a close was Mrs. Oliver, and she too
moved to leave the room. As she was about to close the
door, she returned and said; "I will let Mr. Carmichael
know they are safe."

At that point, the erstwhile silent Maria began to cry.
Charlotte acting as a proxy for Maria as she often did
explained.

"She wants to know if Daddy will send us from here
for being naughty."

A reassuring squeeze from Mrs. Oliver saw an end to
that conversation, and the children were once again safe
in the arms of Mrs. Oliver.

The children were taken to the bathroom and placed
in the bath together, as Mrs. Oliver, busily chatting
about what was for tea, slowly bathed them. Once she
had finished, she knelt beside the bath and smiled at
Maria, who was gathering up the bath bubbles and
putting them on Charlotte's head.

Charlotte broke the silence.

"We went to find Robert, but we got lost," she
explained, with a tear running down her cheek. Mrs.
Oliver ran her fingers through Charlotte's soft black
hair.

"Robert is being cared for a long way from here, but
he is alright. What you need to do now is to promise me

that you will never again go off without telling me. I will speak to Shirley Adams and see if it is possible for you to see Robert if that's what you would like."

A smile from Charlotte and Maria was all that was needed.

Meanwhile, Shirley Adams stopped by the Carmichael farm to let them know the good news. As she approached the house, she saw the door open and Edward Carmichael standing there. He was unshaven and looked tired.

He invited her into the house and as they entered the kitchen where Sam Carmichael was sitting she broke the good news about the children.

She was pleased to see the genuine look of relief on their faces but was concerned that neither of them seemed to be coming to terms with the death of Ellen Carmichael.

Sam, who was perhaps the more engaging of the two, explained that they were looking to move out of the farm house as soon as the lease on the farm could be sold-on.

As for Edward, he slumped in a chair by the table, strewn with unwashed dishes. A quick glance around the kitchen confirmed that these two self-obsessed men were simply not coping with having to look after themselves.

Shirley Adams decided tentatively to broach the subject of how and when Edward was going to engage with the social welfare department about the future of the children. Edward became angered.

"I will make contact with you when I'm good and ready and in the mean time I'll thank you to get on with your job and let me get my life in order." She was shocked by his response but undeterred.

"Mr. Carmichael," she pressed, "let me remind you that the best interests of the children will not be served by you taking this sort of attitude. They are young, vulnerable and in need of constant reassurance from you that you will be there for them when this temporary problem is resolved."

Rising to her feet to affect a degree of authority she concluded; "Surely you would agree that their interests and not yours are what should concern us."

Edward also rose to his feet and approached to within a few inches of her.

"There will be nothing temporary about this situation," he bellowed. "I will not be in a position to take the children back until I marry again, and that will not be for another two years. And even then, I will have to find a place large enough for us all to live....so, until that time, your job is to care for them," he concluded, without a care for the sheer arrogance of his statement.

Shirley Adams was taken aback by the comments.

The social welfare department was alert to the possibility that the children might be in their care for a few months until Edward was more settled. But this was the first time that she had heard in such blunt terms that Edward was likely to disengage completely.

But it was the callous, cold hearted nature of his comments that disturbed her the most. It seemed that Edward held the view that because of *his* circumstances, social welfare had a responsibility to *him* and not the children.

A movement outside the door prompted Edward to see who had arrived. But as he was about to open the kitchen door, Sarah hurriedly entered the room.

"And what's she doing here?" she asked, bristling at the prospect of having to discuss the children once again with the social worker.

Sarah was impatient of Shirley Adams and what she saw as the prospect of having her time with Edward interrupted by discussions about his children.

Skipping the episode about the children's disappearance earlier in the day, Edward repeated to Sarah both the social workers comments and his own reply. The already tetchy Sarah made clear once again her own position about the children.

"Edward and I will marry, hopefully in the spring of nineteen fifty once his divorce from Ruth is complete. We will settle into married life and once that is complete, and we have a home, then.....and only then, will those children be returned to Edward. I'm going to be expected to act as their mother, which I will do.... but not before, and let me repeat....not before I'm married, and we have a home."

And Sarah was not finished.

"And if you expect Edward to give up what little time he has with me to travel to Inglewhite and Preston every week to see those children you can put that thought completely out of your mind."

She turned to Shirley Adams and looking her straight in the eye.

She snapped; "I would have thought that you above all people would accept that the children will be better off not being disturbed by frequent visits from their father. My suggestion is that he tries to see them about once each month visiting the girls one month and Robert the next, that way he doesn't lose contact but he also doesn't get in the way of the people who are looking after them."

Sarah moved to Edward's side and in a now softened voice she purred; "That's going to be for the best Edward don't you agree?" Like a lamb to the slaughter, Edward meekly nodded.

Shirley Adams could see that the dye was cast. She knew that if this couple and these children were ultimately to be reunited as a family, she would need to work with the grain of the evolving domestic circumstances. But she also knew that she would constantly need to remind Edward that his duty.... ultimately was to take back his children.

Shirley Adams left Eastbrook Farm pleased that the children were back with Mr. and Mrs. Oliver but recognising that the Carmichael case had now taken on a completely new dimension. She could see that resettling the children with their father was going to be a long and difficult journey for them all, especially the children.

CHAPTER TWELVE

Following Sarah's uncompromising statement of her own and Edward's position about contact with the children, a form of truce ensued. This would see Edward, and occasionally Sarah visit the children for an hour or so every other month.

As the summer of nineteen forty eight drew to a close, September saw Charlotte being excitedly prepared for her first day at school.

A trip was made to Preston with Mrs. Oliver where a school uniform and shoes were purchased. She was also taken to have her hair cut, all essential prerequisites for the proud presentation of a child to the local school.

Despite the austerity of the times, parents were anxious that their child should not be identified as poor. Then as now, how your child looked on that first day when other anxious parents and children would congregate at the school gates was critical.

Charlotte was excited about beginning school and in the days running up to the first school day she could be found alone in the bedroom trying on her uniform.

But to the observant Mrs. Oliver, it was becoming noticeable that Maria was unnerved by the prospect that her sister would be heading off to school. It was also evident that Maria was now to be found alone in the den and that the children seemed to be less close, and tetchier with each other.

Over tea, on the evening before Charlotte would start school, Mrs. Oliver countered the excitement coming from Charlotte by announcing that she and Maria would take Charlotte to school in the morning, and they would then take the bus to the local market in Garstang.

The impact was positive, and both children went to their beds full of excited anticipation for the day ahead.

The first day at the local infants' school took Charlotte completely by surprise. Not being used to the company of so many children and having been for most of her life in the rural setting of a farm, she had experienced very little contact with other children.

Arriving at the school gates and seeing the other small children clinging pensively to their parents only served to increase the worry and fear of what lay ahead for Charlotte. She too began uncharacteristically to cling tight to Mrs. Oliver, and as they reached the point when she needed to go beyond the school gates, the tears began to run down her face.

Maria picked up on Charlotte's emotions, and she too began to cry, imploring Mrs. Oliver to let Charlotte go with them to Garstang.

But displaying the strength of character that would see her through her future life, Charlotte wiped her eyes on the sleeve of her coat. Making sure that she was not seen by the other children, she said goodbye to Maria and Mrs. Oliver and strode purposefully alongside her new teacher, prepared to face whatever lay ahead for her.

As Charlotte entered her brave new world, so Maria found herself in the unfamiliar setting of being without

Charlotte and in her view, entirely alone, and she didn't like it. The four hour round trip to the market at Garstang was taxing for Mrs. Oliver as she began to see a side of Maria she had not seen before.

While there had been examples of silliness on the part of Maria in the past, she had generally used Charlotte to set the behavioural context for all situations when they were together, and for the most part, this had made Mrs. Oliver's job that much easier.

The children had been extremely good, and apart from the time when they had decided to go looking for Robert, they were a delight for Mrs. Oliver to care for. Now, without Charlotte to set a behavioural compass, Maria was proving to be a real handful for Mrs. Oliver.

Their trip had been difficult and while Charlotte adjusted quickly and positively to her new school surroundings, Maria for most of the day until Charlotte came home from school was naughty and ill behaved.

Mrs. Oliver no longer had the support and advice from regular visits from the social worker who by now regarded the placement as sound and had not dropped by for some weeks.

Mrs. Oliver discussed Maria and her changed behaviour with a neighbour who saw nothing out of the ordinary remarking that she wished her two children were as well behaved as these two.... alone or together.

Mr. and Mrs. Oliver, who had one grown up son, currently based in Germany in the army had previously only fostered one child at a time, and those had tended to be children between the ages of eight and ten years of age. Having two energetic young girls around the house was proving to be challenging for Mrs. Oliver, but stoically she persevered.... never sharing with Mr. Oliver her growing misgivings.

A routine of sorts began to emerge whereby Edward and Sarah would arrive at Fellside Farm about once every two month to take one child for a couple of hours, usually into the country or the nearby towns or villages.

The insistence on only having one child at a time came from Sarah, who claimed that one of the children having the undivided attention of their father was preferable for the children themselves. In truth, she was playing games.

Sarah found it hard to share Edward's attention with the children and to humour him had agreed to these *short* visits on the understanding that she too had a trip out.

It was also becoming clear that Sarah, whose ultimate role would be to become a 'mother' to these children, could hardly engage one at a time let alone two or all three. But more concerning, she was also displaying the kind of power-play games that would become her coping strategy later in the lives of these children.

The trips out in Edward's car were looked forward to by the girls, but they never knew until the day which of them would be taken out. The pretence always employed by Sarah was that they would choose which of the girls to take based upon where Sarah had decided they were going on that day. The child left behind was abandoned to cope with the sense of absolute rejection as well as the absence of their soul mate to comfort them; a cruel combination for such young children.

But the girls soon recognised that falling out with each other over who was going out with their father was futile. There quickly developed a private conversation between the two of them when they knew that their father and Sarah were due to visit.

On the morning of the visit, they would both excitedly dress, and then one would ask the other as they saw their father's car entering the farmyard: " *I wonder who's in favour today.*"

They would rush to the front door and wait expectantly and excited but knowing that the excitement would fade quickly for one of them.

And as Sarah stepped from the car one of the children would be utterly ignored, and the other warmly called over, embraced and taken away.

The sister left behind would never reveal the impact of Sarah's decision. She would simply wait until they had left the farmyard and return to the bedroom, change out of her best clothes and eagerly await the other's return.

These visits continued but with rather less enthusiasm on the part of all involved. Being taken to the countryside on a cold winter's day was far from what either the children or Sarah wanted.

Thus, the visits tended to be no more than a trip to a local tea shop for tea and cakes and a swift hand over to Mrs. Oliver before Edward and Sarah moved on to somewhere warmer and more convivial.

~

December saw Edward move from Eastbrook Farm to a small flat in the Deepdale area of Preston.

This move coincided with Sam Carmichael also moving-on. He was still finding it hard to cope without his wife, and worryingly his whereabouts were unknown for some time to Edward or any member of the family. But Edward's preoccupation with Sarah meant that his father's deep depression didn't even register.

Sam Carmichael left Lancashire and wandered the country in search of work, staying for a few weeks anywhere where there was a job. He lived in bed and breakfast accommodation and cut a very lonely, distant figure to those who employed him for his varied skills and those who came into contact with him. He turned to drink in the hope of neutralising the sense that everything that was remotely dear to him had gone.

For Sam Carmichael, this dark period of his life was spent utterly alone.

In the period since Robert had been taken into the childrens home, Edward had visited only once. Sarah accompanied him, but upon seeing the inside of the institution, with its lingering smell of stale food and sweaty bodies, coupled with the long dormitories which housed twenty or more boys, she left before even setting eyes upon Robert.

Edward's visit lasted little longer, given his obsessive concern for Sarah's wellbeing.

Edward spent a few minutes with one of the many priests who ran the orphanage and was taken to a small room where Robert was waiting. The twenty month old boy was nervous and confused. While he recognised his father he neither recognised him as a father or as someone who cared.

As Edward moved towards Robert, he recoiled as any child would from a relative stranger. He stood upright and to attention as an enlisted man might when a senior officer entered the room. Robert was not frightened; rather, he was pensive and uncertain about how to engage someone he was expected to be fond of, even to love.

But there was nothing between these two people both of whom were playing out a part they felt ill at ease with. Both sought nothing from each other, and both gave nothing. The emotional gulf between Edward and Robert was symbolised as much by the fact that they sat at some distance from each other as it was by the complete lack of contact.

Edward asked after Robert's health in much the same way he might greet a relative stranger; Robert didn't answer. Instead, a soft voice with a distinct Irish brogue replied from the shadows of the room.

"The boy is healthy and eats well Mr. Carmichael so have no concerns in that regard." The response came from Monsignor Monaghan, the priest, nominally in charge of the younger boys section of the orphanage.

The towering authoritative figure of the Monsignor was instantly identifiable by the red lining on his cassock.

"He is now old enough to understand what's right and wrong, and we ensure he does. He can be naughty, and we will punish him where this is seen to be appropriate, but we certainly won't let him give voice to his unruly side," he reassured Edward, being careful to ensure that Robert was in direct eye contact.

Another figure also emerged from the shadows, introducing himself only as, "The Diocesan Bishop."

His entry into the room prompted Robert to spring again to his feet. The tiny figure rushed toward the Bishop, knelt and dutifully waited for the hand of the Bishop to be held out for Robert to kiss the signet ring.

Robert returned to his seat only when dismissed by a slight movement of the hand from the Bishop.

Robert remained silent throughout.

He sat on the edge of a large wing back chair nervously anticipating any instruction that may come from the Bishop or Monsignor Monaghan. He never once looked towards his father and Edward only briefly glanced in Robert's direction.

As the conversation began to come to an end, Monsignor Monaghan turned to Robert.

"So what do you have to say for yourself boy?" he enquired. There was no response from Robert other than to spring to his feet and stand nervously to attention.

"There, you can see the makings of a good boy Mr. Carmichael…. attentive and silent unless he needs to say anything."

Monsignor Monaghan was impressed by Robert's response and with the merest gesture from him, Robert ran towards the door to leave.

"Do you have anything to say to your father?" he asked. The answer, as Robert left the room bowing towards the Bishop was a simple and sad…"No."

Edward was to leave the childrens home that day, only returning on a handful of further occasions during the years in which Robert was placed there.

Edward's ability to place his own interests, or perhaps more correctly, Sarah's interests above the needs of the children would baffle the social welfare department. They were struggling to chart a course that would see these children being reunited with their father for some years to come.

~

In the meantime, Edward and Sarah were very much the young couple in love, taking every opportunity to be together going to the cinema, the theatre and in particular dancing.

Their carefree singleton lifestyle drew little comment except from those who knew Edward well, and they were scornful. But that only served to speed up the distancing by Edward of such people in favour of those who knew little of their past. Sarah and Edward were to most of their new friends, people with a future and no past.

The evolving story for the new found friends was one of tragedy; a father with three 'orphaned' children who was eager to get them back as soon as Edward and Sarah were married.

Sarah basked in the portrayal of her as a modern day saint willing to marry and take on a readymade family at some sacrifice to herself. The narrative was only to build and grow, and the perceived future sacrifice began to take on biblical proportions.

CHAPTER THIRTEEN

The winter of nineteen forty eight and early forty nine, though not nearly as harsh as the previous year, proved to be a struggle for Mr. and Mrs. Oliver. There were regular snow falls over the Pennine Hills, and the freezing temperatures outside meant that for the most part, the children needed to be entertained indoors.

This was beginning to become difficult for Mrs. Oliver, who, alongside her parenting duties to the children, also had responsibilities to the farm and her husband. She slowly began to find the challenge of coping with the constant demands of the two boisterous and active young children was affecting her health.

Mr. and Mrs. Oliver decided that it was time to discuss their concerns with Shirley Adams their assigned social worker for the children who they had not seen for some months. They were unsure about what they would say, but they were sure that they needed, to be honest about the burden the two children were now becoming on Mrs. Oliver.

It was agreed that Mrs. Oliver would telephone Shirley Adams the following day when the children were playing and out of ear shot.

By now, Mr. and Mrs. Oliver had managed to get a telephone installed at the farm though for the time being this was a *party line*.

Today, the prospect of sharing a telephone line with a neighbour where every time you sought to use the telephone it might be in use by your neighbour would be unacceptable. Even more unacceptable would be the prospect that the neighbour could listen in on your telephone calls should they so wish.

But, in the trusting and polite society of the late nineteen forties, a simple, 'I'm sorry,' would suffice, when one party picked up the telephone to make a call to find the other was already on the line.

On the following morning when the children were playing in the kitchen, Mrs. Oliver, still somewhat fearful of the telephone went into the small living room and rang the social welfare department, asking nervously to be put through to Shirley Adams.

Unfortunately, Mrs. Oliver, who believed that it was necessary to speak loudly on the telephone, alerted the children to the fact that she was on the phone which was very much a novelty to everyone in the house.

The children, who were always interested in the conversations of others, stood by the part open kitchen door where they were able to hear Mrs. Oliver clearly in the sitting room.

At first, they were unaware of who she was speaking with but quickly, a glance from Charlotte to Maria said it all; she was speaking to Miss Adams.

Alert to every word, they overheard Mrs. Oliver ask; "Mr. Oliver and me need to speak with you quite soon about the girls; are you able to come over to the farm this week?"

Charlotte drew Maria to her side and putting a finger to her lips implored her to be quiet.

There was obviously something said by Miss Adams before the children heard; "No, we need to see you this week it's urgent, and it can't wait."

The girls froze.

But they then realised that the telephone call was coming to an end.

They heard Mrs. Oliver saying, "I will see you tomorrow morning then, and we will get Tom Masters to entertain the children in the barns so that we can talk in confidence."

The children were momentarily frozen to the spot. They had developed an antennae that would immediately signal any shift in the equilibrium of their lives, and they were now on full alert, and concerned.

They heard Mrs. Oliver approaching the kitchen and immediately rushed back to the table where they had been drawing. But now, instead of one of them at each end of the table, they were sat so close, that it was immediately obvious to Mrs. Oliver.

"Are you alright you two, you look as though you have seen a ghost," she said, noticing that Maria was now even closer and pulling nervously on Charlotte's sleeve.

"No, we're fine thank you," came the less than convincing response from Charlotte.

With that, the girls excused themselves on the pretext of needing to get something from their bedroom.

Once there, and when they were satisfied that Mrs. Oliver could not hear them, they squatted on the floor between the two beds. Occasionally they peered like Meerkats above the beds to ensure nobody had entered the room, and they began their examination of why Mrs. Oliver had asked to see Miss Adams so urgently.

Their immediate thought was that one or both of them had been naughty. They forensically examined their conduct over the past few days and with an understandable bias they determined that it couldn't possibly be that.

They wondered if Daddy was coming to the farm to see them, but eliminated that on the basis that Mrs. Oliver wouldn't need to speak urgently on that subject either.

Charlotte mused if there was going to be another war, but neither could answer that question, and so it too was dismissed.

And then, with alarming clarity, Charlotte whispered, "She wants to get rid of us. Perhaps we *are* too much trouble, or perhaps we eat too much, or perhaps we don't do enough around the house."

Their speculation was brought to an abrupt halt when the figure of Mr. Oliver could be seen in the doorway.

"What are you two scallywags up to?" he asked, clearly oblivious to the deeply concerning conversation the girls were having.

The girls went back to the kitchen for lunch each looking for the merest sign of what might be wrong. But what they found was, if anything a rather less anxious Mrs. Oliver and a somewhat more attentive Mr. Oliver.

It was clear to the girls that an answer to their question was not to be found around this table.

After they had eaten, they put their warm coats on and retired to their den in the garden to ponder and further explore the many, and often bizarre possibilities only to further depress their already anxious minds.

Their day went slowly as they used every moment alone to examine further why Miss Adams was being called to the house.

That night, and not for the first time since their arrival at the farm, Charlotte and Maria insisted on climbing into bed together. At any other time, the sharp eyed Mrs. Oliver would have taken this as an indication that the girls were upset about something, but she missed the signals.

Preoccupied by her thoughts for the following day, Mrs. Oliver said her goodnights and left the room.

The whole household slept poorly, awoke early and assembled as usual in the kitchen as Mrs. Oliver set about her morning routine of cooking porridge and a hearty fried breakfast for everyone.

This being the February half term break; the children were at home together and would, therefore, take on light chores, which they generally enjoyed. Slightly out of character, Charlotte suggested to Mrs. Oliver that she and Maria might wrap up warm and go and let the chickens out and at the same time see if there were any eggs for collecting.

With this agreed, they ran from the house to be greeted by the semidarkness of the winter morning and a severe frost.

As they walked across the farmyard, they could hear the familiar sound of Tom Masters whistling in the milking parlour.

The chickens, particularly the cockerels were already noisy and ready to be let out, and Gertrude the pig could be heard grunting contently in her warm sty beside the milking parlour where she would certainly stay until the sun was up.

The children's thoughts were immediately drawn to the prospect of the meeting Mr. and Mrs. Oliver would have today with the social worker, and that they would be looked after by Tom Masters while this meeting took place.

They swept into the milking parlour and were immediately spotted by Tom Masters, who was busily wiping the teats of the next batch of cows to be milked. He was, as always thrilled to see the girls...but to see them at this hour.....he was somewhat taken aback!

"I thought you were going to be with me later in the morning," he shouted over the noise of the milking machine. Charlotte smiled at Maria and began to quiz Tom about what he had said.

Realising that he had probably said something he shouldn't have, he compounded it by revealing more, under pressure from intense questioning by Charlotte.

"Mrs. Oliver wants me to look after you while she sees the social worker, and that's all I know," but that was all the children needed.

The secret service would be proud of Charlotte's interrogation skills, having educed in minutes enough information to now legitimately return to the kitchen and interrogate Mrs. Oliver.

Forgetting the original purpose in leaving the house earlier, on her return empty handed, Charlotte was immediately sent back into the farmyard to open up the chickens and look for eggs.

But on Charlotte's return, Mrs. Oliver was looking sternly at Maria.

Turning abruptly to Charlotte she snapped, "I understand that you and Tom Masters have been having a conversation?" she asked as the sheepish Maria looked on.

Unaware that Maria had already confessed to the conversation with Tom Masters *and* that they had also overheard the telephone conversation the previous day, Charlotte began desperately to try to dig them both out of the hole they were in.

Mr. Oliver came to the rescue.

"Yes, we are going to see the social worker to discuss your futures. You have been here for some time now, and we want to discuss what happens next," he said, rather hoping that the icy impasse might be resolved by being straight with the girls.

A rather worried looking Mrs. Oliver passed off the opportunity to add further to the comment other than to say; "Shirley Adams will be here at ten o'clock and yes we have asked Tom to keep an eye on you while we have a '*confidential*' conversation with her."

Stressing confidential a second time she looked sternly at Charlotte making sure she knew she was not to listen in again to their private conversations.

The children were sent down to the barns with Tom the moment that Shirley Adams arrived, looking rather concerned and not even waiting for her customary chat with the girls.

Charlotte looked back at the house as the group entered and closed the door. Taking Maria's hand, they reluctantly went with Tom.

After no more than about twenty five minutes, the children heard the sound of the car leaving and ran into the farmyard to see it speed off in the direction of Preston.

Charlotte and Maria were called back to the house as though nothing had happened. They anxiously looked for signs to reassure themselves but, apart from a call to lunch at twelve o'clock, all was as though nothing had happened.

The children examined the events of the day that evening in the privacy of their bedroom and surmised that indeed; all was as normal......but it was far from normal.

Meetings with Shirley Adams and the familiar routine of Tom Masters looking after the children was to be repeated twice more that week before, ominously, on the following day, another car arrived, and two people emerged. That car was followed by yet another as the girls were being taken on the familiar journey down to the barn by Tom Masters.

The children recognised the last car to arrive and its occupants. It was their father and Sarah. These were worrying signs for the ultra-sensitive children whose survival instincts had developed well over the past year.

Nothing could now persuade them from the belief that there was something very serious going on. Indeed, for Charlotte, her memory swiftly went back to the day her grandmother had died and her sense of utter confusion.

She spent the morning anticipating the very worst with great foreboding.

Two and a half hours later, and with the arrival of yet another car at the house, and after many trips to the barn door to look to see if anyone was coming to fetch them, the girls heard the sound of voices approaching.

The first to enter the barn was Mrs. Oliver, holding a small handkerchief to her nose looking extremely distressed and uncomfortable.

She was followed by Mr. Oliver, who was also looking awkward and ill at ease as he signalled that the children should follow him back to the house.

Tom Masters sensed that all was not well and as Maria passed him by, he touchingly stroked her worried face.

"Twill be alright my dear," he said; but how wrong he would be.

The children entered the house where they found Shirley Adams the social worker, another lady and a man sat at the kitchen table looking pensive and quite obviously avoiding eye contact with the girls.

They also saw their father and Sarah, whose only acknowledgement of their arrival into the room was a weak smile before they turned to look at the officials sat at the table.

Maria immediately rushed to Charlotte's side and began to cry uncontrollably, and so she might.

Over the course of the next ten minutes, Shirley Adams clinically set out for the girls that they would be leaving Mr. and Mrs. Oliver's home the next day. She explained it was time for the children to move on and that they should spend tonight saying their goodbyes, thanking Mr. and Mrs. Oliver for looking after them and packing their few belongings together.

There were no explanations just facts; clinical unadorned facts. The usually sensitive Mrs. Oliver was also avoiding eye contact as she occasionally glanced at the isolated figures of Charlotte and Maria clutching onto each other, tearful and afraid.

What the children were not to know was that the moment their father was drawn into the conversation about the children's future, their fate was to take a surprising and very unusual direction.

~

Having established that Mrs. Oliver could no longer cope with the two children, consideration was given by the social welfare department to finding another foster family who might immediately take both children. This proved difficult but was considered to be a possibility.

However, Edward was having nothing of this. He was increasingly concerned to separate the children suggesting that two different Catholic childrens homes, one in the suburbs of Preston the other on the outskirts of Lancaster should be approached to take the girls. He arrogantly dismissed the established wisdom that the girls should be kept together, instead arguing that the two girls were becoming overly dependent upon each other and that this was holding them back emotionally and developmentally.

So persuasive was his argument, supported by Sarah's influential contacts within the Catholic Church that the social welfare experts were won over by the immediate and permanent solution being offered to *their* problem.

The Catholic Church was able to move with remarkable speed when faced with the prospect of *embedding* The Faith in these recently converted children, and within days, places were made available in the preferred childrens homes.

And so it was that these two confused and shocked young children would spend the following hours packing their few belongings and trying to reconcile in their own way what was happening to them.

Coming to terms with the news was not helped by Mrs. Oliver, who every time she saw the girls rushed away in floods of tears to deal with her emotions. She felt that she was the architect of this terrible catastrophe and guilt, combined with a genuine love for the girls left her heartbroken.

The night was long for everyone, but it eventually gave way to a cool and misty dawn.

The household rose and set about addressing the tasks of the day as though this day was to be as normal as any...but it was to be far from normal.

Breakfast was taken in an uncommon silence, interrupted by the occasional attempt by Mr. and Mrs. Oliver to see positives where they frankly didn't exist.

It was hard for the girls to acknowledge the feeble attempts from Mr. Oliver that they would be better off by moving-on.

"You'll be able to meet new friends and be in the company of lots of other children," he insisted, as he poked and prodded the tobacco at the bottom of the bowl of his pipe.

The girls were far from convinced when they were perfectly happy with their current life and friends.

Understandably, any attempt to suggest that there were positives were simply shrugged off by Charlotte and Maria. They had by now developed a deep mistrust of Mr. and Mrs. Oliver, the people from the social welfare, especially Shirley Adams, and most of all...... sadly, their own father and Sarah.

The girls returned to their bedroom after breakfast where they waited until they heard the sound of cars in the farmyard.

Without a word said, they carried their few personal possessions down the stairs and into the hallway.

A tearful Mrs. Oliver greeted the deeply emotional children and kissed each child, as Mr. Oliver looked on not knowing what to say or do.

They gathered their emotions, and all four strode purposefully toward the cars in the farmyard.

Shirley Adams stepped from one of the cars into the chilly mist and beckoned Charlotte to her side. Dutifully, Charlotte took a couple of steps towards her and turned expecting Maria to be right behind her.

It was at that precise moment that Mr. and Mrs. Oliver and Charlotte and Maria were to realise that the children were heading off in different cars to different destinations.

Shirley Adams, impatiently gestured once again for Charlotte to join her, but by this time Maria, Charlotte, and a protective Mrs. Oliver were locked together as Mr. Oliver sharply intervened.

"Why are the girls being taken in different cars, are they not going to the same place?" he enquired, by now becoming red faced with anger.

This was a genuine enquiry as he and Mrs. Oliver had not been privy to any of the detail relating to the plans for the children, except to be told that they were going.

Shirley Adams' voice was drowned out by the officious and superior intervention from her evidently irritated colleague.

"Now, now," she rather patronisingly interjected. "Your role as foster parents to these children is at an end, and it is for us to take the children and place them as *we* see fit."

"I repeat, are the girls not going to the same place?" questioned a now very angry and protective Mr. Oliver."

The second social worker became visibly angered at her authority being questioned and moved toward

Maria, wrestling her from the grasp of Mrs. Oliver and Charlotte.

"You madam are going with me to Allenby, near Lancaster," she snapped grabbing Maria by both arms, " and I'll take no trouble or tantrums."

Pointing to Charlotte, she continued; "And you young lady can stop your crying and be a little more grateful that there are people out there who are prepared to look after you. You are going to a very nice childrens home and will go to a convent school nearby. There, you know everything," she spluttered, by now bundling the distraught Maria into the car.

Further tussles and protestations were futile; the fate of these children was sealed as the calm of the morning was infused by the uncontrollable emotions of Charlotte, Maria, and Mrs. Oliver.

Even as the cars were leaving, the children could be heard screaming.

That was to be the last direct contact Mr. and Mrs. Oliver were to have with these children.

CHAPTER FORTEEN

Charlotte arrived at St Agnes childrens home for girls an hour later, an emotional wreck. She had long abandoned her protestations, and her will to fight was broken.

She stepped from the car quietly and was led obediently by the arm through the ornate wrought iron pedestrian gate and down a long straight pathway towards the imposing building that was to become her home. The path was bordered on both sides by Rhododendron and Laurel bushes that cast deep, dark, frightening shadows.

As every step was taken towards the large double doors of the childrens home, so the sheer size of this rural grey-stone, Victorian building imposed itself upon the small child inside Charlotte.

Charlotte could see that the main orphanage building had an equally imposing second, adjoining building and attached to that was a single spire church which beckoned the good folk of Preston to its daily services.

To Charlotte, now fully indoctrinated into the Catholic Faith, the spire was the ultimate symbol of supreme authority on earth and a place to be feared.

"You'll be seeing the inside of that church on a regular basis," quipped Shirley Adams, picking up on Charlotte's fixed gaze as they neared the front door of the orphanage.

A sharp pull on a bell cord and Charlotte could hear footsteps slowly approaching the door from within. The turn of a key on the other side of the door and the creaking of the door being opened revealed a slim, young postulant nun.

"This is Charlotte Carmichael; I believe you're expecting her," announced the social worker as they were beckoned into a large, shadowy hallway.

The nun seemed to communicate through simple hand gestures as she ushered the pair into the hall while closing and locking the entrance door behind them. She silently glided passed them and was soon lost in the darkness of this foreboding hallway.

As they stood waiting, apparently for someone to *clerk* the young Charlotte, she glanced around the cavernous hallway.

Wherever she turned, wherever she looked, she was confronted by symbols of the Catholic Church. Paintings of religious icons adorned the walls, and three statues held pride of place in the centre of the hallway.

The first and largest was that of a kind and comforting Christ with children at his feet. On a plaque were the words; *'Suffer Little Children to Come Unto Me, for of Such is the Kingdom of God.'* Alongside this was a statue of the Virgin Mary holding the baby Jesus in her arms and alongside that, was a statue of St Agnes, the patron saint of girls.

To Charlotte, these almost life-size figures were terrifying, looking down on her as though they saw into her very soul, and she feared that they didn't like what they found.

After waiting for some time, a door opened, allowing a shaft of light to penetrate the hallway. The young postulant emerged from the shadows and genuflected as the Mother Superior walked towards Charlotte.

The Mother Superior was a person who would be difficult to age but certainly she was in her late sixties and someone who clearly commanded and expected unwavering respect and attention. She received both from all present.

"You have been crying girl......I don't tolerate crying that's for the weak. Jesus never cried, did he? And look at the suffering he went through," she urged with the authoritative and commanding voice of an archetypal Mother Superior. Charlotte trembled; Shirley Adams trembled, and the postulant.....well she seemed to tremble constantly.

"You are a fortunate young girl to have a father and a future step-mother who have the foresight to place you in God's hands until you can join them when they are married. You won't like St Agnes's.....none of the girls like it here, but we're not placed on this earth to like things. While you are here, you will serve God by being good, clean, tidy, quiet, and obedient, devout and if you are all those things you will not incur my wrath."

She completed her well-rehearsed monologue by drawing herself close to Charlotte and bending very slightly in her direction to be sure her words were clearly heard.

"And, if I have to speak to you for being naughty in any way, I will punish you....mark my words," she menacingly threatened; "now take her away and clerk her," she snapped at the still trembling postulant.

The young postulant was joined from the shadows by another nun, Sister Benedict. Charlotte was taken from the side of Shirley Adams, the only person she knew and her last link with her father and family.

In the blink of an eye, Charlotte lost her identity as a daughter, sister, a niece or member of a family and became a *boarder* at the orphanage, a place she would now call home for many years.

Clerking was an undignified experience for Charlotte, one in which all of her few possessions were taken from her.

Her treasured two dolls were taken from her grasp.

"We don't have things of our own here, we share.... so mind that you heed this rule quickly, or you will be in trouble before the day is out," she was warned, as the dolls were discarded into a box along with others.

Charlotte's few clothes, neatly packed in a small linen bag were also taken and would be reunited with her later in the day when one of the Sisters had sewn a label into each. Each label carried the name, *Carmichael*.

Underwear, socks, handkerchiefs, hair ribbons, gloves and hair clips were not labelled; these were regarded as being for the use of any girl.

As with all institutions, there were endless formal rules. But there were also the less formal, but equally important social and hierarchical means by which the home functioned.

Firstly, the children were categorised.

There were *orphans*; formally defined as having no parents, but further refined by the orphans themselves as those the home was *really* there for. They were the highest status children especially in the eyes of the orphans themselves.

Then there were the *boarders*; seen by the home as being there until a parent took them back. Some of these children were daughters of a very sick parent, others of a parent currently serving a period of time in prison.

The orphans saw boarders as imposters, not worth getting to know because they would be leaving soon, but most particularly they were seen as privileged. Privileged, because occasionally they had family visitors, and some were even taken out for trips by their family.

Charlotte was a *boarder* and would carry that ignominious label for the rest of her stay in the home.

Finally, there were the *Bastards*. The children could spot them a mile away, perhaps because of the distain the Sisters, and the clergy had for them; perhaps because they really were different. But more than anything, they were distinguishable because they were singled out for the deepest indoctrination by the ever present, all pervasive priests. They had the Catholic welfare of everyone to care for in the childrens home.....Mother Superior, the Sisters, the Orphans, the Boarders and yes, the Bastards.

Routine in this institution was seen as the way that idle hands were prevented from falling into those of the Devil. From dawn to dusk there were routines from bed making, washing, and bathing to laying the refectory table, dish washing, cleaning, sewing, and mending. And when those routines were complete.....there were always Catechism lessons and Mass.

The children were brought up on a rich diet of religion; not a religion you were drawn to but one you were sent to. It was a religion that cast all other religions aside; drumming into these young minds that even to walk across the threshold of another religion's church would bring down the wrath of God.

Inclusive, interdenominational religious tolerance was unthinkable in the late nineteen forties, particularly in a Catholic Church that saw itself as superior to all others.

Sunday in the orphanage was a busy day.

At eight forty five the children were walked in single file the short distance from the landmark childrens home to the adjoining church. Several pews at the very front of the church were reserved for the orphanage children. From this vantage point, they fully participated in a full Latin Mass with Catholic hymns and a fire and brimstone sermon.

The children were taught the many Latin responses that dominated the Catholic Mass, and as they progressed in years, they were expected to be able to recite them from memory.

Also, as they were 'Confirmed' into the Church, one of the seven sacraments through which Catholics pass in their religious upbringing, they were expected to take Holy Communion at any Mass they attended. This meant that because of strictly enforced fasting rules, there would be no breakfast...a particularly punishing routine to these ever hungry young girls.

But there were also the Holy Days of Obligation when once again the girls would be trooped to morning mass at seven o'clock before dashing off to school at eight thirty with their buttered toast, wrapped in brown greaseproof paper to be eaten hurriedly before their classes began.

Sunday lunch was perhaps the most relaxed and cheery meal for the children.

Dressed in their 'Sunday best,' the children sat at the large refectory tables, always in strict age order. A table monitor directing the children who fetched and carried the food to the table and cleared away afterwards.

Reflections always followed lunch. This was a time when the children were expected, to be exceptionally quiet, regardless of age and when they were always asked to consider the importance of this, the holiest of days and how "God's mercy" had made them so fortunate in life.

The afternoon was always spent in Sunday school that was held in the Nun's Chapel in the small convent building.

The schooling was a mixture of teachings from the Catechism, learning the meaning behind the Ten Commandments and the singing of hymns. Sunday school was entrusted in its leadership to the older girls but always under the watchful eye and tutelage of one of the senior Sisters.

Patronage was the currency in the home. As children became older and wiser so they realised that good patronage from the senior nuns provided access to untold benefits.

The children were wily and resourceful and realised that to be seen by the orphanage hierarchy as willing and compliant gave them access to additional food, occasional sweets, the first choice of clothes and less arduous duties. Conversely, the naughty, wilful and disruptive child would have nothing and would find life until they were compliant very unpleasant.

~

The childrens home where Maria had been placed was St Theresa's. The imposing building was constructed in the Victorian era in the tiny village of Lune Meadows, in the tiny hamlet of Allenby, now an outer suburb of Lancaster. The two institutions were operated in much the same way, but St Theresa's was considerably smaller.

The children who were of school age would attend the City Cathedral School but in all other ways, the way of life was the same.

But Maria was nowhere near as resourceful as Charlotte, and this, coupled with a rebellious streak and her exceedingly sensitive nature saw her frequently bullied. She was often blamed for the wrongdoings of others and regularly being scolded by the nuns.

How life had changed for these small children.

Their personalities were now shaped by an institutional lifestyle and regime, and that essential ingredient of growing up, a sense of belonging was gone as were love and compassion.

Whist, the children, were cared for, and their wellbeing was uppermost in the minds of their benefactors, the once burgeoning happy, individual personalities were now being manipulated and shaped.

But the most important change for Charlotte and Maria was that they had lost each other, and they were losing touch with their father, and their brother, Robert.

CHAPTER FIFTEEN

A year has passed, and it is now February nineteen fifty. The previous year had seen Charlotte, and Maria settle into a semblance of normality in the environment of their respective childrens homes.

Like so many children in the care system at that time, they had showed remarkable resilience, displaying few outward signs that their new lives as boarders at the childrens homes near Lancaster and Preston was impacting them adversely. The characteristic stiff upper lip of the time had rubbed off on these innocent children to the point that normal emotions were utterly suppressed.

But the girls yearned inwardly for each other. Their memory of Robert their brother was now a fading image of a baby they loved and who once shared a bedroom with them at Eastbrook Farm, which was also a distant memory.

Charlotte had just celebrated her sixth birthday. But birthdays could hardly be described as celebrations in an institution.

Hardly a week passed without at least one child being brought to the front of the refectory at breakfast where her name and age would be announced.

The one thing every child hoped for more than anything was that they would at least not have to share their birthday with one of the other children.

Having been brought to the front of the refectory, one of the senior Sisters, or if you were *lucky,* Mother Superior would give you a gift.

The gift would always have a religious significance. For example, a child might be given a small, brightly coloured, and heavily embossed devotion card with the picture of today's saint and a prayer for that saint. A small crucifix cross might also be given as a gift from the orphanage, to be placed above the girl's bed at night. Alternatively, the child might have bestowed upon them a rosary, particularly a child of Charlotte's age as she would spend the next year in preparation for her first Communion.

But the gift was never something of a personal nature. In the case of those children with a family outside the home they were encouraged not to give any gifts other than perhaps a 'donation' to the home in celebration of '*God's gift to these young children.*'

Charlotte's birthday had an air of predictability about it as her name was the fifth to be called. As the eldest of these birthday girls, she was given the inevitable rosary and sent back to her seat encouraged to use her year in search of God.

Charlotte and Maria had each seen their father and Sarah on a handful of occasions over the previous twelve months but had not seen each other. Though they longed to ask after their sister and their brother, they knew that to do this would irritate either their father or the still distant Sarah and so they avoided the subject.

Maria, who had celebrated her fourth birthday in the October of nineteen forty nine, had spent a couple of hours on that day with her father and Sarah.

Charlotte, always seen by her siblings as their father's favourite, but certainly not Sarah's, had also spent a couple of hours out on trips with her father and Sarah.

On the last of these visits, she was given the surprise news that in the summer of nineteen fifty, her father and Sarah planned to marry.

~

What Charlotte was not to know, was that her father had filed for divorce in nineteen forty-seven on the grounds that his wife Ruth had deserted him, and abandoned the children. The children had been told that their mother was dead, a terrible lie that would be repeated whenever it was necessary for the children to be placed in no doubt as to the fate of their mother.

While it was certainly true that Ruth had indeed abandoned her children in nineteen forty six and had left their father, what was far from the truth, and an absolute legal prerequisite for the granting of a divorce was that Edward had not seen Ruth during a period of three years following the application.

He had not only seen Ruth in nineteen forty-seven when he took Robert from her but for a short time during the late summer of the same year, they had been seeing each other regularly.

Edward was two-timing Sarah and had tried to string Ruth along, allowing her to believe that there was the prospect of a reconciliation.

In truth, all that Edward was looking for was to have sex with Ruth; something denied him before marriage by the devoutly Catholic, Sarah.

Edward finally managed to bed Ruth at the end of that year.

When Edward was later confronted by Ruth with the news that she was again pregnant, he became extremely threatening, finally revealing his hand that there was never any prospect of reconciliation and that Ruth should once and for all get out of his life; despite the fact that she was pregnant with Edward's child.

This frightened Ruth so much that she speedily left Lancashire in the hope of putting Edward Carmichael behind her.

On the second of September nineteen forty-eight, Ruth was to give birth to her fourth child, who she named Huw.

She was later to return to her beloved Wales, with Huw, and she would mature a relationship with her friend from childhood, Dai Evans, who was twenty years her elder and also escaping a fraught marital relationship.

Dai took Huw as his own immediately, as Ruth returned to the close knit village of Senghenydd in Wales. Some years later, they would cement their relationship by becoming life partners moving to live together when they bought a house in Bridgend. They also became business partners in the motor trade, becoming well known in the town.

Dai would later become the father to five children with Ruth before his death in December nineteen sixty two.

CHAPTER SIXTEEN

News that Edward and Sarah were finally to marry brought excitement to Charlotte and a renewed hope that she may one day move out of the childrens home and be with her father again.

But once again, Edward's secretive nature resulted in him telling Charlotte not to tell anyone, with the threat that if she did, the prospect of her becoming a bridesmaid at the wedding would be withdrawn.

And so it was that Charlotte held secret the news of the planned marriage until, one day in May, Charlotte was hurriedly taken from the childrens home to a house in Prince Street in Preston by Edward and Sarah. Here she was told that she was to be fitted for a bridesmaids dress by Sarah.

Sarah had previously worked as a trainee seamstress from the age of fifteen to the age of eighteen in a large department store in Preston and was, therefore, a competent seamstress. However, on the one or two occasions in the past when Charlotte and Maria had been given something to wear that Sarah had made, the children were less than impressed. While the tailoring itself was good, her choice of material and design for children left much to be desired.

On one occasion, before the girls had been taken to the childrens home, she delivered to Fellside Farm identical white and blue polka-dot dresses with a vivid yellow sash at the waist and with a large bow tied at the back.

The children disliked the dresses intensely, and when asked why they were never seen wearing them, there was always the same answer, "they are in the wash."

As Edward brought the car to a halt outside number thirty-seven Prince Street, Charlotte was immediately struck by the utter greyness of the surroundings.

Prince Street was long and narrow with terraced houses on either side. The road rose steeply to the crest of the hill where the car was parked and at this point, all that Charlotte could see were further terraced houses stretching out before her.

The road itself was cobbled and as Charlotte stepped from the car she could hear the unfamiliar sound of clog shoes on the pavement. Small children were running up the street in their clogs to see the still unusual sight of a car in their street and investigate what was going on.

Charlotte's senses were also bombarded by the smell of cooking emerging from the open front doors of the houses where women could be seen 'stoning' their front door steps, something Charlotte had never seen before.

Donkey Stones were used to rub a coloured edge onto the stone doorstep and were given to the householder by the rag and bone man in return for whatever he collected from them.

The Donkey Stone, so named because of the trade mark donkey imprinted on them, came in a variety of colours. As Charlotte looked along the street, she saw an array of wonderful colours on the edge of the steps providing a proud and warm entrance to each home.

The pride with which the housewife stoned her step and washed the pavement in front of their home marked her out in a street of people who had very little except the pride of knowing their home was clean and their welcome was honest.

Charlotte noticed that in contrast to every other house in the street whose front door was open wide, the door to thirty seven Prince Street was closed.

Sarah skipped from the car to the house and slipped a key into the lock. As the door opened, she could be heard calling; "It's Sarah mother, I'm here with Charlotte and Edward."

Charlotte was surprised. She had imagined from all her grand airs and graces that Sarah was on the verge of nobility, and yet here she was living in a terraced house in what was clearly a working class and poor neighbourhood of Preston.

The entrance hall was narrow and dark with a door to the immediate left of the front door leading to the living room. There was also a door through which Sarah was walking that led to the kitchen and on the right were very narrow stairs leading up to the bedrooms. There was a continuation of the dark greyness from the hallway into the rest of the house which felt cold and unwelcoming.

As Charlotte was ushered to the kitchen, she was met at the doorway by Sarah's mother with her arms crossed across her chest, and a rolled cigarette wedged between her lips with at least half an inch of ash waiting to fall from it. Her hair was hidden beneath a head scarf which was rolled into a knot at the front. She wore a wraparound apron and to complete the ensemble; she was wearing faded and well-worn slippers with holes in the toe.

Charlotte was shocked by the sight that confronted her and to hear that this considerably less polished figure was Sarah's mother.

But Charlotte was consumed by the sight of a small girl, standing on a kitchen chair, silhouetted against the light flowing into the kitchen from the window.

"So you're Charlotte are you?" asked Sarah's mother, brushing the ash from her jumper. "You must be hungry, all children are always hungry.... your sister was hungry when she arrived, and she has nearly eaten me out of house and home," she joked, gently placing a hand on Charlotte's shoulder and guiding her into the small kitchen.

As Charlotte entered the kitchen and her eyes adjusted to the light, she was able to see that the slim young girl standing on the chair wearing a calico dress pattern, obviously in preparation for a bridesmaid's dress was indeed Maria.

It had been sixteen months since that traumatic day in nineteen forty nine when the two sisters had last seen each other. They looked at each other now, and with a learnt emotional distance, acquired in the childrens homes they simply acknowledged the presence of each other and showed no other sign of recognition or feeling.

There was none of the feeling and love that so characterised their previous relationship; these two girls were acting as acquaintances rather than sisters.

Sarah's mother was surprised by the coldness these sisters displayed towards each other.

"Well, aren't you going to speak to each other or has there been a falling out?" she anxiously enquired, turning to the girls for some reaction.

"She never came to see me since they sent me to Lancaster so why should she be my friend?" blurted Maria as she shifted her stance on the chair to show her back to Charlotte and the others.

Edward angrily responded trying to defuse a potentially awkward moment.

"Now, now, you two, let's not have any fallings out, you're here to be measured for your dresses let's not spoil the day."

But Charlotte was incensed; "I would have come to see you, but *they* wouldn't bring me, would you?" she said, pointedly turning to face her father and Sarah.

Sarah's mother looked genuinely shocked. She was completely unaware that the two girls had not seen each other, and this only served to add to the condemnation she had previously expressed when she discovered that the girls had been separated and put into different homes.

She was also unaware that the decision to do this lay entirely with Edward and Sarah. But she swiftly moved to defuse a situation that was best pursued on another occasion and outside the earshot of the children.

Putting a gentle arm around Charlotte, Sarah's mother, now with the rest of the cigarette ash having fallen onto her fulsome bosom, moved her to a chair by the fireside.

"Come on Charlotte, let's have a cup of tea and some sandwiches whilst Sarah or should I now be saying 'your Mummy' deals with Maria and then she can measure you."

Charlotte felt the explosion in her head as she held back and forced herself not to say anything as the full glare of her father dared her to do so.

As Sarah busied herself with Maria, oblivious to the now receding tension in the room, Charlotte sat obediently on the chair by the fireplace. As her eyes scanned the room, she could see that it was small but very cosy.

The fireplace enclosed a large black range which dominated the room and at the centre was a coal fire with the kettle now beginning to sing on the iron shelf above. There was an oven to the right and the mantle shelf which was high above the fireplace and covered with a white crochet frill. And above that was a picture of Jesus on the cross with a palm leaf cross left over from Palm Sunday carefully hanging from it.

A further glance around the room with its many icons and pictures of saints only served to confirm that she was in the house of a devout Catholic.

As Maria stepped down from the chair and carefully removed the calico pattern, trying hard not to have the many pins scratch her, Charlotte noticed how thin, she looked. She had remembered Maria as chubby, not fat but certainly not this thin.

As Charlotte removed her dress and stripped down to her liberty bodice in preparation for her fitting, she caught herself in the mirror and was equally taken aback by how thin she too looked.

The childrens homes that Charlotte and Maria were placed in shunned mirrors because, in the view of the Church, they encourage vanity. This was, therefore, the first time the young Charlotte had seen just how thin she looked. While the children ate three meals each day, they were hardly sufficient for active young children, but for any child to suggest they were hungry brought the wrath of the nuns upon them.

And as Charlotte ate her sandwiches and drank her cup of tea with Sarah's mother, hence forth to be called *Grandma*, she was struck by the contrast between the generosity and eagerness of this total stranger to feed her, and the abiding sense that in the childrens home food was regarded as a necessary indulgence; not to be enjoyed or taken for granted.

It was also obvious that Maria, who was sitting down for a second plate of sandwiches, was, frankly, starving.

As Sarah busied herself with the fabrics from which the dresses would be made the children were encouraged to go outside into the back yard to play. This was a very small space but an Aladdin's cave for the inquisitive children.

The yard was surrounded by high brick walls that to the small children looked like a castle's battlements. On one wall were an array hose pipes, a washing dolly, and a washboard and on another wall was a tin bath. And to one side was a dolly tub with steam belching from it like some sorcerer's cauldron.

Sarah's mother caught the children's inquisitive look and immediately came to the back door. She slipped into her clogs and asked; "Do you want to help me with the washing?"

The children suddenly came to life and with great enthusiasm listened intently to 'Grandma' explaining how she used the dolly to agitate the sheets in the tub before they were taken out. There was also great hilarity as she also explained how she and Sarah still used the galvanised tin bath, bringing it into the kitchen every Friday where they would bathe in front of the fire.

The children were allowed out of the rear gate by their grandma to a long rear pathway where they could hear other children playing. But when they entered the company of the local children dressed in their tidy dresses and shoes Charlotte and Maria were immediately mocked as being, 'two-penny toffs,' and as one child put it for being, "posh buggers."

As the other children ran off down the back alley many wearing clogs, Charlotte and Maria walked a short distance to where they found a gap between the terraced houses, known locally as a *ginnel*. The ginnel enabled them to walk from the rear alley into Prince Street and once there they felt they had entered another world.

As they stood on the pavement close to their father's car, they saw immediately in front of them but on the other side of the street, a flat-bed coal lorry delivering sacks of coal to a neighbouring house; this fascinated the girls.

They watched the two strong looking men, who were dressed in dark trousers, a coal blackened white singlet vest, over which was a leather waistcoat, and they wore distinctive heavy clogs. Their bare hands and rugged faces were blackened from the coal dust, but their ivory white teeth sparkled as they laughed and joked with the children in the street.

The girls watched as firstly they would lift a bag of coal from the stack on the lorry, walk to the edge of the lorry and with a smart twist and dip of the shoulders the sack of coal was swiftly emptied onto the pavement below.

After they counted twelve sacks being off loaded, one man jumped down and collected payment in cash for the delivery as the other drove the lorry the short distance to the next customer.

As the lorry pulled away, the fascinated children were able to see the man of the house remove a small metal cover from the pavement into which he began shovelling the coal which disappeared into the cellar beneath the house.

"Eh lass, haven't you seen coal being put down a coal hole before?" shouted the man from across the street, much to the amusement of the passers-by.

"No, we haven't," called Maria as she crossed the street with Charlotte following close on her heels to watch the completion of the job.

As the man swept the last of the coal and dust down the hole and replaced the cover, so his wife arrived with a bucket of water, drawn from the tap in the back yard to wash down the pavement.

The girls were fascinated to watch how quickly she washed away the evidence of the coal delivery. With the cleaning completed, the lady returned into the house as the warm sun quickly began to dry the pavement.

As the girls walked back to the ginnel, they could overhear a group of women at their side of the road speaking about the coal delivery slightly further up the street.

"See that bloody prossy at forty six?" snapped one woman, as she and the others in unison folded their arms across their chests in disgust. "Look at her; twenty bags of coal, no money and they shove it down the hole for her too," she shrugged turning to leave.

"Aye lass, but the way she's *at it* that bloody cellar will be full in weeks," quipped another neighbour, much to the amusement of the assembled company.

The girls found themselves back in the ginnel leaning against the red painted walls, and it was Maria who broke their silence.

"What's yours like?" she asked knowing instinctively that Charlotte would know her meaning.

"It's alright, but the Sisters are not nice, and the food is awful," she replied and in a sentence, their relationship was again restored.

"Mine is the same.....and I never see Daddy what about you?" "

Same," she said as the two of them held hands on their short walk back to the house.

They entered the house to a hive of industry with Sarah and her mother busily cutting out material and deep in conversation about the wedding. Sat in the only comfortable chair by the fire was their father, smoking a cigarette and reading a broadsheet newspaper, oblivious to the conversation or the return of the children.

The room was filled with the grey haze of cigarette smoke, as once again Sarah's mother had a cigarette in her mouth with the ash hanging precariously, looking as though it would drop at any moment. The children had not seen their father smoking before, and it was also something they were unused to in their cloistered world.

"Sarah ....sorry *Mummy*, what's a *prossy*?" asked Maria, innocently.

The ash did fall from their grandmother's cigarette possibly at the same time that she exclaimed, "Where the bloody hell did you hear that word?"

Sarah, momentarily forgetting the original question exclaimed, "Mother....not in front of the children."

Their father sprung from his chair; his half empty cup of tea now evenly distributed between his crotch and his shoes. Charlotte looked at Maria; Maria began to cry and what had been a calm afternoon had now descended into a farce.

"We heard a woman in the street saying that the lady in number forty six was a prossy....is that something like a policeman?" asked an equally innocent Charlotte.

"That's a bad word," cried Sarah, offended by its meaning and embarrassed by its use, "and you mustn't use that word again," she demanded from the bemused and surprised children.

The day away from the childrens home came quickly to an end when Maria was asked to say her goodbyes before leaving with her father to return to Lancaster. The attempt by Sarah to show any sincerity in her goodbye to Maria was abandoned despite a genuine caring hug for Maria from Sarah's mother.

Maria's new found grandmother swept her into her arms being careful that the cigarette hanging from her mouth didn't make contact with Maria. Taking the cigarette momentarily from her lips, she kissed Maria on the cheek.

"Now you come back to see me again little Maria," she insisted, making it quite clear that the message was intended as much for Edward and Sarah as it was for Maria.

Maria walked towards Charlotte but despite the short time they had spent together earlier, neither could find the thread that would draw them together. The institutions they now lived in and the need for self-preservation in their respective homes was now so strong that despite a small urge to hug each other they could not. In their world, this would be seen as a sign of weakness and to be avoided at all costs.

Maria slipped out of the house to return to her own world and the continued uncertainty about her future.

Once Maria had left, Sarah told Charlotte that she was to go with her back to the childrens home that was a fifteen minute bus ride away.

On their journey to the bus stop, Sarah stopped and spoke to several people she knew, not once introducing Charlotte to them. Even when she briefly stopped to speak to a friend who was walking with her children, Sarah ignored the presence of Charlotte preferring to discuss the latest film in the cinema and the previous week's visit to the Tower Ballroom in Blackpool with Edward.

The protocols of the times dictated that these children would simply not engage each other until they were encouraged to do so by their parents and so they stood there, fumbling with their coats making sure they did not make any eye contact.

Following a silent bus journey, Charlotte and Sarah approached the gates of the childrens home where Sarah stopped. She turned to Charlotte and placed one hand on her shoulder. Looking directly into Charlotte's eyes, her parting comment was simple and to the point.

"If you're good, and I mean good, we will take you out of here for the day of the wedding. But if I hear that you've been bad, you will stay here, do you understand?"

She went on. "And let's be clear on another matter. While I'm not your mother, you must understand that when I do become your stepmother, you will do exactly as I ask of you, and that will include being less demanding of your father's time. Do you understand me, Charlotte?"

Charlotte nodded obediently, oblivious to the subtext of Sara's comments as she reached up to open the gate.

Having turned the large gate handle, she turned to say goodbye only to see Sarah, now some twenty or so yards down the street returning to the bus stop without a backward glance in the direction of Charlotte.

For her part, Charlotte dawdled up the long drive, savouring the sense of freedom in being alone on this warm late spring day.

She lingered by the laurel bushes, stopped to smell the perfume on the early roses and momentarily imagined she was back at Fellside Farm. For all that those parting memories were traumatic; Charlotte had been at her happiest in the loving company of Mr. and Mrs. Oliver.

Charlotte was not to know that in the frenetic discussions that led her to this childrens home, Mr. and Mrs. Oliver had asked the social welfare department if they could broker the possibility of them adopting Charlotte.

Edward was informed and though he gave some serious thought to the offer he had indicated that he would have been considerably more amenable to the suggestion if it had been Maria they wanted. But it was Charlotte that Mr. and Mrs. Oliver wanted, and it was Charlotte who as the first born still had a place in Edward's heart.

Sarah was never to know that her arch rival for Edward's attention and affections might so easily have been dealt with.

CHAPTER SEVENTEEN

Robert was by now three years of age and had spent most of his young life in the care system. He remembered no other way of life and the near absence of visits from his father, particularly in more recent months, only served to deepen his dependency upon the home and the institutional way of life.

But because he knew no different, he was, for the most part, a contented child oblivious to what might have been. He mixed well, had several friends mainly amongst the other *boarders* and was regarded by the home as being obedient and good.

He was, however, a sick child, suffering very acute bouts of asthma that established itself almost immediately after the eczema which he had suffered from birth subsided. When these attacks took place, it was frightening for the young Robert and equally distressing for those around him.

An asthma attack could occur without warning, though the home had observed a particular pattern that would suggest the attacks were clustered around periods of emotional upset and there were also the usual environmental factors, such as the pollen season, exposure to damp surroundings and over exertion.

On the last occasion when Robert had seen his father, he had returned to the home in desperate need of calming down and urgently needing his medication.

Edward, when pressed, by the staff, reported that Robert had been excessively demanding while they were out and had been scolded by Sarah, which he took very badly.

He explained to the disbelief of the nuns that having cried for some time the asthma attack came on aggressively which only served to frighten the young Robert more. On several occasions, this was not helped when Sarah insisted that Robert was simply feigning the attack and should not be humoured.

These terrible asthma attacks were to continue for Robert for many years to come.

Charlotte and Maria waited several weeks before they were advised by their respective childrens homes that they would be taken out for a day to attend their father's wedding to Sarah. Robert, on the other hand, was completely oblivious to the plans for his father's marriage and blissfully unaware that this was an essential milestone in him one day being reunited with his sisters and his father.

On Saturday the third of June nineteen fifty, Maria eagerly awaited her collection from the childrens home to be taken to Preston to be a bridesmaid at her father's wedding. The time for collection was set for eight o'clock in the morning and so by seven thirty, she was dressed and waiting for her father to arrive. She sat pensively in the dormitory she shared with eleven other girls, anxious, excited and concerned that she should not do anything wrong in the eyes of Sarah on this her special day.

As eight o'clock chimed on the chapel clock, the nervous Maria began to worry that her father had forgotten. This was eagerly pounced upon by the other children as evidence that they had indeed forgotten and that she would not be going to the wedding.

Maria was teased unmercifully by friends who were jealous that she would be the centre of attention both here at the home and in a few hours' time at the wedding. But eventually at eight twenty, Maria was quietly called by the Sister to come downstairs. Excitedly, she walked quickly alongside her, being careful not to break into a run.

"Now Maria," whispered Sister Josephine, a favourite of the girls for her soft spoken kind approach and her impish Irish humour, "you must be seen but not heard," she advised the attentive and by now over excited Maria.

"You must be respectful at all times, and you must remember that God has brought your father and your new mother together for a purpose and that His Will is that you will all live happily together in God's grace in a house as a proper family. Don't under any circumstances do anything to upset this happy day....do you hear me?" Maria nodded, but the messages were lost on her.

They passed along the landing and down the sweeping stairs into the hallway. As Maria did so, she was taken aback that she could not see her father where he would usually wait for her alongside the vestibule door.

But at that moment, she was startled to hear; "Maria, it's Granddad; don't you remember me?"

Maria turned and was confronted by an older looking, slimmer, and now balding Sam Carmichael acting as though it were just yesterday that he had last seen her.

Maria recoiled when he tried to draw her close to him, something that initially alarmed Sister Josephine, who, dressed in her all black habit cut a formidable figure in the dimly lit hallway.

Sister Josephine, known for her forthright views on the world outside the gates of the childrens home, believed that Maria would instantly recognise Sam Carmichael and even welcome seeing her grandfather again. She was about to take charge of the situation but stopped.

As Maria looked more closely at the elderly figure, so her memory slowly drifted back to photographs she had seen taken at Eastbrook Farm and the grandfather who, though not close to her, was said by Charlotte to be kind and giving.

Sam once again tried to engage Maria, this time holding out a hand encouraging her to hold it which she did. A few minutes passed, and it became clear to Sister Josephine that Maria was surprised but increasingly comfortable in Sam's company.

As Maria clasped the hand of her grandfather, Sister Josephine wished her well for the day, reminding Sam that Maria must be back at the home by no later than six thirty so that her routine would not be interrupted.

Sam and Maria climbed into a small Austin van which to the inquisitive Maria seemed like Aladdin's cave.

From her vantage point in the seat next to her grandfather, high up at the front, she was able to observe that the cavernous space behind was largely empty except for a suitcase, and a few boxes. Above these was an overcoat and trilby which were neatly hanging on a makeshift hook directly behind Maria.

They said very little to each other on their journey, and what they did say was confined only to the occasional observation from Sam who would point out various meaningless landmarks to the utterly bored Maria.

She was, however, taken by the apparently endless fields of black and white Friesian cows and the occasional flock of sheep. Otherwise, her journey with this virtual stranger, who was taking her to her newly acquired grandmother, in a very strange street in Preston, was utterly tedious.

But then, thinking of the street in which her new grandmother lived, she remembered the conversation that she overheard between the ladies in the street.

"Granddad," she asked inquisitively; "what's a prossy?"

Without hesitation, and certainly without acknowledging who had asked the question, he replied as he might to a work place colleague.

"It's a prostitute......someone who sells her body to men," her grandfather replied, trying hard to concentrate on where he was going as they entered the outskirts of Preston.

"Oh," she replied, in an equally matter fact way, "well, you would think your body was worth more than twenty sacks of coal wouldn't you?" she asked, now absorbed by the busy streets and the people going about their daily chores.

"Hmm, I suppose you're right," concurred the entirely unfazed Sam. And with that, they pulled into Prince Street and stopped outside number thirty seven.

Charlotte's short journey to her new grandmother's house could not match Maria's for the scintillating conversation, and she was in the house already dressed in her bridesmaids dress when Maria and Sam entered the house.

Charlotte didn't immediately see her grandfather and was about to say something to her sister when Sam called to her.

"Well, aren't you going to give your old granddad a big hug?" he asked, taking a step towards the shocked Charlotte.

Charlotte hesitated but could not contain herself.

"Why did you leave us too?" she asked with tears rolling down her face. "Where have you been and why haven't you come to see me?" she cried, now sobbing as the grief and pain of the past two years began to release itself.

Maria moved quickly and instinctively to Charlotte's side as the shocked Sam began to withdraw.

"You have visited all this upon yourselves you Carmichael's, and I have no sympathy with any of you," quipped Sarah's mother as she moved to sweep the two crying children into her arms.

"And by the way, I'm Sarah's mother. And I can see it won't be hard for me to do a better job of being a grandparent to these two than you have done," she snapped, as a stony faced Sarah and a distinctly angry Edward crept in on the tail end of the exchange.

"You know nothing about what I've been through this past two year so keep out of my business," snapped Sam, who by now was making a hasty retreat from the room.

"Been through....been through, you miserable bloody man, look at these two children and ask yourself what they've been through," she shouted, as the ash from her cigarette fell to the carpet accompanied by the customary, "bloody hell."

"Mother, I knew I could rely upon you to spoil my day," blubbered the sobbing Sarah as Edward rallied to her side in a vain attempt to calm his bride to be.

By now Sam was back out in the front street drawing deeply on a Capstan full strength cigarette, actively questioning why he had made the effort to be there.

Sarah's mother had taken the children upstairs into her bedroom, and Edward was left with the unenviable task of placating both Sarah and his father.

By eleven o'clock, Sam Carmichael had been allowed into the house again, invited by Edward to apologise to Sarah's mother which he grudgingly did.

Sarah's mother was now dressed for the weeding and was apologising to no one!

The children were not moving from their new grandmother's side which meant that despite constant requests to moderate her language, she was cussing and swearing at anything that either Edward, his father or her daughter did that didn't meet with her approval.

Having received what passed for an apology, from Sam and having been calmed and mollified by Edward, Sarah was now the centre of attention, an attention she would revel in over the coming few hours.

The car to take Sam, Edward and Sarah's mother to the wedding arrived. Without a word said out of place, Sam elected not to use it deciding instead to drive himself and Edward in his van to the church.

Sarah's mother, therefore, left the house alone in the wedding car bound for the church clutching her pack of Woodbines and continuing to mutter disapproval even as she closed the front door behind her.

As she stepped into the black wedding car, trimmed with white ribbon she drew the attention of the near neighbours who pointedly stuck their noses in the air as one of them called; "Look at lady muck there, mother of the posh bride with all her airs and graces."

She laughed and called back, "I ...but she'll bed tonight as a virgin, more than can be said for your two."

The street banter continued as she glided down the street waving to all as though she were the Queen herself.

Sarah's father had died several years earlier and so rather than being escorted down the aisle by someone else, she chose to make the walk alone.

Charlotte and Maria, the two bridesmaids, had strict instructions to look down and manage Sarah's veil as she looked up and out to the congregation gathered to witness the veneration of this young woman of the parish to a position of near sainthood.

She was keen to be seen as giving her life to caring for a new husband and three children, and, as she would never be able to have children of her own, this was indeed a big commitment.

Sarah looked every bit the beautiful virgin bride she was, dressed in a full length wedding gown in the purest of white materiel, trimmed with lace and exquisitely edged in hand sewn beadwork.

Their marriage was solemnized in her Catholic parish church before God, her family and for the most part their friends.

The ceremony and the wedding breakfast that followed fulfilled the glittering expectations of the young and beautiful Sarah. She had eventually secured the marriage she so dreamed of.

Sarah was indeed a beautiful young woman whose great deportment enabled her to sway slowly down the aisle at a half beat pace, milking the *princess* moment for all it was worth.

She looked stunning which she knew, and as she eventually caught the eye of the expectant Edward she coyly smiled as though to say, 'I'm now yours.'

Edward's thoughts as he prepared to make his marriage vows returned to the commitments he also made to Sarah before he left the house for the church; to always remember that he should place her needs above those of his father and the children's unless they were ill or in danger.

"I'm marrying you for you, not those children," she forcefully insisted, "and remember that Edward Carmichael." These were her parting words as she sent him on his way to the church, firmly establishing where the power would lay in their marriage.

The wedding was every bit the triumph Sarah had planned. Her sister and husband were there alongside her mother, and that was the extent of her family. Her friends amounted to fifteen people she had worked with but who were not close friends.

For Edward's part, his father was there along with Aunt Dorothy and Aunt Matilda, who were deputed by Sarah, to inspect the children constantly to ensure they were presented well and were well behaved.

A similar number of friends were invited by Edward, and again these were nothing more than acquaintances.

Both Edward and Sarah had shed friends as they devoted their time exclusively to each other. But there was also a keenness on their part to develop themselves as people with a future and no past.

Having people from their past who could fill in the gaps for their new found friends was not something they wanted to happen. Their past and the circumstances that had led to the three children being in separate childrens homes complicated the new narrative they were both so anxious to develop.

The wedding reception was held in a local hotel. Guests were entertained to a buffet as Sarah circulated amongst them, in between the endless photographs with the prescribed groupings of family, family, and friends and with the children.

Rapidly, boredom set in for Charlotte and Maria, who found refuge in the cloakroom where they sat in a window seat watching the comings and goings in the street outside while eating sausage rolls, vol-au-vents, fish paste sandwiches and Victoria sponge cake.

They chatted about their respective childrens homes, their friends and the wedding guests they liked and those they didn't care for.

Neither of the girls could see the enormity of what was happening that day and the implications it would have on their future lives. What mattered most, and they were told this constantly, was that they didn't scuff their white shoes or get their bridesmaid's dresses dirty!

Absorbed in their own world, and as detached as they could possibly be from the wedding, they were suddenly disturbed by Aunt Dorothy and Aunt Matilda whose sharp eyes had seen the girls retreat to the cloakroom earlier.

Apart from a momentary hello outside the church as they left for the wedding breakfast, these two Aunts had hardly registered the fact that they too had ignored the children in all the time they had been in the childrens homes.

Aunt Dorothy asked Maria to go with her on the pretext that Sarah was apparently looking for her for yet another photograph. As they left, Aunt Matilda saw the dejected look in Charlotte's eyes.

"The problem you have Charlotte," she began, sitting down alongside her; "is that you look too much like your mother, and that will never do. Your mother had the same colour hair, the same facial features and dare I say the same mannerisms. And remember; Sarah knew your mother, and every time she sees you, she sees that woman. And every time she sees you with your father, she sees him with that woman."

The six year old Charlotte understood every word.

"Where is mummy Aunt Dorothy?" she asked, by now fearing that she had again broken the golden rule not to speak of her.

"You ask too many questions Charlotte that simply can't be answered," she replied, looking sternly at the inquisitive face of Charlotte. "One day...maybe when you are older, you will begin to understand that bygones should be bygones and things like this should be left in the past."

Charlotte was about to speak when she felt the gentle finger tips of Aunt Dorothy touch her lips.

"I'm not proud of my part in all of this Charlotte, and perhaps my best gift to you is to be your friend. And as a friend, and your Aunt, listen hard to me young

Charlotte; don't ever get between your father and Sarah, and don't ever mention your mother in front of either of them…do you hear me?"

As they rose and walked back into the reception, Charlotte met the full glare of her new mother penetrating her mind and soul to understand what had passed between Aunt Dorothy and herself.

But despite the promise of friendship, Aunt Dorothy would not meet Charlotte again until she eventually left the childrens home some years later.

By four thirty, the children were being taken back to Prince Street to take off their beautiful dresses, and like Cinderella, get back into their day clothes, a poignant symbol and a reminder of their place in this complex life.

By six, o'clock the fairy tale was over. Charlotte and Maria were back in their familiar worlds leaving behind the few hours of princess existence, the company of other people and what little family they had.

Today had seen the children replace a maternal mother who had abandoned them with a self-obsessed stepmother who was far from maternal and who in truth didn't like them. She would ultimately care for them but would never love them.

And Charlotte, who was a constant reminder of Ruth, her mother, would never forget the warning and the caution from her Aunt that the burden of looking like her mother would have on her in the years to come.

CHAPTER EIGHTEEN

Throughout the years from June nineteen fifty when Edward and Sarah married, through to the summer of nineteen fifty two, they lived the lives of newlyweds; carefree and without responsibility to burden their lives. They lived in Edwards's flat in Deepdale, Preston and became a thoroughly modern couple, each going out to work in highly regarded jobs.

Edward was a very capable engineer and through a series of restless moves had progressed upwards in his career ambitions and was now beginning to earn the salary that went with the middle class life he had imagined for himself and Sarah.

For her part, Sarah was back in the couture business, working as an assistant manager at a well-respected fashion house in the centre of Preston.

Their joint income supported a post war lifestyle of cinema, dancing and the occasional meal out that could only be dreamt of by many of their contemporaries. They were also saving money for the deposit to buy a house, but they were unconvincing in this regard when confronted with their responsibilities for the children by the social welfare department.

Several meetings had been called by the long suffering social welfare managers and staff and begrudgingly Edward, who was occasionally accompanied by Sarah, attended. Edward's demeanour was always the same;

belligerent, uncompromising and that of a victim. When asked when he could be expected to resume his responsibilities as a father to provide a home for his children, the response was always the same; "I will take them when I have a home large enough for the three of them….and not a moment before."

This arrogant attitude annoyed the social welfare department who had gone much further with the Carmichael's than could reasonably have been expected.

But now they were faced with the significant problem that the childrens home in which Robert was housed, was pressing for him to be moved on as he was now about to attend school and they needed his placement for younger children. This finally galvanised Edward into action.

Edward and Sarah had long decided that Preston held too many links to the past with ghosts and memories that needed exorcising. Their preference was to live in the Lancaster area, close enough to visit Preston but far enough away that some of the more challenging questions would not follow them.

Edward, an already secretive man, was obsessed by the need to keep up the pretence that Ruth was dead, not just in the minds of the children but also symbolically to please and placate Sarah. Even two years into their model marriage, any reference to the past that might have links with Ruth, would spark Sarah into a rage, underpinned by an insecurity that began to surface regularly which saw many arguments.

These blast furnace rows, marked by their heat and intensity were pure theatre; staged by Sarah and always with predictable outcomes.

Sarah's insecurity needed feeding with commitments from Edward to increase the time he gave to her and assurances that she was the centre of his universe. These assurances were always accompanied by a need to know that he was not seeing another woman.

The onset of a row was always predictable, preceded by a short period of moodiness in which Sarah would ignore Edward unless he lavished her with time, gifts or both, and was always followed by a period of intense closeness on her part towards Edward.

Sarah always felt that Edward was cheating on her, an obsession that never seemed to have the underpinning evidence. But between the rows they were happy and attentive towards each other but wary of the impact having the three children in their lives would have on their firebrand but deeply loving relationship.

Sarah was a deeply complex person, riven by personal insecurities about her body shape, image, and her appearance. She craved attention and increasingly needed to be told that she stood out from her contemporaries as the beauty in the room. In truth, she was a beautiful woman and very much a head turner. But this was insufficient, and her ego needed constantly feeding.

In her work, she was defined by her fashion sense, her subtle use of makeup and her refined style. In the burgeoning post war local fashion industry, she was the face and figure of the future to the women who brushed with her world.

For many women, theirs were lives shaped by being homemakers with no status; no independence; little or no money; endless house work; parenting and endlessly pandering to the needs of their misogynistic husbands.

For those women who were fortunate enough to have jobs, many worked in local weaving mills in noisy unglamorous roles. On weekends when they were able to 'window shop,' these hard working women were able to peer into Sarah's world and only imagine what it might be like to look and dress as she did.

And when Sarah came into contact with these very real people, she was contemptuous; using her experience of being able to better herself as a blueprint that others could and should copy.

~

In the June of nineteen fifty two, with Edward having secured a good job in Morecambe, he and Sarah moved into a house in the outer suburbs of Lancaster. The arrangement they had with the owner who was trying to sell the property, was that they would rent it for three months with the option to buy it, a practice that was not unusual at that time.

The property was a three bedroomed semi-detached house, in the southern suburb of Southmead on the outskirts of Lancaster and now seen as a fashionable place to live. This was very much a step up to upper middle class living for Edward and Sarah.

Fuelled by the need to be successful and be able to demonstrate the material trappings of success, this house met all their every needs.

By the January of nineteen fifty three, they purchased the house and began to furnish it slowly.

While Edward was happy in his job in Morecambe; Sarah knew that she would need to work locally to help towards the mortgage costs and the increasingly expensive middle class lifestyle they had adopted.

Edward had purchased a newer more reliable car to go to work, and there was the need to budget for the expense of having the children come to live with them.

Sarah quickly found a job in Lancaster working as a designer and buyer in a women's fashion shop. For Edward, this was the necessary turning point for considering bringing the children to live at the house; there were two wages; a modest size house with a garden and *good* neighbours.

But in truth, the social welfare department were exasperated by the years of prevarication and were now openly discussing a deadline for the return of Edward's children or they would start proceedings for their adoption.

At the age of five, and having experienced a short period in foster care and almost four years of institutionalised life in a childrens home, Robert was the first to be brought to the new family home.

Plans were made for a date when this would happen and in the weeks before he was due to leave the home, Edward and Sarah would spend a couple of hours with Robert to attempt to rekindle a relationship that had been all but non-existent in the previous years.

It was evident in the first of these meetings that Robert was apprehensive when in the company of his father; an authority figure with whom he had no relationship. But, Robert was already savvy enough to work out for himself that he needed to make these meetings work.

Sarah also tried hard, and slowly a relationship was built though Robert was wary and fearful of crossing a line that might see him loosing favour with both his father and Sarah.

When in their company his eyes would constantly dart between each of them, as he sought to reassure himself that what he said and how he said it found favour with them both.

Robert was finally told that he was to move out of the childrens home the week before he was to be collected by Sarah. When told, he was cautious in his reaction, having seen this process with other children many times before. He had seen children wild with excitement only to find that their day passed by, and their adoptive parent would not show up. He had also see boys returned to the home within weeks when their new parents couldn't cope.

In the late July Sarah travelled by bus to Preston and collected Robert from the door of the orphanage.

Like a character from Dickens, he stood there in faded short grey trousers and an off white shirt that was far too large and with a collar that was frayed from constant washing. He wore a grey neck tie, a remnant from the school he had been temporarily attending and the school blazer that also looked far too large. He wore grey calf length socks and a pair of sandals that were old and badly scuffed.

His dark black hair was neatly parted on the left, and his nose had a reflective glow, evidence of having been washed down ready for the handover. His brown eyes ringed with dark lines beneath the eye lids looked sunken in his cherub like face, reflecting the years of broken sleep and the worsening asthma. Under his arm, Robert carried a small box of personal items and a package of clothes.

Robert knew only that he was going to Daddy's house with Sarah, who he now must call Mummy. He was unaware if this was a trial visit or if he was to stay with this woman and his father. Robert placed enormous trust in this near stranger as he strode purposefully down the pathway away from the childrens home, and into an unknown future.

He endured a difficult bus journey from Preston to Lancaster being sick on several occasions until the bus eventually left the suburbs of Preston and set off along the main trunk road to Lancaster.

Sarah faced the challenge of Robert's motion sickness by simply stepping away from him and shouting, "Stop... please stop will you?" much to the amusement of the other passengers.

But the bus conductor stepped in, wiping Roberts face and reassuring him.

"Don't you worry lad," he quipped, "the way your mother's looking I'll be wiping her pretty face in a moment and giving her a squeeze." The passengers roared with laughter as Sarah squeamishly returned to the seat next to Robert.

It should be no surprise that Robert was motion sick. In all his time at the childrens home, he had never been out on a bus trip and had only travelled in a car on one or two occasions and then only for short journeys.

Buses were also poorly ventilated and old. The suspension was either too soft causing the bus to wallow or too hard resulting in passengers being sprung from their seats whenever the bus hit one of the many potholes in the road.

These journeys were also lengthy, not always caused by the number of stops they made, but largely because the bus simply didn't travel at any speed. They were slow and very uncomfortable but for many, they were the only means of travel apart from trains that often offered the same slow, uncomfortable characteristics and were generally more expensive.

As the bus settled into its journey and passed through the suburb of Fulwood, neither Sarah nor Robert were to note the significance as they passed Sharoe Green hospital. It was here in nineteen forty seven that Ruth gave birth to Robert. She was later to become very unwell, and Robert was to be united with his father and the sisters who knew nothing of his existence.

The bus trundled along through the villages of Broughton and Bilsborrow and on to the market town of Garstang.

Between taking fares, the conductor attempted to distract Robert from the nausea by encouraged him to name any makes of the cars that they passed.

"That's a Vauxhall Wyvern, and over there is an Austin Six," rambled Robert, with an encyclopaedic memory that fascinated the conductor, and the few people sat around them.

"So where did you learn so much about cars?" asked a lady sitting opposite, "does your daddy run a garage or something?"

Sarah suddenly tuned into the conversation, but she was too late...far too late. Politely, and in a courteous voice Robert replied.

"I'm not awfully sure what Daddy does; all I know is that I'm going to live with him and..." Robert paused for a moment while he ordered his thoughts and words, "and this lady who is now my Mummy is taking me to meet him."

Head's turned as everyone on the lower deck of the bus attempted to make sense of the information, but Robert was there to help yet again!

"You know, I'm a *boarder* at a childrens home, and I think they are letting me go. So you see.....I'm awfully excited, and perhaps that's why I'm throwing up so much."

The conductor looked at Sarah, looked at the bewildered onlookers and tapped Robert on the head.

"You'll do lad," he said, giving a sideways glance and raising his eyebrows to the passengers, who were quietly gossiping in whispered tones.

Robert was by now standing to attention saluting the passing AA motorcycle and side car, and he leapt for joy as the AA man smartly returned the salute.

Sarah and Robert left the bus after a journey of more than two hours, both grateful for the fresh air. But their journey wasn't over yet. They faced a fifteen minute walk to Lodge Drive during which there was no conversation other than the repeated, "Are we there yet?" coming from the ever more bored and tired Robert.

Sarah had no idea how to entertain a bored little boy and didn't even hold his hand. Instead, he meandered behind her stopping to speak to anyone who would engage in conversation, or simply stopping to look at a parked car or a child playing in a garden.

But he also couldn't walk fast because his already challenged breathing simply would not allow his body to move any quicker.

Eventually, Sarah turned to Robert and triumphantly announced; "Well now Robert, there is your new home."

But Robert was considerably more impressed and preoccupied by his own achievements, having managed to kick the same small stone from where they had stepped from the bus to this point. He certainly was not going to be distracted from his challenge by what looked like a perfectly ordinary house that looked like all the other houses they had passed on their dreary walk from the bus.

As they approached the modest house on the corner of Lodge Drive, a tree lined road of similar brick built semi-detached properties; Robert became increasingly excited but not before he bent down to pick up the stone and place it in his pocket.

Looking up, Robert could see that the house had double wooden gates at the head of a short driveway leading to a garage; a rarity in the nineteen fifties.

Fewer than three million of Britain's fifty million people owned a car though a car was one of the most aspirational purchases of Britain's growing middle class. But a new car might easily cost the equivalent of what a person earned in a year. However, a house with a garage was seen by the car owning Edward as marking it out as superior to others in the street by being the only property of its kind.

The house also benefitted from a very large rear garden because of its location on the corner of the street completing the must have's on Edward's middle class list. The symbolism that gates could be closed meant that Edward would be able to keep people outside his secretive and private world.

The rear of the house also overlooked a large expanse of common land with a gate from the garden providing access to an essential shortcut pathway that led to the city. The large rear garden was laid mostly to lawn but had apple and pear trees along the boundaries on both sides which themselves were defined by six foot high privet hedges.

A magnificent espalier of copper beach formed a separation between the recreational part of the garden.....the lawns and shrubberies nearest the house and the vegetable garden on the other side.

There was also a small brick built garden tool shed attached to the rear of the single garage, an essential place to escape from domestic chores for the less than modern man.

The interior of the nineteen twenties brick built, bow fronted property included an open plan living and dining room with a door leading off into the very small kitchen and pantry and another leading into the hallway.

A ceramic tiled open fireplace formed a central focal point to the otherwise featureless living space. The floor covering was a dark linoleum which bore the evidence that many stiletto heels had walked across it over the years. The indentations formed a distinctive pattern leading from one doorway to another and were almost preferable to the utterly bland expanse of highly polished flooring.

A window from the living end of the room looked out onto the small lawned front garden with its high privet hedge, creating an effective privacy screen between the house and the street and any inquisitive neighbours or nosy passers-by.

But as if that was not enough to screen the occupants of the house from prying eyes, there were also heavy net curtains at every window doing an admirable job of also blocking out much needed light from an already dark room. A similar window at the dining end of the room looked out over the westerly facing rear garden.

The upstairs had three bedrooms and a bathroom. The large master bedroom looked out over the front garden as did the small single bedroom, and the third bedroom and bathroom looked over the rear garden and the field beyond.

To Edward and Sarah, this property was both a statement of having arrived in the burgeoning world of the post war middle classes, and it was also a sharp reminder of their newly assumed responsibility to provide a home for Edward's children.

In truth neither wanted to step away from the idyllic life of the unencumbered newlyweds and so the house also symbolically noted the end of an era of independence and the beginning of responsible married life.

Robert was taken to the rear door of the house, and as they entered, Sarah stopped and turned to him.

"Now Robert," she started in a rather schoolmarmish way. "When you come into my house, you take your shoes off there, and you hang your coat up there," she insisted pointing to a piece of newspaper on the floor and a hook on the wall.

Obediently, Robert took off his coat and climbed onto a small stool to put the coat on the hook.

"Now look at what you've done," she snapped, pointing to a small piece of dirt on the stool that had come from Robert's shoes.

"I'm sorry...it's my fault," exclaimed the visibly unnerved Robert. "It's my fault," he repeated trying hard to hold back tears as he wiped the cuff of his shirt over the dirt to clean it off the stool.

Robert dutifully removed his shoes and placed them on the newspaper, but not before Sarah noticed the holes in the toes of both socks.

"You're going to have to be more careful with your clothes now that you're living here; money doesn't grow on trees you know," she scornfully commented as she bent down to obsessively straighten Roberts shoes in the obviously well-ordered kitchen.

"Cleanliness and tidiness are important in this house as are respect and doing what you're told, do you understand?"

Robert nodded and again apologised; "I'm sorry Mummy it's my fault, I'm very sorry." He didn't cower, but his demeanour verged on total dejection.

He had learned and had drummed into him at the childrens home that he must obey. He had learned subjugation, and he had also learned that it would be others who would free up his personality, shaping it into what *they* wanted. His personality for what it was came from mimicking the other boys in the childrens home and from reflecting back what authority figures told him they wanted of him.

Robert was by now already worried that the predictions of his less charitable friends at the childrens home that he wouldn't last a week were ringing true.

Apologising, even when you were not in the wrong, was a learnt behaviour and a defence aimed at defusing a situation. The boys had learned that the punishment for owning up to something that you didn't do attracted a swift, sharp rebuke and brought closure. This was much preferable to being treated by authority figures as an unrepentant liar even when you knew you had done nothing wrong.

Sarah moved towards the door that would take them into the living room. Still clutching the bunch of keys she had used to get into the house, she opened her handbag and took out another key which she used to unlock this door.

Seeing a bewildered look on Robert's face, Sarah explained.

"When we are out of the house the downstairs interior doors will also be locked to stop anyone who breaks down the back door from progressing any further into the house; you can't be too safe," she said as she carefully rechecked that the back door was now locked behind them.

Sarah failed to pick up the immediate signs of distress on Robert's face. He had never feared for his safety in the childrens home; the only doors that were locked were the outside ones and those of rooms they were forbidden to enter and now, here he was confronted by fear and the prospect of burglars and bad people.

They moved into the living area, and Robert was struck by how tidy and ordered everything seemed. He looked quizzically at the highly polished oak dining room table and the small vase of roses perfectly placed at the centre. As they passed by a petal fell, and almost before it landed Sarah was there to pick it up and take it to the kitchen.

While she was briefly out of the room, Robert took the moment alone to look around the rest of the room in what for him was his first experience of being in a *real* house; a home and the place of dreams for his contemporaries in the childrens home.

The room was sparsely furnished with the table and six chairs at one end beside the window overlooking the garden, and two lounge chairs and a small sofa were arranged around the fireplace. In the corner of the room was a large piece of highly polished furniture which to the inquisitive Robert, resembled a rather uninspiring box. Robert couldn't start to imagine what was inside the roll fronted doors.

It was, in fact, a television, something that was a rarity still in the homes of the nineteen fifties and also something that Robert had not seen in his cloistered world at the childrens home. And it would be some months before he would get the opportunity to view a programme on the television as both Sarah and Edward saw the one channel television as something for adults and not children.

In the other corner of the room was a standard lamp with a large brightly coloured floral lamp shade. Otherwise, the room lacked any personality; there were no pictures on the walls, no photographs and only a handful of ornaments on window sills and the mantelpiece above the fireplace.

The linoleum floor covering was a familiar sight to Robert, but he was not used to walking on carpet which he swiftly skirted around as he walked past the fireplace and moved towards the big piece of furniture for a closer inspection, but was stopped in his tracks.

"You must not touch anything in this room; remember that this all cost hard earned money," commanded Sarah, who by now had unlocked the door into the hallway and was ushering Robert through it.

They went through the small hallway and up the narrow stairs with its slightly threadbare runner carpet on the centre of the treads and on reaching the landing Robert was urgently guided to the bathroom.

"Now there you are...go in there and go to the toilet," Sarah urged, as she gently pushed Robert through the half open door, "and don't forget to put the seat down," she reminded him.

The concept of toilets with seats was entirely new to Robert, who was used to a toilet that had two narrow strips of wood moulded onto the porcelain pan, making for uncomfortable ablutions in what were always cold lavatories.

Robert didn't want to go to the toilet but decided to dawdle in the bathroom to look around. Once again, he was struck by the tidiness. There was a mirrored cabinet on the wall out of his reach that looked interesting....and on the window ledge, there were two glasses each with tooth brushes standing proudly in them. There was also a rather interesting mirror that hinged out from the wall.

Looking around Robert saw there was a large bath, and as his eyes looked up the half tiled wall, he was taken aback by the sight of a shell shaped bracket on the wall hanging from which were several pairs of Sarah's nylon stockings.

Robert had not been in the regular company of women in all his six years, so these flimsy stockings intrigued him. He guessed they might be stockings because he had seen a film where the baddies wore them over their heads, but still he was unsure.

"Are you finished in there Robert?" called Sarah, "I haven't heard anything yet; have you *been*?"

Robert quickly flushed the toilet, ran the tips of his fingers under the tap water and decided to wipe them on his shirt rather than disturb the towels that were neatly folded over the rim of the bath.

Robert was taken along the short landing past a bedroom on his left where he saw two single beds. Sarah moved him swiftly along and pointed to the next bedroom door.

"This is the bedroom where me and your daddy sleep and as you can see it is locked and will always remain locked. You and your sisters will never go into this room.....do you understand me, Robert?"

Robert nodded; to him, this was probably the norm for people who lived in houses, he was more interested in the door facing him which he worked out was where he would sleep.

Sarah opened the door and showed Robert in.

The room was very small, previously used as a box room in what was ostensibly a two bedroom house. To Robert though it looked like a den, a place to be alone, a place where for the first time in his life, he would sleep on his own, and he relished the thought of this.

The room which was above the hallway and staircase had a small bed, a tiny wardrobe, and a large shelf which boxed in the slope of the stairs that rose beneath the room. The window overlooked the street outside which was immediately of interest to Robert as he saw a car come down the street.

"That's a Morris Minor you know, and they were first made the year after I was born," exclaimed the excited Robert, who had certainly not captured a similar enthusiasm in Sarah.

Sarah paused in the doorway, bemused by the unrestrained excitement of Robert, who knelt on the bed peering through the window eagerly naming even more of the makes of cars as they passed by.

"That's a Vauxhall Wyvern, and that's a Triumph Mayflower; I've only ever seen one of those before, but I know I want one when I grow up," enthused the knowledgeable Robert.

Sarah found the unguarded enthusiasm of Robert a complete surprise which she found even endearing.

"That's a Bond Mini," exclaimed Robert. "My daddy used to own one of those, and this is a new Austin A Thirty; it's from Preston because it has an RN registration."

Sarah leant against the door frame for several minutes, enthralled by Robert's excitement and her momentary connection with this little boy who she hardly knew.

Sarah left Robert in his bedroom with instructions to remain there until his father returned home from work in about an hour.

Robert looked around his new bedroom and was happy. To him, this was a dream come true and despite the size of the room and its sparseness, he was content. He was rather less enthusiastic, though, with the picture of Jesus on the wall, overhung by a set of rosary beads and the familiar catechism placed by his bed. This was too much of a reminder for Robert of the childrens home he had only just left, but still, it was infinitely better.

Robert remained at the window, idly watching the comings and goings of people walking along the street.

He imagined where they were going and where they had come from. He saw men in long raincoats wearing trilby hats and carrying a briefcase walking with purpose on their way home from their day's work. He saw the occasional children walk by, and as they did so, he waved from the window but received few responses. But occasionally, an adult, noticing his disappointment would enthusiastically wave which thrilled Robert.

At about six o'clock Robert saw a large black Hillman Fourteen saloon car carefully negotiate its way into the driveway with his father at the wheel. Robert knew the car well as the Monsignor at the childrens home could be seen driving the same model.

Despite Robert's enthusiastic waving from the window, his father didn't acknowledge his presence and simply stopped the car in the driveway and went out of sight. Robert could hear the sound of the garage doors being opened and assuming his father was going to park the car he dashed down the stairs with the aim going outside to greet him. But Sarah was having nothing of this.

"I made it clear to you earlier that you were to stay in your bedroom until such time as I called you downstairs; now go back and wait there," she snapped, very obviously angry. Robert did as he was told and with a shrug of the shoulders he dragged himself back upstairs.

As he slowly climbed the stairs, he could hear his father in conversation with Sarah and decided to sit on the top step of the stairs to hear if he was in trouble. Their quiet conversation continued for fifteen minutes or more before Robert heard the handle of the living room door turning a signal to slip back quietly into his bedroom.

There was an expectant silence until the door to his bedroom slowly opened. There, framing the open door stood his father.

Robert's emotions were confused.

Though his contact with Edward had been limited, Robert nonetheless had an emotional connection. However, the urge to run to his father and embrace him was suppressed; in part, because he had never done this and perhaps more importantly because the invitation from his father was simply not there. Robert felt the need to show gratitude, but even that emotion was not strong enough to move him from the spot where he was riveted.

They looked at each other for a little while before Edward broke the silence.

"Well, now Robert, this is your new home, and I hope you like it. Your sisters will join us very soon, and we will all be very happy here won't we?"

Robert nodded believing this to be the right thing to do.

"And before we go down stairs, you and I need to talk Robert, don't we?" questioned Edward.

Robert was at a loss as to quite what to say or do. His father looked stern, and Robert was scouring his mind to recall what he might have said and in particular what he might have done wrong.

"I'm told by Mummy that you have been naughty already. And what's this about you waving to strangers as they pass by the house? This will never do; this simply will never do. They are strangers, and we don't wave at or talk to strangers, do we?"

Robert once again nodded.

"And when Mummy tells you to do something, you do it without question don't you Robert?" Once again, the confused Robert obediently nodded tears welling up in his eyes.

Robert's thoughts were simple. Here he was, on his first day in his new home, in trouble with his father and his new mother, and hovering over him like the sword of Damocles was the ever present prospect in his mind that he would be sent back to the childrens home.

Robert was a child who dwelt upon things; constantly evaluating if he was being good, or bad, or if he was simply in the wrong. His nervous disposition and his deep sense of wanting to please made him vulnerable to those who would exploit his innocence and his deeply felt fears.

He was about as vulnerable as a child of six could be.

But, despite the guidance from the social workers that they would need to treat Robert with great emotional sensitivity, Edward and Sarah chose to orientate him quickly to *their* needs of him.

This became a journey of strict discipline where neither of them acknowledged the emotional rollercoaster Robert was on. They could not see beyond *their* needs and their obsession that once the three children were living in *their* home, they should integrate into *their* way of life, without any quarter being given to the trauma that they might be experiencing.

Robert meekly followed his father down the stairs and into the living room. The look of dejection on Robert's face met with the approval of Sarah, who busied herself putting the evening meal on the table.

"I told you to be good Robert and you will, hopefully, learn the lesson that if you are not good, your father will always deal with you firmly once he gets home." The flood of tears so skilfully held back by Robert now ran down his face.

He stood alone, an experience he had never before known. In the childrens home, you at least had the unspoken support of your peers when adults brought you to book.

Robert was directed to a seat at the table.

"This will always be your seat at the table," the chirpy Sarah explained, running a hand through Edward's hair as she passed him by, signalling her approval of how he had dealt with Robert.

The tears ran down Robert's face, but the uncontrollable quiet, subdued sobbing went unnoticed by Edward and Sarah.

The meal was eaten in silence other than the occasional polite conversation between Edward and Sarah about the events of the day. Even comments about the journey Sarah and Robert had taken from Preston, made no concession to include Robert. They ignored the utter despair and continued sobbing from Robert, and they also failed to register that he had eaten little or nothing.

Robert, Charlotte, and Maria came to recognise this behaviour on the part of Edward and Sarah as normal and essential if their father was to placate and humour Sarah. She needed unfettered attention, and seeing the children being chastised by their father was a powerful symbol of her control over Edward.

Robert went to his bed that night tearful and without consolation.

But the following morning he awoke with the memory of the previous evening less painful in his mind. This was hardly surprising when he was enthusiastically embraced by Sarah when he entered the living room at eight o'clock for his breakfast. Indeed, throughout that day and for the several days that followed, Robert discovered that Sarah could be nice if she tried and that he could enjoy her attention towards him even though it was fragile and likely to be short lived.

CHAPTER NINETEEN

Two weeks after Robert arrived at forty five Lodge Drive, he was told that on the following Saturday he, Sarah and his father would go to a childrens home where Maria was living and bring her home.

Robert met the news with mixed emotions. Though wary and cautious about the protocols and tensions in his new home, he was also beginning to settle. He had the feeling that the Sword of Damocles that hung over him; that sense that he could be returned to the childrens home at any time was at least receding. Now he would need to discover what it would be like to have a sister and not just one.....but two.

The Saturday arrived and rather than a palpable excitement in the house, Robert detected an ice cold breeze sweeping through. Sarah deliberately delayed dressing and when dressed, fussed about small unimportant things much to the annoyance of Edward though he contained his feelings, at least to some extent.

It was an hour after they were due to leave the house that Sarah slowly emerged from the bedroom. The more that Edward urged her to hurry, the more that she found yet another thing that needed to be done. This continued until Edward found the right words to placate and reassure her.

He told her that she looked beautiful, that it didn't matter if they were late in picking up Maria and that she should take whatever time she needed. This was all Sarah required to be placed once again at the centre of his thoughts, and she was willing to go to any lengths to achieve this.

Two hours later than originally planned, the three of them climbed into the ageing but large Hillman Fourteen. Robert sat in the back behind the sliding glass screen that separated the driver and front seat passenger from passengers in the rear. The car, though old oozed opulence with its leather seats and wooden interior trim. However, the smell of the leather soon made Robert feel nauseous.

He managed to open the door windows and soon began to feel less uncomfortable, soaking up the late summer warmth and the views on their short journey to the childrens home.

On arrival, Robert was told to remain in the rear of the car and await the return of Sarah and his father. He remained there for more than twenty minutes peering through the sliding glass divider at the instruments and levers on the dashboard and the large steering wheel. He so wanted to slip into the driver's seat, turn the knobs and switches and press his foot on the brake and accelerator peddles.....living out his constant dream that one day he would be old enough to drive.

Robert heard the sound of voices approaching and quickly slipped back into his seat. Through the open window, he first saw Sarah emerge from behind the heavy oak front door of the building followed by his father and then, some paces behind followed the shy, apprehensive Maria.

Though Robert had seen her infrequently, he immediately recognised her. Maria was by now approaching seven years of age and looked taller than Robert had remembered. She was a freckle faced child, with a cherub nose and auburn, almost red hair in contrast to Robert and Charlotte whose hair was a rich dark black.

Maria was crying as she approached the car, and she tried hard to hide this from Robert. As Edward opened the rear door to the car, Maria paused and looked back at the Nun hovering in the main doorway of the childrens home. This seemed to irritate Edward, who tried to hurry the distraught Maria by saying that they needed to leave immediately.

Sarah was far less subtle.

"Frankly, if you like this place so much, we should consider leaving you here, you ungrateful little madam," she snapped.

This served only to upset the sobbing Maria further, and it was only the intervention of the Nun in her black habit and calming voice that finally won the day.

"Maria, you are welcome to come back and see us here and to meet your friends here at any time, and remember that you will see many of the girls when you go back to school in September."

Maria finally stepped into the car her eyes swollen from crying and her face blushing from the embarrassment of causing such a scene in front of Robert.

"Well, aren't you going to say hello to your brother," snapped the now visibly angry Sarah. There followed a rather wooden, "Hello Robert," and, "Hello Maria," from two near strangers as Maria stepped into the car.

Once in the car, they each sat at the extremes of the rear seat with their backs turned to each other where they stayed for the entire journey home.

Maria, unlike Robert, had viewed the prospect of leaving the childrens home with mixed emotions. On the one hand, she longed for that sense of belonging and being part of a real family, but she was also wary of the role that Sarah would play as her step-mother. Maria was also unsure about how she might now relate to Robert, who she hardly knew. Charlotte was older than her, and she wondered how she would get on with her too.

While the childrens home was not a family home, it was *home* to Maria, and its sense of caring, its predictable firm rules, and her many friends had helped Maria to come to terms with this as a way of life and above all, she felt as though she belonged.

The car eventually pulled into the driveway at the house, and Maria perked up a little though remained wary about letting her guard down. Sarah took her through the ritual of unlocking the doors with the same explanations that were given to Robert.

As they walked through the living room and Sarah produced the key for that door, Maria turned to Robert who shrugged his shoulders as though to say,' don't ask'.

As Sarah began to go upstairs with Maria following behind with her two bags of belongings, Robert was instructed to remain downstairs.

Maria was put through the same ritual of being told to go to the toilet which she shrugged off with a curt but firm response. "I think I'm old enough to know when I want to go to the lavatory and at this moment I don't," she smarted still wary and unsure about Sarah.

Sarah passed off this remark as she opened the door to the rear bedroom. Without going in, she pointed to her right indicating where Robert's room was located and then gave Maria the same commentary she gave to Robert about never entering her parent's room.

Maria noticed the lock on the door.

"Why do you have a *lock* on your bedroom door mummy?" she asked, emphasising the words 'lock' and 'mummy.'

She was swiftly pulled into the bedroom that was to be hers.

"Now look here madam," Sarah snapped, "you might be able to get away with your smart quips in that childrens home, but you won't here. I'm your step-mother and at some considerable sacrifice to me personally, and I will not tolerate you questioning me or trying to outsmart me," she snorted.

Maria waited for a moment.

"Mummy," she started; "Mummy, I only asked why you lock your bedroom door because I'm interested. Are there secrets in there that you don't want me to see?"

Sarah went red in the face, holding back her anger sufficiently to make her final warning shake Maria.

"However smart you may think you are *little girl*, remember that *I* rule this house, and *I* say what happens....not your father. I say what you eat, I say what you wear, and I judge when you are good, and I judge when you are bad. Do you understand and do you realise that your future is now in my hands? Get on with me, and I will get on with you; cross me, and you will regret it, do you hear me.....*little girl*?"

Maria was shaken and silenced by the venom in Sarah voice.

All she could do was to drop her head and acknowledge that Sarah was right. If she was to survive the coming years, she knew in an instant that she would need to play to Sarah's rules.

Having set the boundaries, however, unconventional her method, Sarah stepped to the doorway and as a passing and closing remark to Maria she said; "We all have secrets, Maria. One day you will discover all our secrets, but that day will be a long time off and until then, we can at least be friends, can't we?" Maria smiled and nodded.

Sarah's comment about secrets was to become one of many deliberately planted and carefully calculated hints that she would drop over the years; hints that there were indeed secrets and deceptions in the lives of her and Edward that one day might be discovered.

The children became wise to these, never overly probing; never asking for more but always gathering and synthesising the merest shred of new information. The children, even at this early age, knew that everything was not as they were being told it was.

Maria settled quickly but was distinctly wary of doing anything that might be seen as a challenge to Sarah. Deep down Maria was far from happy and was now fretting about the imminent arrival of Charlotte. But in the meantime, Maria was slowly getting used to having a brother and even more slowly, she was getting used to the new rules and routines. More than anything, she found the close proximity of people in what was a small house, quite stifling, feeling that she could never find space and time to herself.

The rules of the house never included closing the bedroom door unless you were changing or sleeping, making a snatched private moment alone almost impossible.

Maria liked time to herself, and in the absence of time in her room she could often be found under a bush in the garden or peering over the wall at the children playing on the recreation ground.

And therein lay yet another rule; not to speak to anyone over the wall. Sarah and Edward were obsessed by secrecy and a need for privacy; constantly seeking to protect themselves from questions that might shine a light into the dark corners of their past.

Maria was also chastised for engaging in a lengthy conversation with the next door neighbours.

The neighbours on the right of the house were a Mr. and Mrs. Monaghan, a fact established by Maria before she was sternly called back into the house by her father. But that was not before she had given her life history in a two minute monologue.

"*My* mummy's dead you know," announced Maria to the attentive and inquisitive Mrs. Monaghan, "and I know she will be in heaven," she said with the conviction of youth.

"My daddy has a new wife......and she is called Sarah, but I have to call her mummy or she gets very angry. My brother has lived here a long time and my sister is coming tomorrow....."

Edward was furious. In an era of polite, reserved distance, when a close relationship with a neighbour was still limited by the formal use of surnames; when a really good neighbour might lend you a cup of sugar when you ran out but would certainly not be invited into the house, such familiarity outraged Edward.

But the damage was done, and any hope that Edward and Sarah might have had of living a private life here in suburban Lancaster was now gone.

On the following day, Maria and Robert slipped out of the house and into the small brick tool shed in the garden.

"Do you know if we're going?" asked Robert.

"No, I don't," snapped Maria, still trying to acclimatise to the incessant inquiring mind of a younger brother. "All I know is that Charlotte is coming to live here today, that's all they have said, and I only know that because I heard Sarah, sorry mummy, say that she couldn't see why *she* should have to go with daddy."

"What's Charlotte like?" enquired Robert, who had no recollection of his eldest sister at all.

"She is bigger than me; I think she is eight, and I think she might be nice, but I'm not sure," responded Maria as though they were discussing an acquaintance rather than their sister.

"Anyway," insisted Maria, "you know what daddy says; you'll know on a need-to-know basis and not before."

With that the wooden door to the small tool shed swung open to reveal an angry and red faced Sarah.

"You're father has been looking high and low for you two, why have you decided to hide in here?"

Robert was about to mount a 'we're not hiding,' defence when a tug on his sleeve and a wary glance from Maria signalled that this was not the right tactic.

"We're sorry mummy; we were just talking to each other and getting to know each other as you asked us to do yesterday," explained Maria, rather pleased with her speed of reaction.

Sarah was unimpressed.

"And that's enough of your *smart Aleck* comments young lady or you'll spend the night in here," she threatened as she hurriedly herded them back into the house, pausing only to brush cobwebs from Robert's jumper and insisting that they leave their shoes on the door step outside.

Once in the house, their father announced: "We are going to Preston today in the car to pick up your sister Charlotte and to bring her home."

Again a sharp tug on the jumper and a wary glance from Maria prevented Robert from saying that he already knew this.

Maria was sharp and wise beyond her years when dealing with Sarah and her father and was already protecting Robert from his own inexperience in such matters.

"I have already told you there is no way that I'm going to that dreary place to collect Charlotte," exclaimed Sarah whose demeanour offered sufficient evidence that she mean it. "Take your other children so that I can have a few hours to myself in the garden," she urged, already finding the challenge of two children taxing enough.

A look of disapproval flashed from Edward and was immediately dealt with by Sarah.

"Don't look at me like that," she snapped; "I'm here aren't I? I'm prepared to look after *them* aren't *I?*" she snapped, "and I would ask you to consider *me* for a moment rather than putting those children first every time."

Edward said nothing but Robert and Maria absorbed everything and once again, uncertainty about his future and the possibility of being sent back to the childrens home was too much for Robert.

Robert, now wheezing badly with an asthma attack slowly walked towards the back door for air; his body hunched over as he tried desperately to get air into his lungs. Maria had heard Robert wheezing throughout the morning but was now alarmed and frightened.

"Can't you do something for him?" she asked, appearing to be the only one present to be concerned by Robert's now alarming asthma attack.

Edward followed Robert into the kitchen and took an adrenalin vaporiser inhaler from the cupboard and carefully began to draw a small amount of adrenalin chloride fluid from a tiny medicine bottle. He put this into the double bubble glass mouthpiece that sat on top of the rubber nebuliser.

Maria was intrigued but frightened by the speed in which the asthma attack had taken hold. Edward gave the nebuliser to Robert, who by now was sitting on a stool at the kitchen door bravely struggling for air from the short, shallow breaths he was taking from which a loud wheeze could clearly be heard.

Robert took the nebuliser and began to squeeze the rubber ball at its base; the intention being to vaporise the adrenalin chloride fluid into what small amount of air he was able to gasp.

He loathed the process, knowing that if a droplet of the fluid were to fall on his tongue, the taste would be horrible. But slowly and perceptibly the treatment could be seen to work and Robert's breathing, though still challenged and still wheezy became easier.

Throughout all of this effort on Robert's part, Sarah took only a passing interest, sufficient to be assured that something was being done but nothing else.

When the attack had subsided sufficiently for Robert to be able to breathe without being too hunched up, Sarah returned to the prior conversation as though nothing had happened.

"Well, you had better get on your way," she declared ushering Maria to the door.

Turning to Robert, she glared with disapproval.

"And we could have done without this little drama, couldn't we?" she demanded, dismissing the whole event as contrived and totally unnecessary.

Edward, appearing to show some sympathy for the boy expressed concern that he might be better off staying at home, after all, resting in bed until he felt better.

"What you mean is that you want me to look after him," she shouted, "I told you, I need some rest too you know," she snapped becoming increasingly irritated by the situation.

"Daddy, I will look after Robert; I don't mind," declared Maria rushing to the aid of Robert immediately.

Sarah was furious declaring that the whole sorry saga was attention seeking on Robert's part and that Maria was simply being silly if she thought she could do anything for him.

In a rare show of assertiveness, Edward insisted that Maria should stay with Robert so that Sara could get her rest before what he described as a "busy and important weekend," descended upon them.

As Edward left the house, Sarah squeezed past Maria and Robert and departed to the garden where she gracefully sat herself down in a garden chair and proceeded to read a magazine.

Robert rose from the stool and turned to go upstairs to lay on his bed to rest. As he did, he turned to Maria and whispered, "My asthma comes on when it wants to, and I don't like it but thanks for standing up for me."

Robert slowly climbed the stairs and slipped into his bed, propping several pillows up so that he was almost in a sitting position which he knew would enable him to breath and rest.

It was some two hours later that he awoke to find Maria sitting on the floor.

"Are you alright?" she asked with genuine concern.

"Yep, I am," he replied with little trace of the terrible wheezing that had caused Maria to be so frightened.

They sat chatting for some time before Sarah could be heard calling, "There's some lunch for you on the table."

Robert moved slowly, still hunched over but visibly improved as they set off down the stairs.

Sarah was for once chatty, engaging and reflected none of the angst she displayed earlier in the day. Indeed, she was transformed; appearing to be genuinely interested in how Robert was feeling and thanking Maria for spending time with him.

"I'm afraid that I cannot stand seeing people suggesting they're unwell....for the most part, I just want to tell them to pull themselves together and get on with it," she explained as she busied herself with the soup she had made.

It was later on that Friday afternoon that Edward arrived back at the house with Charlotte. Her homecoming had many of the hallmarks of Maria's and Robert's but being that little older she was considerably more apprehensive.

Like Maria, she was now quite settled into the childrens home and while she and her friends often talked about what it would be like to be part of a family and to live in a *real* house, facing up to the reality of what that might mean, was challenging.

Charlotte had many friends, and while she was still only eight years of age, she was increasingly seen as one of the 'older girls' by the institution. With this came responsibility and status and an increased sense of belonging. Giving all of that certainty up was now beginning to dawn on Charlotte as she prepared to get out of the car and meet her future.

Robert was in Maria's den at the bottom of the garden when he heard the now familiar sound of his father's car. They walked as quickly as Robert could up the path to the driveway and stood waiting for the car doors to open.

Charlotte stepped from the front passenger seat, much to the annoyance of Robert, who had never been allowed to sit there in what he saw as a vantage point from which he could further study how his father drove the car.

Charlotte looked apprehensive as she approached her siblings. Maria was vaguely known to her, but Robert was by now a complete stranger.

Robert stepped forward with purpose.

"I'm Robert, your brother, I hope you're going to like me," he declared waiting for a negative reaction from his father who was carefully watching the scene.

"Well I shall like you if you are good and if you don't play with worms or bring frogs into the house," she replied in what Robert thought was a slightly haughty, refined voice.

Maria, by now standing next to Charlotte asked; "Do you remember me?"

Charlotte nodded and without a word spoken they walked towards the rear door of the house.

With their father having entered the house along with Robert, Charlotte stopped and turned to Maria.

"What's it like here?" she asked, and bending down to Maria's ear she whispered, "and what has *she* been like?" Maria did not have time to answer as her father had by now returned urging them to come into the house.

Charlotte was indeed apprehensive, remembering Sarah's warning to her outside the childrens home that she should not get between her and Edward.

As she entered the kitchen, Sarah threw her arms around Charlotte.

"My dear Charlotte," she gushed, "how lovely that you are here to bring this whole family together at last."

Charlotte was, not surprisingly, taken aback as was Edward, who leapt upon this as a sign that Sarah and Charlotte were to become great friends. But once again Sarah was playing games with the emotions of the children.

"Can I show Charlotte to our bedroom?" asked Maria, who was anxious to enter the bubble of affection that Sarah had created for Charlotte and which she had shown to her and Robert only a couple of hours earlier.

"No" was the curt and angry reply from Sarah.

The response was delivered with a look that even these small children could recognise. They knew Sarah was in one of those moods where she would favour Charlotte to the exclusion of Maria and Robert. Edward also detected the frostiness directed towards Maria and ushered her and Robert into the garden to await Sarah's return.

Upstairs, Sarah sat on the edge of Maria's bed as she engaged Charlotte in warm conversation, explaining the plans for the weekend while she helped Charlotte to unpack her few belongings from her small suitcase.

As Charlotte unpacked, she was not to know that she would in years to come open a much similar suitcase from which she would retrieve the secrets of her birth mother's extraordinary life.

Charlotte was cautious, even wary of Sarah and far from comfortable with this woman she knew was capable of turning unpleasant at any time. Nonetheless, it was nice to feel welcomed, and it was good to feel that someone cared.

This was particularly so as she was unable to strike up any conversation with her father on their journey back from Preston, something that Charlotte took to mean that she was not entirely welcome back into the family.

Charlotte could not have been more wrong.

Her father had always favoured her above the other two children, but he found it hard to know how to strike up a conversation with her and even harder to show his feelings towards her. Charlotte was also a wise eight year old, and Edward knew that of the three children she remembered more about the past, and from their previous meetings, he knew that she could remind him of this at any point.

The evening meal was eaten in an atmosphere of understandable tension made worse by Sarah's preoccupation with singling out Charlotte for conversation while totally excluding the other two children. Worse still, she manipulated Edward into that conversation, making the feeling of exclusion total for Robert and Maria.

But Sarah failed to reckon with the experience and resilience of children whose survival in the past years was built upon an inane mistrust of most people and an ability to expertly measure people and situations.

Robert and Maria remained quiet, only occasionally looking towards each other for reassurance. And at no time did they feel any ill towards Charlotte. They already knew that tomorrow it could be one of them that was *in favour* with Sarah and that Charlotte would be where they were right now.

After the evening meal was eaten, the children were immediately sent to their bedrooms by their father to prepare for bed. This was a routine that Maria and Robert were becoming accustomed to as it signalled in a rather formal way the end of the day for the children and the end of contact with their parents.

Edward would move from the supper table to a chair alongside the fire place; turn on the wireless to listen to the news, open a newspaper or take papers from his briefcase. He would acknowledge the departure of the children with a nod and a simple, "goodnight."

For her part, Sarah would move into the kitchen to wash the dishes but in so doing she would say; "I will call up to you in fifteen minutes time when I expect you to have washed your faces and been to the toilet."

Charlotte entered the routine with good grace but could see no justification that being the eldest she needed to conform to a routine aimed primarily at the younger children. But tonight she would share a room with Maria for the first time in many years, and she was keen to hear from her what life was like under the same roof again with their father and now with Sarah.

CHAPTER TWENTY

Despite being told on two occasions to be quiet and go to sleep, Charlotte and Maria spent several hours chatting before they both wearily and reluctantly succumbed to sleep.

They awoke only when there was the evident sound of movements outside their bedroom door signifying that it was morning. There wasn't a clock in the room, but the chime of the one in the hallway beneath announced that it was seven o'clock. This was late for the girls who both had been used to rising at six o'clock being awoken by the Angelus Bells, which were rung daily by the church in their institutions.

The Angelus Bells were rung after the chimes at six in the morning, twelve noon and six in the evening and were a constant reminder to the orphans of the Catholic lives they led. The lengthy peel of the bells placed a duty of devotion on everyone to pray.

Maria explained to Charlotte that they must always wash and dress before going downstairs for breakfast and that they must be quiet as *mummy* liked to sleep late on a Saturday. She went on, explaining that they must not use the bathroom before their father had shaved and dressed and they must not go downstairs until the door into the living room had been unlocked.

"We will know this because you will be able to hear the boring sound of daddy's wireless which is always tuned to the BBC Home Service with people talking," she explained, listening intently at the bedroom door for the subdued sound of the radio drifting upstairs.

"There are rules about clothes and washing too," she authoritatively explained. "Knickers.....but mummy insists they are called panties," could be changed daily, as could socks, "but dresses, blouses, and skirts have to last and be worn until they are visibly dirty."

"However," explained Maria, "if you are leaving the house to go out with mummy you must put on clean clothes and have clean shoes."

But rules were the norm for these two girls and so for Charlotte, it meant simply exchanging one set of ridiculous rules for another.

The girls washed and dressed, but before they went downstairs, Charlotte asked Maria about tooth paste.

"At the childrens home we cleaned our teeth using soap on our tooth brush, but what do you do here?" she asked, remarking that there was a tin of Gibbs toothpaste on the window sill.

"Oh, I don't know," she said. "I saw it but didn't dare ask if I could use it, so I used the soap," explained Maria.

"Well, I have used it, and it's nice, and I'm going to use it until I'm told not to," advised Charlotte, embarking on her big sister career with some style.

Maria was struggling to brush her hair when there was a gentle knock on the door.

"Go away," whispered Maria, explaining that Robert was very nervous about going downstairs in the morning without her and that he would wait until she was ready.

"Oh, let him in," rebuked Charlotte, who quietly opened the door.

Robert stepped back when he saw Charlotte unsure about how to engage her.

"Come here, silly," she called, holding out a hand and gently encouraging him into the room.

He came in and sat on the floor by the door, interested by the hair brushing and bed tidying activities, none of which he had undertaken, save that he had at least washed his face and hands.

"I wonder who's in favour today" he whispered.

"Well, you won't know that until *she* gets up," remarked Maria knowing that the fickle hand of fortune could descend upon any one of them that day, despite the gushing welcome Charlotte had been given the previous afternoon.

"Let's not bother about that now," suggested Charlotte and in that moment, this little band of children, Ruth's abandoned babies had a leader. They had someone who placed them at the centre, and they also had someone who clearly wanted the three of them to be friends and stand up for each other.

In Charlotte, they now had a sister who was already showing that she cared. And all of this was from an eight year old child who had only been reacquainted with her siblings the previous day.

The day had its predictable start with Sarah being deliberately slow to emerge from her bedroom despite the urgency of needing to go to the shops to finalise the purchase of school uniforms in time for the start of the autumn term, which was now only a week away.

When Sarah eventually joined the children and their father, who was by now anxious to get into the car and set off to Lancaster, there was one little matter the children knew had to be decided; *'Who's in favour today?'* But that was quickly resolved.

"Come here Robert darling," called Sarah, crouching down at his side and putting an arm around his young shoulders, "did you have a good nights sleep?"

Maria turned to Charlotte and nothing more needed to be said. An encouraging glance from Charlotte put Robert at ease as he gratefully accepted the invitation that for today at least, he would be the favoured child and offered Sarah's equivocal attention.

The morning in Lancaster was frenetic. The only shop that sold the uniforms for the Cathedral School where the children would attend was busy with parents and children from infant to junior level completing their list of items in an environment that didn't bring out the most charitable side in Edward, or for that matter Sarah.

The girl's tunic dresses were easily resolved though with both of them being terribly underweight for their age, the fit was far from perfect. Blouses offered the same challenge as did the Blazers. However, after an hour of trying on different sizes, the complete list was filled, and the girls were released by Sarah to sit tidily and quietly on the small chaise longue near the entrance to the shop.

Robert presented a somewhat greater challenge. He too was underweight, and the short trousers did nothing to hide the fact that he was dreadfully thin and also short for his age. He under filled the smallest shirt, and the blazer sleeves on the smallest size engulfed his hands too. Short trousers, the required dress code until the autumn looked like under size long trousers on Robeert, but he was overjoyed and couldn't care less.

His smile lit up the dark, grey shop with its equally grey and humourless staff. These were the first school clothes that had not been handed down to Robert, and he felt joy and happiness in abundance.

Sarah, who was an excellent seamstress, confidently saw no problem in making the necessary adjustments that would amount to nothing short of re-tailoring the jacket and trousers, but at last, the purchases were made.

Shoes were quickly purchased from Freeman Hardy and Willis a very popular chain store next door. But there was to be another embarrassing moment for Sarah when all three children became overly excited at having a new pair of shoes.

Maria led the celebration by skipping around the shop showing off her shoes to anyone and everyone exclaiming; "My new mummy has bought these for me, and they are the first new shoes I have ever had."

To the ultra-sensitive Sarah, and to Edward with his paranoia about privacy, this was nothing short of scandalous. The embarassment was made worse because the other people shopping in the store would know that these children were likely to be going to the Cathedral School alongside their children and that they would almost certainly meet again.

With the shopping completed, the family returned home with little conversation at the front of the car. In contrast, there was quite a deal of giggling in the rear with the glass screen dividing the front of the car from back giving some anonymity to the light hearted commentary from the children in the back of the car. Maria's parody of Sarah in the shoe shop was the centre piece of their laughter for most of the journey.

On arrival back home, Sarah resumed her exclusive contact with Robert alone. This approach to communication with the children appeared to go over the head of Edward, who seemed to view any sign that Sarah was engaging with them, singularly or collectively as positive, and indicative of the *family* coming together.

The children, on the other hand, were very clear about what was going on and, therefore, avoided any direct contact with Sarah except to answer when spoken to by her.

Sarah prepared a late lunch of lentil soup and fresh bread bought while in town. She was a modest cook who knew her limitations. But, in preparation for the arrival of the children to live with her and Edward, she had joined the Women's Institute and enrolled on a course aptly entitled 'feeding a family on rations and a budget'.

While the impact of World War Two rationing was slowly coming to an end, sugar and butter remained on ration, and there were occasional shortages of other food stuffs. But it was not the shortage of foods that drove the ladies of the WI; it was the overhang of the spirit of the wartime years, where women stretched budgets and became supremely creative in the way they used the few precious provisions they were either able to grow, buy or be able to afford.

This attracted Sarah, who wanted to be seen by Edward as a good homemaker and cook, and thrifty with the 'housekeeping' money she was given by Edward each week.

Her earnings paid as a weekly wage were deposited into the joint account at the local Midland Bank every Friday lunch time by Sarah. She, like most women of that era, had no money of her own, other than what she could eek out of the housekeeping budget provided by her husband.

Sarah was consumed by the responsibility placed upon her shoulders for managing the household purse. Everything that was purchased was meticulously recorded in a small book. Every box of groceries delivered by the local shop was carefully checked off against the hand written order list that also acted as a receipt, and any discrepancies were quickly addressed.

While Edward didn't check her housekeeping accounts, he too was obsessed by how much everything cost and how little was left over at the end of each week.

But Sarah persevered with her cooking and baking courses and to her credit, this delivered variety into the modest menus she planned before she set about deciding what groceries would be needed each day.

While she would place a grocery order for delivery every Friday evening, she would augment this by buying fresh produce from the city market during her morning break from work.

Milk was delivered to the house daily by Norman, a chirpy man in his mid-thirties and someone who Robert always waved to and often ran to the gate to meet in a morning when he delivered.

Another home delivery was the 'pop man' who brought amongst other favourites, bottles of Tizer, Dandelion and Burdock and orange juice.

But Sarah's greatest challenge was going to be how she would meet the voracious appetites of these three growing children. And this modest lunch was to be an example of that challenge.

The children ate their lentil soup and devoured the slice of bread, thinly spread with margarine which was placed on each of their side plates.

Noticing that they appeared to be hungry, Sarah returned from the kitchen with four more slices of bread and placed them on a plate at the centre of the table; another of Sarah's cruel games was about to begin.

"Edward darling you must take that nice thick slice that I've cut for you," she said, knowing that he would take it, oblivious to the implications. Now there were only three slices.

"And Robert my dear, you must keep your strength up," she purred, passing a slice of the bread to him. There were now only two slices.

Looking directly into the eyes of the two girls who were, of course, not currently 'in favour' she reached across to the plate.

"And I think I will have this one," she declared leaving one slice of bread between the two hungry but polite young girls.

This was to be a cruel game she would play for many years to come. She would deliberately place insufficient cakes or scones on a plate and attempt to cause the children to react...which, of course, they deliberately would not. Nonetheless, it remained a game she would always win with her well-rehearsed quips and responses. But the children had the measure of her, and though upset and hungry, they never showed it. And as far as the remaining slice of bread was concerned, well.... it remained on the plate uneaten.

Over the coming years, the constant hunger the children experienced in a family environment where you simply couldn't ask for more, as Dickens' character Oliver Twist did resulted in the children resorting to disparate measures.

When they were sent to the local bakers shop for a loaf of sliced bread, the baker, who grew to know the children well would often give each of them a miniature loaf to eat on the way home. If he was not present and the children didn't get their little loaf, they would sit on a garden wall on their way home and carefully un-wrap the bread wrapper.

With increasing skill, they would remove a slice of the bread and share it amongst themselves being careful to reseal the loaf properly. But Sarah became wise to the children's actions and, when they returned with a loaf, she would count the slices!

Hunger was to characterise the young lives of these three children for many years to come. It would be wrong to suggest that their hunger was as a result of Sarah's deliberate abuse; it was more that Sarah was completely unaware of the nutritional needs of three growing children.

CHAPTER TWENTY ONE

The following day, Sunday saw the beginning of a weekly ritual of preparing to attend the Cathedral in Lancaster for the nine o'clock Mass.

Firstly, as Communion was to be taken by Edward, Sarah, and Charlotte, they were required to fast and therefore, none of the family would take breakfast. This presented a challenge to the already hungry children and it also raised the level of tension in the house for the whole family.

The readying by the family had little to do with preparing for the Catholic celebration of the Mass; this was entirely driven by the need in Sarah and Edward to be seen as exemplary middle class 'good' parents in the eyes of their new community and those they would meet at the church. This meant that the children must be seen as models of good behaviour and demonstrate impeccable manners. The fact that the children were all of these things, without a scintilla of input from Edward and Sarah, was considered by them both to be a trivial detail and not to be dwelt upon.

Final preparation for departing to the Cathedral was a far from Christian ritual. Sarah's moodiness was always central to the general demeanour of the family, and today was to be no different. She was simply unapproachable until she had made that final check on her appearance in the full length hall mirror.

Sarah, by now a twenty nine year old slim and very attractive woman was as always impeccably dressed. Today she was wearing a close fitting black dress worn a couple of inches below the knee and a small black hat with a veil that covered the face. A large cameo broach, given to her by Edward during their courting days, adorned the dress, and a single string of pearls, bequeathed to her by an Aunt framed her slim neck, and dainty pearl earrings completed the image.

The black handbag and black gloves lay on the hall table alongside her Missal, a liturgical book containing all instructions and texts necessary for the celebration of a Catholic Mass throughout the year.

The seams on her black nylon stockings were checked and double checked before she lined the children up for their inspection.

Robert's wayward hair was dampened down, and having passed muster, the children dashed out to the car and clambered into the back, heeding the concerned cries from Sarah not to scuff their patent leather shoes or mark their clothes.

For his part, Edward abandoned the grey trilby hat used every day for work and wore a smart fedora trilby made of the finest rabbit hair felt. No matter the time of year, he wore a coat for church. In the winter it would be a heavy black Crombie overcoat but today it was a light raincoat over a charcoal grey suit. Edward would always wear a white shirt, sombre tie, and black shoes for church setting what he regarded as an important standard in a world where in his eyes, standards were already showing signs of slipping since the War was over.

Edward had drummed into him by his mother that he should *"never wear brown in town"* so black shoes were the order of the day. Dressing up for church was the *done* thing. Everyone engaged in the same ritual which always resulted in the same highly un-Christian process of judging people by what they wore, how they spoke or how their children behaved.

The journey to the Cathedral in the car was achieved in total silence with the children and Edward waiting for Sarah to take the lead something which she finally did.

Sliding back the glass partition window she called through to the children.

"Don't any of you do anything to embarrass your father and me, do you hear me?" she asked while at the same time filing her finger nails and checking her face powder and lipstick in the rear view mirror.

On arrival at the Cathedral, Edward parked the car close to the main entrance and quickly ushered the children out. He then moved swiftly to the pavement and to the passenger side of the car where he held open the door for Sarah to alight.

In a well-rehearsed move, copied by studying the starlets of the day at the cinema, she swung both legs out of the car being careful to keep her knees and feet together. Edward put out his hand, and she slipped her arm into his.

The children were then instructed to follow closely behind as they walked up the pathway to the main entrance of this gothic, revival style Cathedral, which was built originally as a parish church in the middle of the nineteenth century and elevated to the status of a Cathedral in nineteen twenty four.

As they walked slowly past other parishioners arriving for Mass, the connection was slowly made that *these* were the children Sarah had so *charitably* taken on.

"Oh, Mrs. Carmichael, how lovely to see you and these must be the children you have talked so much about," came the warm response from one group. "How charming to see *them* all dressed so nicely for church, they are a credit to you, Mrs. Carmichael."

"We do our best," she demurely replied, basking in the near sainthood standing she had already achieved in this high status Cathedral community.

Once inside the Cathedral, Edward led the family group to the dark oak pews in the far left transept. The children were filed in first, but not before they were silently reminded by Sarah to genuflect towards the altar before kneeling to pray alongside Edward and Sarah. The children only took a seat when Sarah and Edward lead the way by doing so.

To these young children weaned on a diet of Sunday Mass, Holy Days of Obligation, Sunday School, catechism and fire and brimstone sermons from zealot priests and nuns, the thought of an hour and fifteen minutes of the same was very much taken in its stride.

But they were not prepared for the priest's sermon.

Deep into Mathew's Sermon on the Mount and lifting his arms heavenly, Father O'Reilly read: "*Blessed are the merciful, for they shall receive mercy....*" His voice faltered. "And here....here amongst us today..... here in this very house of God, sits a woman who has......nay who is the living embodiment of such mercy. A woman who has taken on three children; children whose mother sadly passed away, and a woman who is providing a good Catholic home and upbringing to these children......"

He went on at length, his voice rising ever higher as each glowing statement was made.

Charlotte was the first to realise that the woman with the three children was none other than Sarah.

Sarah had no pre warning of what was unfolding. But far from being embarrassed, she could be seen, almost imperceptibly, turning her head slowly to meet the looks of admiration from those who had also begun to recognise who Father O'Reilly was talking about.

"She is an inspiration to us all. Blessed indeed are the Merciful," he pronounced, his hands still outstretched to the heavens but his eyes now firmly fixed upon Sarah and Edward, who by now had tuned into what was being said about them.

The walk from the alter rails after having taken Communion today was to be Sarah's and hers alone. The eyes of the whole congregation were upon her as she protectively guided the *out of favour* Charlotte with an arm carefully placed around her shoulders, back to their pew.

This was pure theatre, and completely unrehearsed.

But now this congregation was also drawn into the lie that Edward and Sarah had so carefully crafted that Ruth, the children's mother was dead. This was something that the children were already suspicious of and something that over time they would question... and question again.

And there were two people in the congregation, sat only three rows behind the Carmichael family who had heard the priest's words and who also knew them to be far from the truth.

Blending into the background and not wishing to be recognised by the Carmichael's were Mr. and Mrs. Oliver, the couple who had acted as foster parents to Charlotte and Maria when Edward's mother had died. They knew that Ruth had walked out on Edward and abandoned the children, as did many in the close knit community around Inglewhite.

Mrs. Oliver was shocked and angry that this should be the story these children would be hearing, but she held back. She was anxious not to have Charlotte, in particular, recognise her, and she wanted to avoid the possibility of Edward and Sarah catching sight of her and her husband. She tugged on Mr. Oliver's coat and without a word said they stood and eased their way out of the pew.

But their quiet exit didn't escape the notice of Charlotte or her father who both quizzically looked behind to see what was happening.

Edward recognised Mrs. Oliver in an instant, and his look made it clear that he was not happy to make their acquaintance once again. The last encounter, on the driveway of their farm, was etched into the memory of them all and Edward, in particular, knew that they were angry and distressed by his decision to separate the children.

Charlotte felt she knew their faces and stared intensely into the eyes of Mrs. Oliver, who by now was anxious to leave. Maria picked up on the distraction, but Charlotte's cautionary hand on hers stopped her from questioning.

Sarah was oblivious to everything; still basking in the saintly aura that she felt now surrounded her.

As the Carmichael family walked from church to the car, Maria tugged Charlotte's coat.

"Who was that lady who was staring at you?" she asked, making sure that her parents couldn't hear.

"I'll tell you later, now be quiet" whispered the ultra-cautious Charlotte.

"What woman...who are you whispering about?" quizzed Sarah, picking up only on fragments of the conversation. But before Charlotte could reply, Edward stepped in trying to end a conversation on this topic before it began. But Sarah was having none of it.

"Who was what woman?" snapped Sarah, "I'm not stepping into that car until someone tells me what's going on."

Charlotte looked at Edward and then looked at Sarah.

"It was the lady who looked after us before we were sent to the childrens home," she said, knowing immediately that she would regret having said this.

Sarah tugged on the handle of the car stepped in and slammed the door shut; her earlier elegance replaced now by anger and expedience to be away from this place as swiftly as possible.

There was a furious row in the front of the car on the way home much of which the children were unable to hear fully. But on arrival back inside the house, the children were ordered by Sarah to "stand and listen."

"Don't you ever speak to that man and woman if they approach you in the future," commanded Sarah, red faced, angry and by now quite threatening. "They are mistaken if they think they know us and are probably not nice people."

Edward nodded sagely and dismissed the children to change out of their Sunday clothes.

But this was to be only one of many instances where something would happen that the children remembered; a memory that would be revisited time and again as they grew up trying to piece together what was sheer fabrication and what was the truth.

~

Monday morning brought about many more rules that the children would need to adapt to. This was not a school day as it was the last week of the school summer holiday, but it was a work day for Edward and Sarah.

Edward left the house at seven o'clock precisely; movements around the house and the wireless playing downstairs ensured that everyone was awake and aware of his departure.

As Edward pulled his car out of the driveway Robert waved from his open bedroom window but received no response; his father was in a hurry and oblivious to everything around him. However, while he received no response from his father, he did receive a friendly wave from the man who lived next door. He was also on his way to work but walking briskly towards the bus stop. The wave brought a beaming smile to the young Robert's face.

"Good morning Sir, how are you?" he called.

"Tolerable," the neighbour replied chirpily; "tolerable for a Monday morning," and with that, he had gone from view. But as he disappeared Sarah threw open the bedroom door.

"How dare you call to people from the window, you're not to do that again...do you hear me?" she asked, shaking with outrage. "What on earth would our neighbours think, with you acting like some common little street urchin?"

Robert recoiled, knowing that Sarah was really angry and that this would result in his father being told when he returned home that evening.

Despite the passage of time, Robert remained deeply concerned that misbehaviour on his part could see him being returned to the childrens home, a fear that would take many months to subside.

"I'm sorry mummy; I'm really sorry, and I won't do it again," he cried, tears flowing down his face. "Please don't tell daddy, please don't send me back ...please?"

But Edward would be told, and the fear of what was to come would fill the mind of this young boy for the rest of the day.

Eventually, Sarah emerged from her bedroom, a signal for the children to go downstairs. She was dressed and ready for work and busied herself preparing cereals for the children's breakfast. As she dashed from the kitchen back upstairs to her bedroom, all the children could hear were calls for them to hurry and finish their breakfast.

The children were sat at the small table in the kitchen on stools very close to each other which enabled whispered conversation outside the earshot of Sarah.

"If she's going to work, who's going to look after us?" asked Maria, who was always the great worrier amongst the children.

"I don't know," replied Charlotte, who was equally interested but not at all concerned.

"She's coming," whispered Robert and with that, Charlotte gathered the dishes and rushed to the sink to wash them.

They could hear Sarah coming down the stairs and entering the living room. They heard her turn the key in the door from the hallway into the living room before she rushed through the dining area and into the kitchen.

As she entered the kitchen, she held up a key on a piece of string.

"Put this around your neck Charlotte and make sure you don't lose it. This is the key to the back door, and if you step out of this kitchen, you must lock the door, do you hear me? Also, you must not leave the garden while I'm away," she breathlessly instructed.

"Oh, and Charlotte.....you're in charge until I come home at twelve thirty to get you some lunch. If there is a problem, and I'm sure there won't be, Mrs. Herron, who lives next door, will be available, but I don't want you bothering her, do you hear me ... Maria?" she cautioned.

With that Sarah locked the door from the kitchen into the dining room and dashed off on her way to catch a bus to work, only to return just moments later.

Breathlessly and casually she pointed to the side door of the garage. Without a thought to what she was about to say, she casually informed the children: "Your father has put a bucket in there just in case you need to have a wee before I get back."

The children looked at each other and waited for a few more seconds to be sure Sarah had gone before there was a collective cry of excitement.

"We're free," exclaimed Robert as he jumped through the kitchen door into the warm late summer morning air.

Maria turned to Charlotte. "I'm not weeing in a bucket; I'd rather bust myself," she declared with a very concerned look on her face.

"Oh, come on, Robert's right, we're free to have fun let's do that," Charlotte urged as she called the others to the tool shed for a planning meeting.

"What should we do?" asked Charlotte excitedly.

"I want to go into the field and explore the air raid shelters," declared an excited Robert.

"But we don't have a key for the gate to get out there from the garden, and if we climb over the wall, we might not get back," offered the ever cautious Maria.

"But *I* know where the key is kept," replied Robert clambering passed Charlotte to open a drawer under the work bench. "I saw daddy put it there last week when he returned from shouting at some kids for climbing on the wall," he proudly announced.

He slid his hand in the drawer and pulled out a long black latch key. "There I told you so; now can we go to the field Charlotte?" begged an over excited Robert.

Charlotte looked at Maria and with a nod the plan was made.

"You'll have to put some string through the key and put it around your neck with the house key so that you don't lose it," cautioned Maria, always fearful of risk and terrified of getting into trouble.

She was a follower rather than a leader. Robert, by contrast, saw no danger; he saw rules as mere obstacles to be navigated around, and he craved adventure.

Charlotte took the key and deftly strung it onto the string around her neck allowing the two keys to jangle together.

"Now we will need provisions for our journey," announced Charlotte striding purposefully back to the open kitchen door. "We need water, and we need food for our long trek, and we must all put on our Wellington boots," instructed Charlotte as she searched the cupboards for a water container.

Having found an empty Tizer bottle which was set aside to return to the Pop Man, she carefully filled it with cold water from the tap and placed it into a small wicker basket Maria had found on a shelf in the shed.

"Now food," she mused looking at the few biscuits left on a plate for the children by Sarah. Charlotte took a paper bag from the drawer and placed the biscuits in carefully.

"I need a wee," protested Maria, "and I'm not going in that bucket. I'm going to ask Mrs. Herron if I can use her toilet," declared a determined Maria.

Charlotte sensed that any attempt on her part to dissuade Maria was going to be pointless, and so she gathered Maria and Robert now suitably dressed in their Wellington boots and having carefully locked the back door they trooped next door.

A sharp knock on the door from Robert saw Mrs. Herron swiftly answer it as she had already heard the chatter of the children outside her front window as they lifted the latch on the gate.

Mrs. Herron was an instantly likeable figure, with a warm smile and laughing eyes. She was a spritely quite evidently lively lady despite being a sixty eight years old grandmother to six though as the children would hear later, none lived close by.

"Now my dears, what's the matter?" she asked concerned that a disaster had befallen them on the first day that she had been asked to watch out for them.

"We're off on an expedition, and Maria needs to have a wee, and she won't use the bucket in the garage," announced Robert in his finest and most refined accent.

Charlotte was clearly angry at Robert for blurting out far too much. But Mrs. Herron smiled and ushered Maria into the house not remotely interested at that moment in the bizarre background to the request.

"Well, if you're off on an expedition you had all better go to the toilet," she urged, ushering in the wellington booted trio.

"Take off your boots," ordered Charlotte fearful that they might bring dirt into the house.

"Oh, my dears the boots are as clean as my floor, just dash upstairs quietly as Mr. Herron is still sleeping."

Maria and Robert were out of earshot when Mrs. Herron asked; "I'm more than happy for you to use my toilet but is yours not working?"

Charlotte paused; "The toilet... well, it's upstairs, and all the doors are kept locked except the back door into the kitchen where we can play."

Mrs. Herron hid her concern and surprise looking on as Charlotte took the string from inside her blouse and showed Mrs. Herron the back door key.

"And is that the key to the gate into the field?" asked Mrs. Herron, presuming that the expedition was heading in that direction.

Charlotte blushed; "We have borrowed the key so that..."

Mrs. Herron stopped Charlotte with a light touch of her finger on Charlotte's lips.

"Don't worry my dear, your secret is safe with me; now what provisions do you have for your long journey?" she asked looking into the basket.

As Robert and Maria returned, Mrs. Herron was just covering over the basket with a tea towel having put three slices of homemade fruitcake wrapped in grease proof paper at the bottom.

"Now Charlotte, I will keep an eye open for you so can you, please wave to me every now and again so that I know you're alright?" Charlotte nodded slipping out of the kitchen also to dash upstairs to use the toilet.

Charlotte was struck by the homeliness of the living room with its many photograph frames with pictures of Mrs. Herron's children and her grandchildren. There were flowers in vases and bright coloured cushions on the chairs and settee and a large square carpet on the floor made the room feel cosy. She couldn't also help noticing that there were no locks on the doors and in contrast to their house next door, there was light streaming in through the open windows.

Robert was by now beside himself with excitement as Charlotte re-entered the kitchen and thanked Mrs. Herron. "Thank you Mrs. Herron and thanks for allowing us to use your toilet and thanks also for the cake."

Mrs. Herron smiled at their politeness and exemplary manners.

"Now remember to wave to me won't you?" she asked as the intrepid explorers excitedly set off on their journey.

Their morning was filled with laughter and childhood fun as they played in the long grass alongside the five, now disused air raid shelters. These shelters, used during the Second World War as a refuge for the residents were now supposed to be fully decommissioned and bricked up. However, local children had managed to prise away the bricks from what was previously the doorway, making it possible to enter the darkened shelter.

The roof of the shelter had twin peaks with a valley in the middle. The walls were brick built with no windows, just the small doorway which required people to crouch down to enter.

The air inside the air raid shelter smelled musty and damp as they gingerly entered into the darkness. Once their eyes had adjusted to the gloom, it was clear that the large open space was entirely empty.

Maria remained there for a matter of seconds before the smell, and the fear forced her to leave. This was not helped by Robert insisting before they entered the doorway that the bones of German soldiers would be bound to be found in there!

Charlotte was the second to leave holding her nose followed closely by Robert, who was not prepared to go so far as to say he was frightened, but he stuck close to Charlotte for some time after that.

The children played games; some invented on the spot others, like *hide and seek* were favourites of Maria and Robert. But in hiding, they never ventured very far from where they knew Charlotte would be sitting. For all the bravery of the 'expedition,' the children were unused to absolute freedom, and while they enjoyed it, they were also fearful of what they didn't know.

They ran and skipped; they played tag, and they sat in a close circle while Charlotte told them stories.

This was also the opportunity for Maria to ask Charlotte about the lady they saw in the cathedral.

"That lady and man in the church are they really not nice people?"

Charlotte lowered her voice.

"From what I remember, they were lovely people, and they liked us very much," replied Charlotte, as a tear slipped down her cheek, she certainly wasn't unpleasant, and she gave us sweets, but I don't know why she sent us away."

Maria was saddened to see her sister cry. "I can't really remember them," she said.

"I can," chirped Robert. Charlotte called Robert to her side.

"Silly Billy, you weren't even there you were somewhere in Preston. Anyway, we shouldn't be sad; we're having a nice adventure," she insisted as she wiped the tear from her cheek.

"Is our proper mummy really dead?" asked Maria as Robert ran off into the grass to chase a butterfly.

"I don't know, but I don't think so," replied Charlotte, "but don't say anything in front of daddy and her."

This was the beginning of the strong bond that would grow between these children who, like all siblings would have their moments of disagreements and fallings out but would increasingly return to the security of their friendship and their growing common purpose.

That purpose, which grew over the years, was one in which they would adapt to the rules, roles, and oddities of their domestic situation but would take every opportunity to be released to play together and to be together. The serendipity....that what the children wanted also suited Sarah and Edward, was an bonus, as nothing suited Sarah more than to see the children entertain themselves leaving her and Edward to be alone.

The children sat and ate their cake and shared the bottle of water oblivious to the time, though Robert regularly waved to Mrs. Herron, who reassuringly always waved back. But this time, Charlotte was alert to a voice in the distance calling her name.

It was Mrs. Herron who was rushing through the grasses signalling to the children that they should go to her. When they met Mrs. Herron, who by now had a big smile on her face, she asked, "How was the expedition?"

"Oh, very good replied Robert," still excited but by now beginning to wheeze quite badly.

"It's almost twelve o'clock, and I suspect your mother will be home soon to get you some lunch so you might want to get back into the garden quickly," advised the wily Mrs. Herron.

Charlotte panicked.

"We must rush and put our wellington boots back in the shed and tidy ourselves up and be ready for mummy coming home," she urged. But by now, with a combination of the excitement and the rushing around, Robert was having serious trouble breathing and was stooped over walking, always a strong indication that his asthma was bad.

"What's wrong with him?" queried a very worried Mrs. Herron.

"Its asthma," replied Maria in a matter of fact and unconcerned way, "he will need to have his spray and his Do-Do tablets," she continued.

Charlotte rushed ahead and opened the gate into the garden while the others slowly brought Robert back to the house.

In the meantime, Charlotte had removed her wellington boots and slipped into the kitchen where she took out Roberts's medication. When Robert arrived, she sat him on a small stool by the open doorway looking into the garden; a favourite place for Robert to sit when he was having trouble breathing.

As Mrs. Herron looked on with increasing concern, she watched in amazement as Charlotte put the drops into the glass bubble in the mouthpiece and then put this into Robert's mouth. Slowly and gently she asked him to squeeze the rubber bulb that made the atomiser work. Maria was all the time gently wiping the sweat from his brow using a flannel soaked in cold water.

Mrs. Herron was utterly transfixed, watching these young children dealing with a serious asthma attack as though they had done it many times before, which they had not. Her father had instructed Charlotte on how to use the atomiser as a precaution if Robert ever had an attack, and Maria had watched when Robert had experienced his last attack.

Slowly colour returned to Robert's cheeks and though he was still struggling to breathe properly, he was breathing perceptibly better.

Amidst the drama of all of this Robert had the presence of mind to remind Charlotte to remove the gate key from the string around her neck so that it could be returned safely to the drawer in the tool shed. Charlotte also asked Maria to ensure all the Wellington boots were placed back in the shed with all traces of their morning expedition carefully removed.

About half an hour later, Sarah came around the side of the house to witness the aftermath of the earlier drama.

"What's wrong?" she called out to a startled Mrs. Herron.

"It's all fine Mrs. Carmichael. Young Robert had a bit of an asthma turn, but his sisters have been wonderful, administering to him like skilled nurses, and he is most certainly on the mend."

Sarah was palpably angry.

"So what possessed you to disturb Mrs. Herron and what have you been doing to get Robert into such a state?" she asked Charlotte.

But Mrs. Herron came to the rescue.

"They came around to ask if I would oversee Robert being given his medicine just to make sure they were doing the right thing," she insisted, turning to Robert and winking. "Don't you think that was very adult of them?" she asked, her explanation appearing to sound plausible to Sarah, who at no time had sought to reassure herself that Robert was out of danger.

Mrs. Herron slipped away, also giving Charlotte a wink of the eye as she left. Sarah brushed past Robert and unlocked the doors into the living room and the hallway from where she insisted that Robert should immediately go to his bedroom to lay down.

He carefully and slowly climbed the stairs and settled down on his bed in an almost upright position where he could breathe more easily. With the window thrown wide open, he slowly began to recover from this latest attack.

Sarah returned to the kitchen and prepared some sandwiches for lunch announcing at the same time that she would not be returning to work in the afternoons of this week to be around for the children as they settled into their new surroundings.

But her take on being there for the children on this occasion was to take the deck chair out of the shed and sit in the afternoon sunshine on what was a very pleasantly warm day, but not before she changed into a fashionable swimming costume and collected the magazines she had brought home with her. Then she reclined in the chair where she stayed for most of the afternoon. She was disinterested and entirely unaware of what Charlotte and Maria were doing as she soaked up the sun.

Sarah would have been surprised if it had been pointed out to her that her behaviour was hardly that of a caring and responsible adult. She would be surprised because she saw the children as a self-contained functioning unit on the periphery of her responsibility. She didn't deliberately ignore her responsibilities because she would never have seen child minding or caring as central to her role. She would feed the children, provide them with clean, very respectable clothes and tend to them if they needed help. But intervention, like playing with them, or talking to them or entertaining them, was simply not on her radar.

Furthermore, it simply would not occur to Sarah that her place now was to tend to the needs of Robert, even if this simply meant calling in on him every half hour or so to check that he was comfortable. Neither would it occur to her that Charlotte was far too young to be given or to have to assume a responsibility to look after Maria and Robert. She lacked any maternal instincts, and this hardly helped in a situation where the children craved love, understanding and some sense of belonging.

As five o'clock approached, Sarah went indoors and changed, taking the opportunity for the first time that afternoon to drop in on Robert. She found him much improved, with him asking if he could now go downstairs and be with his sisters.

"You will need to stay where you are young man until your father comes home and talks to you about your disgraceful behaviour this morning" she replied.

Robert was taken aback as it took him a moment or two to recall the scolding Sarah had administered at the start of the day. To Robert, this was a matter that was so long ago in his mind to have almost been forgotten, particularly in the light of his terrible asthma attack.

When Edward came into Robert's bedroom, some forty five minutes after returning home he admonished Robert, extracting a promise that he would never again call out to people from the bedroom window. But there was also a fleeting moment of empathy when Edward asked Robert if he was now feeling up to coming downstairs for supper. This met with a beaming smile and an attempt on Robert's part to step towards his father.

But their relationship was still distant and for that matter, Edward didn't entirely agree with the modern liberal view that one should embrace ones children to bond with them. He stepped aside and with the briefest of touches on Robert's shoulder he directed him out of the bedroom towards the bathroom to wash his hands.

~

The remainder of the week presented no further dramas for the children. They did, however, enjoy the mornings they spent together undertaking other expeditions, but none that quite matched the visit to the air raid shelters. Their afternoons were mostly spent playing in the tool shed or in the den beneath the laurel trees which by now was a favourite place of refuge for Maria.

But Monday and the first day at school brought its own set of completely new challenges.

Having dressed in their obviously brand new school uniforms, the three of them set off on foot with Sarah to walk the mile and a half journey to the school. The walk was done in near silence as Charlotte and Robert contemplated the likely challenges of their first day.

For Maria, this would not be a first-day, in the same way, as it would be for Robert and Charlotte as she would be re-entering the class she left at the start of the summer holiday.

But Maria's circumstances had changed markedly. Then she was a boarder at the childrens home with the simply awful stigma and teasing that brought. Now she was an *ex-boarder,* and she knew that the teasing by her former orphanage friends, most of whom were still there, would probe how long her new circumstances would last. So a certain nervousness and trepidation was also being felt by Maria.

For Charlotte, this was a move to a new school, and she knew that there would be questions and interrogation from her new classmates eager to know which school she had been to and why she was coming here.

Charlotte was not prepared for the greeting she received at the gate of the school when she was received by Father O'Reilly and introduced to some of the girls who were eager to know who this *new girl* was.

With no thought to the impact what he was about to say might have on Charlotte, he loudly announced: "This is Charlotte Carmichael, who joins us today from an orphanage in Preston where she also went to school."

The information would circulate amongst her contemporaries within minutes and provide rich pickings for the bullies in that community.

Robert was handed over at the gate of the school to a teacher who interrupted Sarah when she began to explain who he was.

"We know who Carmichael is," he advised with authority, "his *file* has been handed over to us, and we know his background. And Mrs. Carmichael, we also know what a wonderful job you are doing," he continued.

"We will continue to instil discipline, good behaviour and strong Catholic morals in the boy.....be sure of that," he assured her, and the small audience around Sarah. "These orphanage lads can be a real handful if you don't discipline them and do it early," he concluded, swiftly cuffing Robert around the head for good measure.

Robert could hardly believe what he was hearing.

"But I am a good boy aren't I?" he pleaded, turning to Sarah for some reassurance. Sarah avoided the question and went on her way.

Another task and yet another assignment had been discharged by Sarah, who briskly set off on her short journey to work.

But like most children, Robert, Maria and Charlotte dealt with the day and ultimately settled into the school life, and its routine. They were bright and so they at least didn't struggle with achieving the high educational standards expected within the school. And dealing with the social challenges of settling into a new school and making new friends ultimately resolved itself with all three children adapting well.

The Carmichael family slowly settled into a way of life that might not have been described as conventional, nor might it have been described as normal, but it was *their* way of life. They slowly adjusted to each other, and Sarah's utter dominance of the family's emotions continued. She was far from being a good mother, but that was not how she saw her role.

Sarah returned to working full time, and when the school had holidays, the children returned to using the small kitchen for their food and the garage as their play space and their shelter. And the bucket would be dutifully placed in the garage though the children steadfastly refused to use it.

CHAPTER TWENTY TWO

The following few years saw the Carmichael family steadily adjust to each other and their new circumstances. For their part, Edward and Sarah adapted their expectations of each other to recognise that they also had the children to think of.

This was a difficult adjustment for Sarah whose hope for their marriage was that the children would have little impact. The last couple of years served to demonstrate that life would never be the same, at least until the children were off their hands, and at this stage that was still some time away.

It was by now the end of July nineteen fifty five and the schools had begun their six week summer break.

Nineteen fifty five was a year in which Britain had earlier re-elected a Conservative government who were now hoping to take advantage of the end of food rationing and the feel good factor of a nation firmly focused upon a brighter post-war future.

Winston Churchill, Britain's charismatic wartime leader, had resigned as Prime Minister at the age of eighty due to ill health, as the rather less affable figure of Anthony Eden was named as his replacement. But Britain was buoyant, and a mood of unexpected optimism swept the country.

A new era of consumerism gripped the nation with sales of all those items that had previously been rationed or restricted now experiencing record sales. Families wanted homes, a car, washing machines and televisions, and they would have them, stoking unprecedented levels of consumer borrowing.

The youth of the country flocked to cinemas and also discovered pop music, the most liberating force to brighten up a post war Britain. Elvis Presley's record *Heartbreak Hotel* was topping charts across the world. Songs from artists such as Pat Boon, Doris Day and The Platters, were on the lips of most young people who were discovering a freedom of expression that was new, and this was not finding favour with the political establishment and with parents.

Charlotte was captivated by the modern music much to the annoyance of Edward and Sarah. They viewed Elvis Presley's *Hound Dog*, as degenerate and his hip thrusting movements, now copied by every teenage boy, as morally repugnant. But this did not deter Charlotte from listening to her transistor radio, if necessary under the bed covers to hear the sounds of what was to become the beginning of a defining era in music.

But tension was ever present in the Carmichael household, and when Sarah felt she was not getting the attention she needed, blast furnace arguments would break out between her and Edward. Threats by her to leave Edward added the toxic ingredient needed to escalate their rows to fever pitch before Edward would eventually and inevitably capitulate and agree to Sarah's needs.

One example was that Sarah felt Sunday mornings should be *their* time, when they could be together for the morning Mass without the responsibility of having the children in tow; an utterly bizarre concept on her part when other families saw a church service as important family time.

Sarah decided that she and Edward should continue to go to the nine o'clock Mass at the Cathedral but the children, under Charlotte's care and direction would attend a ten o'clock service at St Stephen's Catholic church about a mile away. Therefore as Edward and Sarah departed by car for their service, so the children would also set off on foot for theirs.

Following Mass, Edward and Sarah would be back at the house by ten thirty, but the children would not return until midday giving Sarah plenty of time without the children which was her primary driver.

Sunday afternoon was also taken up by the children being dispatched, again on foot to Sunday school, this time at the Cathedral. They would leave the house at two o'clock and not return until about five o'clock. But there was mutual benefit in this unorthodox arrangement as the children were also grateful to get out of the house and be away from Sarah.

Unsurprisingly, not every Sunday morning was spent by the children at St Stephen's church and many warm Sunday afternoons saw the children disappear to Williamson's Park, with its landmark Ashton Memorial and its acres of parkland in which to play in.

The few pennies intended for the collection plate were also occasionally *diverted* to what the children saw as a greater need, which included sweets and ice cream. The children would recognise that this was morally reprehensible, but they equally saw it as thoroughly enjoyable!

The family also saw the return one Saturday morning of Sam Carmichael, Edward's father.

There was a heavy knock on the door, and the children were immediately curious to learn who was calling. It was most unusual for there to be any visitors at the house. Indeed, visitors were positively discouraged with the exception of Father O'Reilly from the Cathedral. His visits always seemed timed to coincide with family meal times and being the priest; it was considered to be rude not to invite him to stay.

Another visitor to the house on a Saturday was Norman, the milkman. He would call by every Saturday to be paid and following months of begging he succumbed to the pleas of Robert that in the next summer holidays he could go out on the milk round with him.

But the children were intrigued to know who this unexpected caller might be.

Sarah answered the door and for a moment was taken aback.

"Well, aren't you going to invite me in?" Sam asked as he stepped into the house with his small bag clasped in one hand and a bunch of bedraggled carnations in the other.

"What are you doing here?" Sarah demanded, irritated by his presence without prior notice and his presumption that he could simply walk back into their lives.

Since the death of Ellen his wife, Sam had become an itinerant figure, staying where there was work; living in 'digs' in places as far apart as Bristol and Newcastle and rarely writing to let people know his whereabouts.

He no longer had a permanent address; he no longer owned a vehicle, and he travelled everywhere by bus or train with his life's possessions appearing to fit into a single suitcase.

Sam was a weary soul and for a man in his late fifties, he cut a sad, lonely figure, looking years beyond his age, unkempt and slightly dishevelled. Gone was the upright, distinguished head of the family of only a few years earlier, replaced by someone who was still grieving and still angry that life had dealt him this hand.

Sam put his bag down in the hallway and without being asked, walked into the living room where Edward was sat comfortably by the fire place.

The children were playing a game of snakes and ladders on the dining table, but their attention was firmly fixed upon the man in the room.

"What the hell are you doing here?" Edward snarled, irritated like Sarah that Sam had descended upon them unannounced.

"I hope he doesn't expect to stay," quipped Sarah, who flounced into the kitchen slamming the door behind her.

"What sort of welcome do you call that?" smarted Sam, who clearly expected a rather warmer welcome than he had received so far.

He turned to the dining table where the children were agog to understand what was happening.

Charlotte by now a switched on, alert eleven year old turned to Maria and Robert and sarcastically announced in her most refined accent; "Let me introduce you to your grandfather."

The children were dismissed to their bedrooms only to be called back some time later when the heated words downstairs had subsided. Peace or at least a semblance of peace appeared to descend upon the house, and Sam joined the family for tea, but there was a tension in the room throughout.

The children had no relationship with this virtual stranger and try as he might, Sam simply could not engage them. Charlotte was wary; Maria was unusually guarded and shy and Robert, who was drawn to his grandfather, preferred to take a lead from Charlotte and so he too was withdrawn.

The tension between Edward and his father was palpable, with few words being spoken and Sarah..... well she simply ignored him!

Sam remained in the house overnight, sleeping on the sofa, but he departed with little ceremony and the briefest of goodbyes, almost overlooked as the household went about its Sunday ritual of preparing for Mass.

This was to be the nature of Sam's relationship with his son and the family over the coming years, with no one knowing quite where he was living, what he was doing and if he was well. The sadness was that Edward, who now considered himself as head of a 'middle class' family, had no room in his life for a grieving itinerant father and made it quite clear that he was not particularly welcome.

Sam would die only a few years later with only the kindness and concern of his landlady to fall back on, a woman who in the end cared more for him than did his family.

The past couple of years had also seen the family establish a monthly routine of visiting Preston to spend Sunday afternoon with Sarah's sister and brother-in-law,

Elizabeth, and George Morrison. They had one son, Mortimer, who was a year younger than Robert, but the two of them were like brothers when they were together.

The visits were a welcome break from the much resented routine for Sarah, who was extremely close to her sister. It was also a generally happy trip out for the children who found their 'uncle and aunt' easy to get on with, but they also found that Sarah was considerably more at ease when she was with her sister.

However, it was always obvious that Edward and George were not entirely comfortable in each other's company, even though they shared a common interest in cars of which there were always plenty in George's driveway. But that interest was expressed at a remote and cursory level by Edward, with no personal chemistry, not even the common language that men seem to find when they chat together about cars.

His middle class status obsessed Edward; anathema to George, who was a hardworking and a successful garage mechanic and an entrepreneurial car dealer. George found Edwards's behaviour tiresome, but he humoured him for Elizabeth's sake. But the relationship changed when it became obvious to Edward, that George might be able to help with a small matter.

~

Edward and Sarah had discussed openly with Elizabeth and George their desire to have Charlotte attend a Catholic girl's only school in Preston as a day pupil. They felt, probably correctly that the educational standards and attainment levels were better at the school in Preston, but there was also an ulterior and overarching motive.

Sarah was increasingly uncomfortable with the questions and innuendo from the staff and parents at the school the children were attending in Lancaster relating to the children's birth mother. Teachers had pointedly asked Edward and Sarah at parents evenings why it was that Charlotte in particular but also Maria were convinced that their mother was still alive. This was despite the commonly accepted explanation established by Edward and Sarah that she had died some years earlier.

Teachers reported that Charlotte simply refused to accept that her mother had died. This was becoming both a talking point amongst the children and a lightning rod for teasing when friends taunted her for having been in a childrens home.

Sarah and Edward had discussed the prospect of Charlotte going to the school in Preston to defuse chatter and rumours but acknowledged that the journey time and cost of transport on a daily basis were unacceptable.

The solution Sarah was hoping her sister would offer was for Charlotte to live with her and George during the week returning to Lancaster on a Friday evening by bus. And it was today, after many hints and much prompting by Sarah that Elizabeth finally broached the subject.

"You know that George and I would love to have Charlotte stay with us. We have the room, and it would be nice to get to know her a little better," Elizabeth explained.

Sarah could hardly contain her joy. In truth, her primary reason for wanting Charlotte to be schooled in Preston was not about her education, nor was it entirely about removing her from the chatter at her current school. The reason was the same as it had always been; Sarah simply didn't like the competition for Edward's time and affection.

But there was a deeper reason. As Charlotte became older, she increasingly took on the looks and mannerisms of her mother Ruth, and this presented a constant reminder to Sarah of Ruth's continued presence in their home. Packing Charlotte off to Preston for the week was a very elegant solution.

By the end of the day, arrangements had been made with Elizabeth and George that Charlotte would begin the new school term in September as a day girl at St Bernadette's school and would become the new member of their family, at least for the week days. The school was known to be willing to accept Charlotte, and now all that remained was to tell her about the decision.

Robert was in Mortimer's bedroom playing while Charlotte and Maria were outside sitting on a bench bored when Sarah called into the garden for Charlotte to come into the house.

She was somewhat taken aback when she entered the sitting room to find the adults staring at her, all with beaming smiles on their faces.

"Charlotte," began Sarah, hardly able to contain her excitement. "You're to leave the Cathedral school in Lancaster and in September you will attend St Bernadette's girls school here in Preston, and you will stay with Auntie Elizabeth and Uncle George during the week."

Charlotte had no inkling of this move, but inwardly she was overjoyed. She had friends whose parents were also sending their daughters to the same school with similar arrangements to stay with relatives in Preston.

Charlotte listened to what was being said and rather than show her inner excitement she simply shrugged her shoulders and returned to the garden to tell Maria.

CHAPTER TWENTY THREE

The long summer holiday was, to begin with, the Carmichael family taking a week's holiday on a caravan site.

The old Hillman Fourteen car had long gone, replaced with a smart new but smaller Standard Eight car which would have the task of pulling the newly acquired caravan and carrying the family and their provisions for the week, to St Bees Head on the North West coast of Cumberland.

The arrival of the new car some two weeks earlier was a day of great excitement particularly for Robert, who was obsessed by cars. He was emotional about the old car going but stood at the pavement edge outside the house for an hour waiting for his father to return home eventually.

For once there was a connection between Robert and his father, a rarity but nonetheless enjoyable for the very excited Robert. He wanted to climb inside the car which he was allowed to do with the greatest of care. He wanted to see under the bonnet and asked endless questions about what the various parts in the engine compartment did. But it was when he saw the towing ball on the back of the car and was told that they would be having a holiday in a new caravan that his already heightened excitement went off the scale.

Robert ran to see his sisters to tell them only to find that they were less than impressed. This was made worse when later they were told that the caravan could sleep only two people and that the children would, therefore, need to sleep in a bivouac tent.

And it was indeed a bivouac as they later found out when Edward decided to erect it in the garden to make sure he knew how to do so before they went on holiday.

The heavy grey bivouac ridge tent was an army surplus model and made very popular with families discovering the joys of camping. It was large enough for the three children to lie down with some ease but as they found out when a rain shower passed through later in the day if you touched the inside of the bivouac when it was raining, the tent became porous.

Having discovered this Edward realised why the shop assistant had insisted that he also purchased a fly sheet that extended over the tent. Once this was strung above the tent, it protected against both the heat and the rain. However, it did little to improve the enthusiasm for camping in the two girls who saw only the prospect of creepy crawlies and wet clothes.

The following morning the house was in chaos as Sarah struggled to gather the necessary sheets, blankets, and pillows against a backdrop of over excited children who were also gathering toys and their clothes.

Edward returned having collected the caravan from the farm where it was being stored bringing to a halt the packing frenzy as the whole family came to inspect this tiny two birth novelty, hitched to an equally small car.

A further hour of dashing between the house and the driveway eventually saw the car and caravan loaded, with just the family needing to take their place in the already overloaded car. To the credit of British engineering, this small car managed its way out of the drive and the family embarked upon their summer holiday.

The journey was torturous on what was to be one of the hottest days of the summer so far. The heat combined with Robert's car sickness and endless stops for him to be sick resulted in the family not arriving at the caravan site until early evening.

But all memories of the journey were set aside as they finally unhitched the caravan in what seemed to be the middle of a very large field. There were about twenty other caravans and several tents but what struck the children more than anything was the vastness of the open space and the views out to sea.

As Edward struggled to put up the tent in a stiffening breeze, the children ran to the edge of the high cliff feeling the unusually warm air coming off the Irish Sea.

A local man pointed into the far distance saying that on a clear day it was possible to see the outline coast of the Isle of Man against the late evening sun. The children looked on that evening and throughout their stay but saw nothing.

When the children eventually returned to the caravan, Edward already had the primus stove alight with a kettle on top behind a shield against the breeze while Sarah was busying herself inside the caravan preparing the evening meal.

But Maria was already concerning herself about where the toilets were located.

"I want to go to the toilet," she called into the caravan without any response from Sarah.

"Daddy, I need to go to the toilet," she called, exaggerating the urgency to promote a response.

It was at this point that Maria realised that the small wooden building in the far distance, near to where the other caravans and tents were located, just about as far away as they could be from it, was the toilet and fresh water area. It was at about the same moment that Sarah made the same discovery.

An hour and a half later, Edward had completed the move of the caravan and tent to a pitch that was close enough to the toilets for Sarah, though now without the remoteness that had previously been her priority upon entering the site.

The week of camping was thoroughly enjoyed by the children despite the occasional heavy overnight rain which kept them awake. They spent most of their days on the shingle beach with its wooden groins set deep into the foreshore. These acted as a bulwark against the ferocious winter storms that would batter this coastline, but today they acted as excellent wind breaks as well as good hiding places.

When not at the beach the children would go exploring, often for hours at a time returning to the caravan only when they were hungry. They were as always, entirely at ease with their own company and apart from the odd day out with Edward and Sarah, visiting local landmarks such as Whitehaven and Keswick, they looked to each other for company and entertainment.

Edward and Sarah also seemed to be more relaxed which had a powerful impact upon the general mood of the holiday. Sarah was never happier than when she was sitting in a deck chair in one of her many swimsuits taking in the sun. She also enjoyed the attention shown to her attractive figure by the men as they passed by.

Sarah and Edward were never concerned for the whereabouts of the children, and for his part, Edward spent much of his time tinkering with the car, the caravan and anything he felt needed his attention.

The children, who had never been taught to swim, mounted sufficient courage to enter the chilly Irish Sea though never venturing beyond the water's edge. Like all children of their ages, the sea, and what little sand there was held a strange fascination and time simply flew by.

But while the children's days were spent in the warm summer sunshine their nights were often spent with their young bodies being covered in Calamine Lotion to sooth the effects of sunburn.

As the last rays of the sun disappeared way out to sea, parents across the caravan site sent their children out for one last play covered in the chalky white lotion signalling an uncomfortable night to come for the red cheeked youngsters.

Robert spent one splendid afternoon with a newly found 'acquaintance' and the boy's father casting lines into the sea in the vain hope of catching a fish. The boy was from Liverpool here on holiday too, but they were all under canvass in similar bivouac tents.

Robert was transfixed by the relationship and dialogue between the boy, who was his age and his father. They joked together and in between baiting hooks they were often play fighting and giggling over shared interests.

Robert so wanted to get close to his father, but he knew that this would never happen. He was not frightened of his father, but he was wary of him. He knew there were boundaries, and he knew that he must not cross these. As much as Robert yearned for closeness with his father he knew that this was a major fault line in their relationship and could not be crossed.

He knew that his father was increasingly intolerant of him but thought no worse of his father for this. This eight year old boy was wise beyond his years and was building life skills that would serve him well in the years to come. He found emotional comfort in his sisters and learnt tolerance and an ability to measure people from his father.

The fishing yielded three fish. The young boy caught two small whiting, but Robert was to triumph with his catch….a four pound cod.

The boy's father was gushing in his praise of what the lads had achieved. He proudly walked with Robert back to the caravan where Robert was eager to evidence the fact that he and he alone, had caught the fish.

But to his disappointment, the triumph of his day was met with derision especially from Sarah.

"You call that big; I've seen bigger goldfish," she mocked encouraging Edward to do likewise.

"I bet the man here caught that on *his* rod, *his* line, using *his* bait and *his* skill. How can you claim any part in that?" dismissed Edward.

The man was furious. In a broad Liverpudlian accent, he chided Edward.

"Your boy has done well and caught a bigger fish today than I have ever done in ten years; give him some encouragement, I'd be over the moon with excitement if my lad had done as well," he explained putting a supportive hand on the proud Robert's shoulder.

Callously Edward turned to Robert.

"Give the man his fish back and wash your hands," he said as he turned to the man. "And you," he said aggressively, "you can sling your hook and take your advice and your fish back to Liverpool and your own people and your common way of life."

The man smiled.

"Mister, you're a snob who thinks that because I speak like this, you and your kind are somehow better than me. Let me tell you Mister high and mighty, you may think I have nothing, but I have my family, and I have self-respect. Oh, and by the way," he explained, pausing for a moment, "before you dig yourself in any deeper, I own a chain of cinemas and cafe's up and down this coast and....well you might like to know, I also own this caravan site!"

The man tapped Robert on the head,

"You did well young Robert, and when I eat this tonight, I will think of the young lad that caught it."

The short holiday was all too soon over, with the family taking that familiar journey all families take home after a relaxing break together. The exuberance and excitement that so characterised the journey a week ago was now replaced by silence as everyone in the car reflected on their own memories.

~

By the following Monday morning, all thoughts of the holiday were now consigned to distant memories as routine returned to the Carmichael household.

Edward left for work at seven o'clock and at eight thirty, Sarah had locked all the internal doors in the house as she readied herself for work. As she left, she hung the back door key around Charlotte's neck and gave her one shilling to buy lunch for the three children.

She announced that she would not return to the house until six o'clock leaving the children; Robert now aged eight and Maria aged nine in the care of Charlotte, who was herself only eleven.

The children went to the tool shed to plan their day as they would do for the rest of this holiday.

By now they each had a bicycle, and this provided freedom in greater abundance.

Today's plan was to cycle the five miles to Glasson Dock. They had been to the docks on many occasions in the past on short trips out with their father in his car so knew the roads to take to get there. Their plan today was to go and do the things that they were not allowed to do when they went to the docks with their parents!

They gathered the biscuits that had been set aside on a plate in the kitchen filled a couple of bottles of water, climbed on their bicycles and with Charlotte in the lead and set off.

For the girls, this was a tiring ride; for the young Robert on a bicycle without gears, this was doubly hard. But it was a challenge he would stoically meet, made easier because the ride was mainly without hills to climb.

Their planned first stopping point was to be the Stork Hotel at Condor Green. This beautiful former coaching Inn sat alongside the tidal estuary of the River Lune.

This was to be an important landmark because they knew that the rest of their journey to Glasson Dock might be cut off if the tide was in. This had happened before to their father who would now consult the local tide tables before embarking on such a journey. For the children, the prospect of not knowing, and secretly hoping that the tide might be in was far more preferable.

They arrived at the Stork Hotel and found to their disappointment that not only was the tide out, but there seemed little prospect of it coming in, in the near future. Nonetheless, they had decided that this should be where they would have a biscuit and so settled down on the grass to do so.

The landlord was busily fussing over the geraniums in pots around the windows and was fascinated to see these happy youngsters resting from what he deduced had been a tiring ride.

Having established that they had ridden from Lancaster and were on their way to Glasson Dock, he warned them to be out of the dock area before four o'clock as the tide was due to be in-flood by five o'clock cutting off the road back to the Stork Hotel and higher ground.

"Can I use your toilet please?" asked Maria politely.

"Of course, you can and if you need to do the same on the way back you tell people here that Mr. Harding the landlord said you are his guests."

One by one the three of them trooped into the hotel toilets, much to the growing amusement of the locals and guests who by now were aware of the adventure these children had embarked upon.

They thanked Mr. Harding and climbed upon their bikes waving to their new found friends as they turned right and headed towards Glasson Dock where they arrived filled with a spirit of adventure.

Their plan was to visit the railway sidings where they knew there were some old steam trains and passenger carriages. But this would need to wait until the shilling Sarah had given Charlotte had been spent.

They stopped at a small shop, close to the road and went in.

"We need to get something for our lunch, and we have one shilling to spend," announced Charlotte to the obvious amusement of a couple of locals who were idling away the time inside the shop.

"Well," said the shop keeper; "when I was your age, I would have wanted a meat and potato pie and sweets for my lunch, and I suppose that you'll be expecting the same won't you?"

Charlotte had no idea what to expect she could buy for a shilling and so was pleasantly surprised when she was given three large warm meat and potato pies, a bag of mixed sweets and six pence change.

"Thank you, sir," replied Robert, "we're off on an adventure," he confided to all that would listen.

"You'd best not go clambering on those trains I keep seeing you looking at," warned the shop keeper.

"Oh, don't be so foolish," laughed one of the regulars, "that's the very place you'd go if you were these kid's age and no doubt about it."

There was much laughter as the children went to leave.

"Now mind you.....Old Tom Higginbotham, the security guard, does his rounds at about three o'clock, so you'll need to be out of there by then," quipped another of the locals, much to the amusement of the rest of the jovial and somewhat mischievous company.

The children clambered back on their bicycles, their politeness, their openness and their tremendously engaging personalities having once again captivated another group of people. Their new found friends saw them cycle to the railway siding as expected and into an Aladdin's cave of surprises and excitement.

The children settled down to eat their lunch on the footplate of a soon to be scrapped GWR Castle Class steam engine, of one of Britain's finest leviathans of steam.

The policy adopted by British Rail in this year would see all steam engines cast aside within twelve years in favour of dieselisation. But this elegant old lady; this goddess of the rails was to feel the power of steam thrust through her veins on one more journey as it's firebox was to be stoked with the imaginations of these three children who knew only the destination, but not the route.

"We're off to see our real mummy," announced Charlotte as Robert struggled to open the firebox door and fill it with the fuel of imagination.

"Are the points set?" cried Maria hanging precariously from the footplate, checking that the way ahead was clear.

"We're ready to go," cried Robert, fully immersed in the journey of their imagination. "Mummy, we're coming to find you, choo-choo... choo choo," cried Charlotte, feeling the wind already blowing through her long dark hair.

Their imaginary journey took them through villages and hamlets, through towns and cities and their cry to the good folk of all those imaginary places was always the same; "Have you seen our mummy?"

Their journey took so long that they were only able to bring it to an end when they heard the cries of the shopkeeper calling, "Kids ...hey kids, Tom Higginbotham the security guard will be here soon."

They slowly brought their train to a stop and met the voice of reality.

"Tom will kick up a stink if he finds you here; you'd better get on your way; you can always look for your mummy on another day," he said, choked by what he had seen and heard as he and others from the shop were silenced by what they witnessed.

The children climbed back onto their bicycles and began their long journey home with a smile and a wave to their new found friends.

"Come back soon," they cried as the children sped off still waving. And so they would do, on many occasions in the future; always making the same journey on their train, carried out to the increasing bemusement and interest of the locals.

As they passed the Stork Hotel, Mr. Harding the landlord still messing about with the pots of geraniums called out to them.

"You made it before the tide came then? Come back and see us again won't you?"

Charlotte smiled; "We will; probably next week," and with a wave, they were gone.

And they did visit Glasson Dock several times that summer, and for several summers to come.

Over the years, their *friends* were always pleased to see them cycle into the village, and while the number of steam engines seemed to increase over the years, their favourite, now named 'Ruth' by the children remained. She had become a symbol of hope that one day they may well find their *real* mother.....Ruth.

It was the last week of the summer holiday; a holiday that saw the children explore the countryside, and the parks when it was dry and the museum and library when it was wet. They had enjoyed exploring and being together and rarely were to be found with other children except in the evenings in the hour before bedtime when they would spend time with the few children of their age that lived at the bottom of their street.

The children would tell their stories of adventure and travel to an audience of children and occasionally a parent who would listen in awe, to stories that might come straight out of Victorian novels. To the parents, they were simply stories from children with over active imaginations. But the final adventure of the summer holiday was not to be told to anyone.

~

Charlotte called a planning meeting in the tool shed at about seven thirty, not long before the children would be ushered off to bed. In whispered tones, she announced her plan.

"Tomorrow we are off on our biggest adventure yet. You must tell nobody, but we're going to try to find the lady from the church....the lady who looked after us a long, long time ago," she revealed.

Charlotte explained that she had been saving the change from their lunch money and now had enough to buy tickets for the bus from Lancaster to Inglewhite. She instructed that they were to get a good night's sleep and, "*be ready to march*," as soon as Sarah left the house the following morning.

Little sleep was to be had that night as the children excitedly thought about the journey they would take the following day.

For Robert, Mr. and Mrs. Oliver in Inglewhite were just people who Charlotte thought might help them find their mother. For Maria, it was a similar excitement though she continued to convince herself that she had a sharp and thorough memory of her time with Mr. and Mrs. Oliver. But for Charlotte, her memory was strong, and she was convinced that if anyone knew about their mother, Mrs. Oliver would.

The following day saw Sarah leave at her usual time of eight thirty, blissfully unaware of the plans and journey the children were about to embark upon.

Having ensured that Sarah was out of sight, the children rushed along the shortcut that would take them to the main road between Lancaster and Preston. There they waited for a bus that would take them to Garstang where Charlotte knew they would need to change onto another local bus to take them to Inglewhite.

As the Preston bus stopped, the children clambered aboard and sat on the nearest seats to the rear door where Robert could get as much air as possible.

"So, where are you three going with such secretive looks on your faces?" asked the cheery bus conductor.

"We're going to Inglewhite near Goosnargh, and we need three children's returns please,' requested Charlotte, trying her hardest to look and sound much older.

The Conductor pressed buttons on his machine which spat out six small square tickets. "That's your return to Garstang; you'll need to get the Inglewhite tickets on the next bus," he advised as he gave Charlotte the change.

"And what, might I ask are three youngsters doing going to Inglewhite on their own?" he posed, completing the question on the lips of several passengers who were also intrigued to hear the answer.

"We're going to find our Mummy," replied Robert, leaving the conductor and passengers none the wiser, as the bus trundled its journey south out of Lancaster stopping several times before they eventually pulled into the bus station at Garstang.

Charlotte gathered her charges around her and set off in search of the bus for Inglewhite. She quickly established that the next bus would not be leaving for thirty five minutes, and so the children sat on a bench quietly waiting.

It was Thursday, market day in Garstang and so the bus station was unusually busy with people from the outlying villages making their weekly trip into town. Robert found the whole experience fascinating seeing people dashing from the buses eager to visit their favourite market stalls or simply to catch up with friends.

There was a cattle market very near to the bus station and with time to kill, Robert persuaded Charlotte that they should walk across the road and see the animals. When they arrived, they were met by smells that were strangely familiar to Maria and Charlotte whose memory of living on a farm was at best faded if non-existent.

The children settled down on seats overlooking the auction arena where Frisian cattle were already being sold on a day of brisk trade. They were fascinated by the language of the auctioneer which Robert tried unsuccessfully to mimic, much to the amusement of the local farmers who were intrigued by the presence of the children.

Maria was rather more taken by the way that the farmers indicated their bids. Some quite obviously raised a hand, but others, especially the man standing next to them simply tugged on his left ear, and she could see that the auctioneer recognised this as a signal for a bid.

Maria decided that she should also tug her ear to see if the auctioneer might acknowledge her. Eventually, with a wry smile on his face, the auctioneer announced, much to the amusement of the crowd, "Arthur, you've been out bid by a bunch of kids." There were taunts and jokes as the auction carried on, and the children turned to head back to the bus station.

But as they did, Charlotte felt a tap on her shoulder.

"You're one of the Carmichael kids aren't you?"

Charlotte turned to meet the vaguely familiar face of Tom Masters.

"Don't you remember me, girl? I'm Tom Masters; I worked for your Dad and Granddad, but I also worked for Mr. Oliver at Fellside Farm."

Charlotte was dumbstruck. She did vaguely recognise the face, but slowly she remembered Tom from Fellside Farm.

"What are you doing here?" he asked looking around to see if he could eye another familiar face.

"Oh, please don't tell Daddy we're here?" she pleaded, tears running down her cheek. Maria picked up on this and also began to cry.

"Now, now my dears....I'm not after telling anyone ....but I am concerned for your safety."

Charlotte gathered Robert and Maria and began to walk quickly towards the exit.

"If you don't want your dad to know, you'd better let me know why you're here, presumably on your own so that I can help," he said, now crouching down to meet Charlotte's eyes.

"We've come to find Mummy; that's why we're here, and we need to get a bus to Inglewhite," announced Robert, keen to feel a part of this conversation with what to him was a complete stranger.

Tom guided the children to a bench seat away from the hustle and bustle of the market.

"Now tell me what this is all about?" he asked.

Charlotte turned to Maria and Robert and with a nod of approval from them she explained.

"My Daddy and our new mummy Sarah, say that our real Mummy is dead, and we don't think she is. We wanted to find the lady who used to look after us to ask her where our Mummy is."

Tom looked at the children knowing that if anyone knew about their past, it was him. He had seen the comings and goings at Eastbook Farm when Ruth and Edward had lived there with Sam and Ellen Carmichael. He had also been present during the period when Ruth had left the children, and he had also experienced the joy of seeing the children again at Fellside Farm, only to see them being wrenched away and taken to the childrens homes.

After some reflection, Tom took Charlotte's hand in his.

"My dear," he began, "Mr. and Mrs. Oliver have left Fellside Farm, and I think they have retired to become *townies*." He went on; "There are many folk hereabouts who will know you like I do, but they aren't about to gossip....especially to young whippersnappers like you."

Tom cupped Charlotte's face in his hands.

"You're too young to meddle into the past, and anyway, there'll be time a plenty in the future when you are old enough to ask your questions and to understand the answers. But there's no one hereabouts who is going to tell you today or anytime in the near future," he concluded.

Charlotte began to cry again.

"My dear," he said, trying to wipe her tears with his handkerchief. You will one day know everything, mark my word, but till then, we'd better get you home afore your Daddy really does find out."

They walked slowly across the road to the bus station as Charlotte explained to Tom Masters where they lived. Tom was concerned that he must get these children on a bus as soon as possible, knowing that if he had recognised Charlotte, there would be plenty of other people who could easily do the same.

They were fortunate that a Lancaster bus had just pulled in and would be leaving in ten minutes.

"Now jump on the bus while I get you something to eat for the journey home," Tom instructed ushering the children through the open door.

He returned a few minutes later with three meat pies purchased from Singletons, famous for its Dinky pork pies, and as a treat, he also gave them each an Eccles cake. He handed over the food to Charlotte and with nothing further said; he brushed his fingers through her dark black hair and stepped off the bus.

But he swiftly stepped back onto the bus with a smile on his face.

"I liked your Mummy, she was a nice lady, but she left you; that's all I can say. One day, my dear, God will guide you, and all your questions will be answered, but not now.....not whist you are so young."

The return journey to Lancaster was subdued, despite the valiant efforts of Charlotte to lift their sprits. Maria was particularly downhearted as she had firmly expected that on this day she would find her real mother.

But soon they were back in familiar territory and with a pact to never reveal a word of what had happened that day, they slipped back into their surreal lives with Edward and Sarah.

CHAPTER TWENTY FOUR

The school holiday was all too soon over for the children. Thoughts of the many adventures they had undertaken were consigned to memories, to be drawn upon over the coming months every time they were alone or needed to have their spirits lifted.

But it would not be just the children who might have fond memories of that summer. There would be the many people whose lives had come into contact with the Carmichael children and who were touched by their extraordinary bond, their character, and their spirit.

On the Sunday before the new school term started, the family climbed into the car and set off for Preston to visit Auntie Elizabeth and Uncle George's house.

Charlotte had packed her new school uniform and other clothes and was ready to begin yet another new chapter in her life.

The plan now agreed with Elizabeth and George was that Charlotte would return to Lancaster by bus on Friday afternoon with the other girls who either stayed in Preston during the week or who commuted daily. The routine would also include an increasing number of weeks when Charlotte also returned to Preston on the early Monday morning bus allowing her a slightly longer weekend at home.

Saying goodbye to Maria and Robert was difficult but was met with the same spirit of stoicism that would so characterise the lives of these children who, at such a young age had learnt to adapt to so many changes.

Charlotte settled to the school and to her new way of life with some ease. She would have wanted to remain with Maria and Robert, but that was not to be.

The autumn term gave way to winter and the Christmas holiday which was as enthusiastically approached in the Carmichael household as it was in any other with overly excited children. Though the family relationships in the Carmichael house were very different and despite the continued distance Sarah kept between herself and the children; she did her best to make Christmas enjoyable for them.

But for the children, the best part of Christmas was when everyone had returned to work, and there was time for the three of them to be together again.

The children who had previously been confined to the kitchen and the garage when Edward and Sarah were at work, now only had the garage as their play space. Banishment from using the kitchen was brought about because the constantly hungry children were helping themselves to what little food was to be found in the refrigerator or the larder. The culinary concoctions they invented were many and varied!

A favourite was sugar sandwiches, starting with lashings of butter or margarine on fresh bread topped off with a good helping of white or brown sugar, whichever was plentiful at the time. The children also had a taste for mixing sugar with anything. Sugar and cocoa, dry mixed in a cup and eaten with a spoon was a favourite, but sugar and dry cornflakes and sugar and desiccated coconut was also rated highly.

But these excursions into the larder were smartly brought to an end when Sarah came home early one day to see first-hand the reason for unexpected depletion in larder supplies.

The children, who were now confined to the draughty cold garage which had an old carpet on the floor, seemed unaware and certainly unconcerned by the deprivation this represented. They would wrap up against the cold, and when the cold became unbearable, they would set off into Lancaster and head for their favourite haunts, either the library or the museum. The children, who were well known to the staff as being well behaved and very polite, were always welcomed.

Over the course of the holidays, the children became well read. They might spend two or three hours quietly reading and during particularly cold spells they could easily read two or three books in a week.

Their alternative venue, used when even the children considered they might have outstayed their welcome, was the city museum; an imposing building in the heart of the city that was filled with artifacts that simply fascinated the children.

At no time would the children consider their lives to be anything other than normal. They enjoyed the peculiar lifestyle they had, with endless freedom to go anywhere and do anything as essential to their way of life. They always had in the back of their minds that they were different, but that never got in the way of them enjoying themselves.

When they returned to their cold garage, they would huddle together as Charlotte read to them, or they would play with their toys all of which were now kept there. Sarah was obsessed by tidiness and regarded toys around the house as little more than clutter.

~

By the autumn of nineteen fifty six, Maria had also been enrolled into St Bernadette's school in Preston and was also staying during the week with Auntie Elizabeth and Uncle George. She adapted, in the same way that Charlotte had done but was less diplomatic when she showed visible signs of being unhappy.

Maria liked stability, and though she found life at home in Lancaster disagreeable at times it was familiar and she also previously had Robert and Charlotte to fall back on when she felt down.

Maria was sensitive and liked to have the pieces of her life firmly in place and saw the arrangement she now found herself in for what it was. It was Sarah's way of moving her and Charlotte as far away from her as possible.

Robert disliked being the only one at home during the week. He found himself regularly in trouble with his father and Sarah often for what he regarded as trivial matters.

He began to withdraw into himself. Having completed his homework at the bureau in the hallway, he would go to his bedroom and would not be seen again until the morning when he went to school.

Few words were by now exchanged between Robert and his father who seemed to meet any question from Robert as underlying his conviction that Robert was, in his words "thick."

"You stupid boy, don't you know?" was a typical response to a question from Robert. Rather than seeing the enthusiastic questions as an opportunity to help Robert, Edward mocked him.

"You're as thick as two short planks; don't they teach you anything at that school?" he would mock, looking to Sarah for her easily given support.

Robert was far from being *thick*. Like his sisters, he was bright, and his school work reflected this. Robert like his sister sat and passed the 'eleven plus' school examination resulting in him being offered a place at the local Grammar School. Even this achievement was derided firstly by Sarah and then by Edward.

"So how on earth did you manage that," was Sarah's sarcastic reaction? "did you read the answers from someone else's paper?" she mocked turning to Edward for the final word.

"Well, all I can say, Sarah is that they must be lowering the standard if Robert can pass," he said, brushing away in an instant the achievements of his son.

But Robert, Maria, and Charlotte were to prove to be bright, academic children achieving high marks in school exams. However, the constant in their school reports was that each of the children seemed withdrawn from school life and though they mixed well they appeared to have few genuine friends.

One teacher remarked of Charlotte: 'This girl will achieve in any circumstances but must also give herself time to enjoy her youth before it passes her by.' Another wrote: 'She carries a burden that we have been unable to assist her with. She is so driven academically that she has no room for anything else in her life.'

The same themes were emerging in all of the school reports; driven, but detached. One teacher wrote of Robert: 'He achieves most of what we ask of him, but he is remote. If I didn't know different, I might see it as worrisome.'

But it was the school holidays that brought the best out in the children. As each of them moved into their teenage years, they continued to enjoy each other's company. They enjoyed nothing more than to cycle to old haunts and finding new ones.

There were also distractions. Charlotte was by now fifteen years of age and enjoyed spending time on the summer evenings with her friends from school. This would also include meeting boys and so was for her, a venture away from the house without Robert and Maria. They, of course, knew that she was meeting *boy-friends* but were happy to be discreet.

Edward, on the other hand, was not happy! He met Charlotte's requests to go out with her friends with suspicion and hostility.

Like all parents, he was rightly concerned for her safety and wellbeing. But his resistance went far beyond this. His questioning would be bound in complete mistrust. He presumed she was mixing with the 'wrong types' when Charlotte gave an address of a friend's house that he considered to be in the wrong part of town. He saw mixing with girls who had brothers as unacceptable, leading to Charlotte fabricating where she was going and who she was seeing.

Charlotte was now meeting many of her friends in their homes, and this helped her to understand how vastly different her upbringing was, from that of her friends. And her friends were also acutely aware of the very different lifestyle Charlotte had from them, and they too understood.

On one occasion, a friend's father rang Edward at the house to ask if Charlotte could stay at his house for the night with his daughter as he and his wife wanted to take them to the theatre.

Edward's reaction was typically barbed.

"Don't you think she has a perfectly good bed here?" he barked at the man. "Why are people like you trying to get into our lives anyway?" he reacted, always believing that people were trying to peer into his life.

Thankfully, most of Charlotte's friends and families were well aware of the strange ways of the Carmichael family, and many were prepared to set aside Edward's rudeness so that Charlotte could see her friends. Many were also aware, or at least partially aware of the fact that Charlotte and her siblings had previously been in childrens homes but knew that there were unexplained circumstances that simply didn't add up.

But for all of this, Charlotte did manage to see friends, even if in doing so she incurred the wrath of her father.

Like most fathers, he was strict about what time Charlotte should be home at night. She was required to be home by nine o'clock in the evening in the summer months with no exceptions.

To achieve this, Charlotte assiduously ensured that she left her friend's houses in sufficient time to arrive home before nine o'clock. Mostly she was home early, but occasionally she was two or three minutes late.

On the last occasion when she was five minutes late she was firmly told that in the future the house doors would be locked at nine o'clock, and if she were late, she would have to sleep in the tool shed. Charlotte knew this was no idle threat and was extremely wary of breaching her curfew. However, she did and with extreme consequences.

Having spent the evening with a friend, her friend's father offered to run Charlotte home as it was raining. The car arrived outside Charlotte's house in plenty of time, but Charlotte and her friend continued chatting for a few minutes before they said goodbye and Charlotte walked to the back door of the house.

Edward had seen the car arrive and had seen Charlotte leave and come to the door.

When Charlotte tried to open the door, it was locked. She knocked on the door several times but received no reply. By now Robert and Maria were awake and could hear Edward calling to Charlotte from behind the door.

"I gave you ample warning that I would lock the doors, and I have done so. You will have to sleep in the tool shed."

Robert was horrified and pleaded with his father to let Charlotte come into the house.

"How dare you question me?" came the chillingly, frightening reply.

Robert sobbed as he saw his sister slowly walk to the tool shed. She looked back at Maria, who was at the bedroom window as she stepped into the shed and closed the door.

She remained there for the whole night.

Edward would not relent. He showed no regard to the fact that it was his fifteen year old daughter that he had stood on principle over, and had left to spend the night outside.

A fault line was created that night that impacted upon all three children. They were old enough to know that whatever the circumstances this was no way to treat an adolescent girl.

The already distant relationship each of the children had with Edward and Sarah was now damaged further.

CHAPTER TWENTY FIVE

At the age of sixteen, Charlotte completed her O-level exams in fine style achieving above average in all the subjects she had taken. A-level exams were the next natural step leading on to university. But a combination of several factors saw Charlotte leave school at the beginning of the summer and seek employment.

Edward and Sarah had made it very clear that they felt the children should not go on to university. Edward argued that no one in the family had been to university in the past, and they had all done well, so why should his children.

The underlying reason was more simple. Edward and Sarah wanted the children to leave home and make their own way in life as soon as possible. They saw Charlotte's strong O-level results as good enough to get her a job and with some energy they set about identifying suitable roles.

But Charlotte was very clear about what she wanted to do with her life, and that was to become a journalist. She had long viewed the newspaper industry as exciting, and she knew that women were increasingly being taken on as trainees. Her English Literature and English Language results at school were very good, and she felt certain that this would serve her well in making job applications.

To her credit, Charlotte had written to a number of editors in national and local publications asking for an opportunity to work on their newspapers. Her ambitions were set high and amongst those she wrote to were the Times, the Daily Telegraph and the Manchester Guardian. She had also written to some local newspapers in Lancaster, Preston, and Morecambe. And her perseverance paid off when she was called to interview at the Preston Recorder only days after leaving school.

On the morning the letter arrived at the house Edward called Charlotte into the living room. He held in his hand the opened letter and Charlotte could see from the letterhead that the letter had come from the Preston Recorder.

"What are you doing opening my letter?" she asked, indignant that he should be so presumptuous.

"I might well ask you what you are doing writing to some newspaper asking for a job without seeking my permission. Where you work and who you work for will be my decision not yours young lady?" he retorted.

A horrible row ensued, bringing Edward to the point where he almost struck Charlotte, who had never seen him become so angry.

"I'm sixteen, and it is you who is insisting that I get a job rather than continue with my education so perhaps you might afford me the chance to at least do something I want to do," she snapped, snatching the letter from his hand.

Edward ran after her, but she made her escape to the bathroom where she locked the door before he could reach her.

The argument continued from both sides of the locked door until Edward needed to leave for work. Charlotte knew that his blustering was more about control than anything else and that by the evening he would have calmed down. Moreover, she knew that getting the first of his children off to work and on a journey to independence was ultimately far more important to her father than a simple matter of principle.

The interview for the junior reporter role in Preston was to be held in Lancaster at the sister newspaper office of the Lancaster Recorder on the following Friday.

Charlotte prepared well and entered the imposing building with confidence. But that was soon to be put to the test when she was shown into the office of the Editor, Peter Thomson.

He was in his late fifties, portly and looked and sounded stressed and angry as he barked instructions to his staff.

As he looked up, and before Charlotte had reached his desk he had already begun the interview.

"They've asked me in Preston to interview you for this role; why should we take you on when there are plenty of other applicants who, I grant you may not be as pretty as you but who could probably make as good a hash of the job as you?"

Without a moment lost, Charlotte responded; "I write well, I can spell, and I will be hard working."

The editor laughed, mocking her response.

"So *pretty girl*, you think that's what journalism is all about do you?"

Charlotte was beginning to become embarrassed and uncomfortable, by the way in which he was looking at her with his leering eyes and his drooling stare that left her feeling that he was undressing her.

"Well, I think that well written stories must have an enticing beginning, a well-researched middle and a strong ending," she replied now feeling completely naked before his lecherous eyes.

"You're full of yourself aren't you Charlotte?" he sneered, his eyes continuing to scan her young body.

She stood her ground continuing to smile but feeling increased confidence before this drooling chauvinist.

He pondered for a moment before asking, "I wonder if you might be better suited to working right here in my office rather than going to Preston each day?" slapping his leg with a gesture that she might sit nicely on there.

Charlotte paused for a moment.

"No," she said with some authority, "I think it would be wrong. I applied for the Preston job, and I think I should see that through don't you?"

Looking him straight in the eye, she continued.

"I know you would be a lovely man to work with because I've been going to school with your daughter Melissa, Mr. Thomson, and she thinks you're the best daddy in the world."

And with the experience of a woman twice her age Charlotte concluded her rebuttal of his advances. "And I think I also met your wife when I came to your house a few weeks ago."

He got the message and backed off but not before one final lingering leer. "Alright," he said; "You've got the job in Preston, and you start a week on Monday."

And thus began Charlotte's career as a journalist and writer.

Independence and freedom beckoned for Charlotte and despite the serious misgivings of her father, she began the new job and her new life in Preston on the lowest rung of the journalism ladder.

It was a male dominated existence, but Charlotte persevered. She made the tea; she ran errands, and she light heartedly accepted the jokes and pranks played on her as the youngest and newest on the paper.

Charlotte accompanied experienced journalists on assignments ranging from lost pets to weddings, births, and deaths. She saw news stories being written by experienced journalists, only to be sub-edited by wily old hacks that checked and revised their copy, scribbling in the margins unintelligible code and commentary, the various changes that needed to be made.

And as part of her apprenticeship, Charlotte was released for a day each week to go the Harris College in Preston where she began to learn the craft of reporting.

She learnt shorthand, she learnt to type, and she studied how good research underpinned good journalism.

CHAPTER TWENTY SIX

Maria, who was always the most sensitive of the three children, found Charlotte's new found independence difficult to deal with. She and Charlotte were close and confided in each other on almost every matter. But with Charlotte choosing not to stay with her Uncle and Aunt in Preston after leaving school, it meant that Maria felt an increased isolation from her family, especially her other siblings during her final weeks of term time.

But Charlotte was also not around during the school holiday, and this placed a new strain on Maria, who looked forward to the familiarity and routine that Charlotte brought to the holiday.

Maria was a follower, and the loss of Charlotte to a new career, new friends and a new way of life, left a hole in her young life.

Though Charlotte slept at the house in Lancaster at night, to Maria, Charlotte was slowly slipping away from her. To compensate, Maria spent the majority of the summer of nineteen sixty in the company of a friend she knew from school.

Like Maria, her Ukrainian friend Lyubov known to her friends as Luba was also a loner. She was a second generation British Ukrainian but felt the distance many people placed between the immigrant families and the locals. But she and Maria were close and practically inseparable from then on.

Maria and Luba were so close that Maria shared with her the secret that she felt her mother was still alive. Luba and Maria thought through many plots and scenarios ranging from Ruth being locked up somewhere, to the worst of all that Ruth didn't want to see the children. They would not realise how close to the truth they came when they considered that scenario.

Robert was also missing the summer holiday adventures but at thirteen years of age had found independence of his own.

He spent most holiday mornings being picked up at the house at seven o'clock by Norman, the milkman. Robert would then be out with him on his delivery round until about nine o'clock when they went to the farm for breakfast.

The farm was a largely livestock family business, supporting a significant size herd of Frisian beef and dairy cattle and a specialist herd of Jersey cows, known for their rich, creamy milk. There were also hundreds of laying hens whose eggs were an essential part of the delivery to households who also took Norman's milk.

Breakfast at Hilltop Farm brought the whole of Norman's family and farm workers together around a large table in the kitchen. Food was in plentiful supply, and the ever hungry Robert was able to eat his fill of eggs, bacon, sausage and homemade black pudding.

After breakfast, Robert would spend an hour or two on the farm collecting eggs, or watching milking and then he would collect his bicycle from the back of the milk van and cycle to the Lancaster bypass motorway which had been opened in the April of that year.

During the bypass construction, Robert had earned good money on Saturdays and other holidays by collecting food orders from the workmen, and cycling to the local pie shop and newspaper shop and filling those orders.

Robert had witnessed the slow progression of the construction work resulting in him having to cycle a little further on each visit to find his customers. But today was Robert's opportunity to sit on the bridge above the motorway and watch the cars and trucks speeding by beneath him.

Robert lost himself in thoughts of one day owning a car, perhaps even driving along this very road, and he was entirely comfortable with what others might see as his lonely existence. Having left the house at seven o'clock in the morning, it was not unusual for this thirteen year old boy to not return to the house until six thirty in the evening.

A pattern was emerging as each of the children began to become more self-reliant and less the bonded unit of three that once took on the world.

When the children had eaten their evening meal, Charlotte would often leave to meet friends in town. Maria would leave to meet Luba, and Robert would retire to his bedroom. Strong bonds were slowly being eroded replaced by a growing need in each of the children to be prepared to face the world alone.

The summer holiday was soon over, and Maria returned to school in Preston and the routine of staying with her Aunt and Uncle during the week. But now she was alone without the familiarity of having Charlotte sleeping in the bed next to her and without the chance to simply chat.

On returning to her Aunt's house at the end of the school day, Maria began to isolate herself from the rest of the family spending increased amounts of time alone in her bedroom. Elizabeth became concerned that Maria was sullen, quiet and unapproachable. She wasn't rude; she wasn't unpleasant, she simply found her own company more agreeable than that of the rest of the household.

She began to miss meals increasing Elizabeth's concerns that there was more to Maria's malaise than simply missing the company of Charlotte. When Elizabeth tried to discuss this with Sarah, she dismissed the symptoms as, "attention seeking." But Maria's withdrawn behaviour was repeated at home even when she had some contact with Charlotte. She would confide in nobody, not even Charlotte, who was equally concerned, but understandably consumed by the excitement of her own work and independence.

Maria felt abandoned. She hurt inside for love and affection. She never lost the hope of seeing her birth mother, and this became the one thing that sustained her through her end of year examinations. She became increasingly detached from her father and Sarah, who were by now consumed by their own carefully choreographed journey through middle class life.

The caravan had been replaced by a boat which Edward insisted everyone would enjoy. In truth, even Sarah saw the boat and sailing as something she was more than happy to sit out.

Maria hated the water and was seasick so often that she didn't sail with Edward either. Charlotte exercised her right to independence, so she didn't sail. Therefore, Robert became Edward's only crew member, and even he disliked it because it acted as a further opportunity for Edward to bully him.

While Edward and Sarah engrossed themselves in their middle class lifestyle, of yacht club regatta days and formal dinners, their children were the furthest from their minds. They would describe the children as 'independent spirits' to the few people they would call friends, but outside their earshot, those same *friends* were increasingly questioning this couples attitude towards Edward's children. They were tolerated in social company, but Edward and Sarah were disliked for their arrogance, their snobbery and their treatment of the children.

~

By the summer of nineteen sixty one, Maria had also left school. She too had achieved good results in her O-level examinations but was also deprived of the opportunity to go on and sit the A-level examinations that might set her on a course to university.

Maria quickly managed to secure a job at a local factory in Lancaster. The factory, a textile manufacturer, had premises throughout Lancashire and employed hundreds of people. These people were all paid a weekly wage in cash, a massive weekly undertaking which provided the opening for Maria to join the wage office staff.

Her primary role was to work within a large team and help make up the wage packets each week, and though tedious, Maria was delighted to be employed and independent. This was a labour intensive role and also one that required absolute accuracy.

The weekly pay was distributed to every member of staff on Friday between eleven o'clock in the morning and one o'clock in the afternoon in an industrial scale operation that began on a Monday morning. Maria's role would be to cross check the wage roll with several other young women, and once this was completed, a pay total would be hand calculated by the pay office who would also calculate tax and other deductions.

Maria and her colleagues were then given sheets, each listing the net pay for the workers in different sections of the many factories. Her job was to take each entry on the sheet and decide the denominations of bank notes and coinage needed to make up that individual pay packet.

It required immense accuracy and was tedious, boring work. Every recipient's wage would be broken down into a certain number of five pound, one pound or ten shilling notes. There was then the half crown, florin, shilling, six pence, three pence, penny and half penny coins to be calculated manually. The tabulations and cross checking were endless, resulting in what her supervisor would call the "bank schedule."

The bank schedule had to be ready and submitted to the bank by Wednesday lunch time. By Thursday afternoon, the money itself would arrive at the wage office, and the frantic job of allocating the money to the named pay envelopes which Maria had carefully written would begin.

By ten, o'clock on Friday the call from the supervisor, "wages balance seal the envelopes," would be heard. Envelopes were then sealed, and the wage distribution would begin.

Maria loved the job despite its mind numbingly boring nature and was soon entrusted to undertake more challenging roles with more responsibility and more job satisfaction.

But she was restless and wanted to get out of Lancaster as soon as she could and away from the home she called *the house of horrors*. She was by now deeply unhappy at home where Edward rarely took the time to speak to her, and Sarah simply ignored her presence.

When Maria heard that the company wanted someone to go to work temporarily in the wage office in Accrington, she leapt at the chance. She asked her supervisor if she could be considered, having only worked in her current role for a mere ten months.

Where she would live and how she would support herself were of little interest when she begged her boss to give her a chance. He agreed, but only on the understanding that her father also agreed.

Maria took the Saturday morning bus to Accrington where she had arranged to meet the company's personnel manager. She put Maria in touch with someone who was renting a room in their house and before the day was over, Maria had a job and a room in Accrington. The missing element to her grand plan was to secure her father's agreement.

To her great surprise and relief, her father agreed with very few questions. His only comments were confined to her future behaviour.

In an echo of her own mother's move from the family village of Senghenydd to Cardiff in the nineteen forties, Edward's only concern was to protect his reputation.

"If you get yourself into trouble," his euphemism for her getting pregnant, "don't you come running back to me, because you won't be welcome....do you hear me?"

These were his only comments apart from ensuring that she had a place to live with someone 'respectable.'

And so, with little more than a nod of the head, Maria was the first to leave home, but Charlotte would not be far behind.

Charlotte had met a young man in Preston in the autumn of nineteen sixty one who she had fallen head over heels in love with. A tall, good looking young man, Stephen, a newly graduated mining engineer was aged twenty two. But despite what seemed to others to be a massive age difference, they were both convinced that they wanted to spend their lives together and that they wanted to marry as soon as possible.

Stephen was insistent that they should declare themselves to Edward as soon as possible so that Edward and Sarah knew that his intentions towards Charlotte were as he put it "honourable."

Charlotte was terrified about her father's possible reaction but grasped an opportunity to speak to him when they were alone. Edward took the news with surprising ease and suggested that he and Sarah should meet Stephen.

This formality was necessary because if Charlotte and Stephen were to marry, they would require the formal acceptance and approval of her father as she was under the age of twenty one.

Stephen met Edward and Sarah in the December of nineteen sixty one in a convivial but strained meeting.

Edward became comfortable with Stephen almost immediately finding common ground in their mutual interest in engineering. Sarah was less comfortable with the situation and spent the afternoon in one of her now frequent moods.

The meeting between Stephen and Edward was ultimately a success, and it was agreed that Charlotte and Stephen would marry in the March of nineteen sixty two.

Stephen had already taken up a job in Barnsley in Yorkshire working with the National Coal Board and was planning to buy a small house there which was to become their marital home.

They married in nineteen sixty two in a small ceremony in Barnsley attended by Edward and Sarah, Maria and Robert and a few very close friends.

~

By now Maria was rarely to be seen at the family home in Lancaster and was pursuing her career having stepped out of the monotony of the wages department into the accountancy office. She was still working for the same company and accepting small promotions as she broadened her skills and knowledge, and she too had met someone who had swept her off her feet.

Neil, a motor mechanic, was twenty one and had recently completed his apprenticeship. He was keen to marry and set up home with Maria, and they began to make plans for their future, eagerly putting money aside to form the deposit on a future home. They were measured and clear about the order of things for their future and so a long engagement was to follow.

By nineteen sixty three, Robert had completed his education with good results. He too was told that the prospect of taking A-level examinations should be put from his mind. But like his sisters before him, Robert's only mission in life was to find a job and leave home.

Robert took a single step towards his ambitions when he was selected as a management trainee for a hotel chain with properties throughout the north of England and Scotland. His first assignment was to a hotel on the shore of Lake Windermere where he would spend six months as a commis waiter in their fine dining restaurant.

Robert left his family home never to return. He accepted many challenging roles within the training phase of his newly chosen career all offered with accommodation and all offering him the chance to build knowledge and skills in the hotel industry.

CHAPTER TWENTY SEVEN

Charlotte, Maria, and Robert were to embark upon their own lives with little regular contact with each other or with Edward and Sarah. Their childhood adventures to find Ruth, their mother were a dim and distant memory though there was still a shared sense that what they had been told by Edward and Sarah amounted to a complete fabrication and a lie.

Robert had undertaken some research that established the date when Edward and their mother Ruth had married, and further research provided information that resulted in him obtaining a copy of Edward's divorce papers from the public record.

The revelation that they had divorced came as a complete shock and while in itself was not proof that their mother was still alive, the absence of any death certificate kept alive the hope that they would one day find their mother.

The divorce papers were a turning point. For the first time, Charlotte, Maria and Robert were to discover that the reason why the divorce was granted was on the grounds of *desertion*. Furthermore, what Robert discovered was that there needed to be a period of at least three years between the application for the divorce by Edward and any knowledge of Ruth's whereabouts on the part of Edward, before a divorce could be granted by the Courts.

The children were now certain that the stories of their mother being dead were a cruel and deceitful lie and therefore they saw hope in their continued search for their mother. But it further alienated the children from Edward and Sarah, who, unaware of their discovery, were acting as before, playing out the fantasy that was rapidly defining their lives.

Robert also made a trip to Senghenydd in Wales, the birthplace of their mother but by then no one could remember the O'Connor family. He now felt that he had simply ended up in a cul-de-sac. If their mother was still alive, they acknowledged that she may well have established a new relationship, perhaps even married but for the time being, their search had come to an end.

The most obvious solution that of confronting their father and asking him to be truthful about the past so that they could search for their mother was not even considered by Charlotte, Maria, and Robert.

Edward's children, now adults still felt they could not approach the past for fear of fracturing the already strained relationship they each had with their father and Sarah.

~

Each of the children had now gone on to have families and build careers. But their initial career choice was not always the direction that their lives would take them.

Charlotte and her husband Stephen settled into married life in Barnsley where Charlotte continued her pursuit of a career in journalism. She transferred to a sister newspaper and continued her apprenticeship.

By nineteen, sixty five, she had been appointed to the full time staff of the newspaper regularly reporting on local and national politics. She had several front page stories to place in her portfolio and one sensational 'splash' story involving a local businessman and his attempt to bribe a local politician. She was a good journalist, crafting well researched news stories that were also well written. Her work, unlike that of other junior reporters, received little sub-editing.

Charlotte enjoyed her work, but she wanted to move on to a regional news paper as a route to a national. But these plans were to be placed on temporary hold when in nineteen seventy, Charlotte gave birth to a daughter who she and Stephen named Genevieve. This was a precious child for Charlotte, who had experienced several miscarriages along the way to this happy event.

Charlotte was able to combine a career as a part time journalist and mother which enabled her to broaden her published work by doing feature articles, initially for her own newspaper, but later for regional specialist publications.

She was published in the County magazines in an articles about village life in Yorkshire. She wrote about how little had changed over the years despite the rush to modernism and an increasing trend of city people wanting to own a cottage in the country.

But once again, Charlotte's career was to be put on hold when, in nineteen seventy five, Stephen was offered a very good job in the Hunter Valley in Australia as the mine manager of a new drift mine site. The job was good; the pay was good and to Charlotte and Stephen the chance to enjoy a warm climate with strong English roots, a rich culture and good education for Genevieve could not be missed.

Edward protested that a move to Australia was too far away and that he would not see Charlotte, but she knew that the move was right for her and her family. And the move proved to be good in many ways. They sold their greatly modernised home in Barnsley realising a good profit on the original purchase some thirteen years earlier.

In what proved ultimately to be a shrewd move, they poured every dollar of their money into the purchase of a twenty five acre plot of land with a small bungalow, set in the countryside north of Cessnock, in New South Wales, Australia. The property was near enough to the mine site where Stephen would work but also only about fifty kilometres from Newcastle where the headquarters of the company was located.

The move to Australia proved to be one which once again would end Charlotte's journalist career hopes. In purchasing such a large parcel of land, Charlotte also needed to understand how they could make it pay its way to service the mortgage.

Much of their land was given over to grape vines in a lease arrangement with a large grower, and this provided a modest income. But Charlotte could see that simply providing generic grapes for onward local production was not the way to go.

In an act of extraordinary self-belief, she persuaded the company to relinquish the remainder of the lease a decision that would enable her to go-it-alone in an attempt to grow and bottle their own wine. Every dollar of Stephens's income and bonuses was ploughed into the winery business.

It took six hard years before the income from the modest winery surpassed the contract income they were previously earning. But slowly, '*Charlotte's Retreat*,' the name used for the vineyard, and the brand for the award winning Cabernet and Chardonnay wines she produced would become sufficiently individual and critically recognised. This small 'boutique' vineyard was beginning to receive accolades throughout Australia where most of the small production of Chateau wines was sold.

Their twenty five acres produced on a good year about sixty to seventy thousand bottles of wine, many of which sold before they were bottled with the rest being sold in tastings on the vineyard.

The net income to Charlotte was good, but she refused to entertain the purchase of more land or any affiliation with other vineyards though many offers were made. She felt that the authenticity of the wine as being produced by her and three equally dedicated employees was more important than anything else.

Their daughter, Genevieve grew to love the vineyard and to understand wine and the industry. Charlotte and Genevieve would meet with visitors who called at the vineyard gates hoping to meet the strange, now slightly eccentric '*Pom lady*,' who was producing such exquisite wines. These people consumed some of the profit, but for Charlotte, it was important to meet her growing following of customers.

Charlotte and Stephen remained in Australia earning a living from the vineyard when Stephen retired, and they returned to England once each year catching up with friends.

When they visited Edward and Sarah, he continued to try to persuade Charlotte to return to England, never acknowledging her successes in life and her business or that she now had a rich and fulfilling life in Australia.

Edward and Sarah visited Australia only once and vowed never to return. This rejection of a country that accepts everyone with warmth and humour was due entirely to Edward's stubborn belief that, "No county or country offers more than Lancashire."

But his interest in luring Charlotte back to England was a self-interest as he looked towards old age and his view that his first born daughter should be there to care for him, particularly if Sarah were to die before him.

~

For his part, Robert worked through the education and training phase of the hotel industry as a management trainee spending time in every department of a hotel. By the age of twenty one, he was already recognised as someone who would be a high flyer in the sector.

He took on assignments as a deputy manager in several of the hotel group's fashionable properties making a name for himself as a creative thinker and someone who could easily identify what the clientele wanted and ensuring that the hotel and the group met those needs.

Robert also married his first love, Annette, someone he had met as a guest in one of the hotels. They were both only twenty one but saw no reason why they should not get married when the opportunity presented itself. This soon happened when Robert was appointed to become the assistant manager of a group hotel located in the fashionable town of Aviemore in the Scottish Cairngorms.

The job came with a small cottage on the edge of the hotel grounds and so Annette was able to establish a home quickly for the two of them. She was a trained secretary and soon found herself employed by a company in the town of Inverness about thirty miles away.

Meanwhile, Robert and the manager set about transforming a once grand hotel back to its former glory. Renovation fixed the building's structural decay while Robert set about marketing the now beautifully appointed hotel to a clientele that wanted the finer things in life.

By nineteen seventy one, the hotel was operating at near capacity throughout the year, and Robert's contribution to that success was noticed and recognised in the head office of the hotel group.

At the age of twenty four, he was brought to the group's headquarters in London into a managerial role assisting with the refurbishment of existing hotels and newly acquired properties that had failed.

In the same year, Annette gave birth to a son, who they named Michael, and the three of them moved into a small house in Staines, Middlesex from where Robert commuted to London each day.

Robert moved up the managerial ladder to ultimately become group chief executive by the age of forty; successfully achieving a public listing for the business on the London Stock Exchange. He was successful but by now Robert was yearning to get back to his roots at the front of house in the business.

He and Annette were lured by an opportunity to help a local group of entrepreneurs establish a spa hotel on the coast of mainland Malaysia. Robert's love affair with this beautiful country was to begin.

At the age of eighteen, Michael began university in London, and Robert and Annette moved to live in Kuala Lumpur from where the hotel and spa business was operated. Within five years the group had established hotel and spa resorts on the Malaysian island of Penang, Kota Kinabalu, Sabah and two in Thailand.

Robert and Annette began to discover Malaysia and in so doing they *found* the Cameron Highlands.

The Cameron Highlands in Pahang was becoming one of Malaysia's most popular tourist destinations. This was no surprise to Robert as he and Annette explored the collection of peaceful townships perched high on a nest of serene mountains.

They visited the tea plantations and strawberry farms which sprawl lazily across lush valleys and meandering hill slopes, and they recognised that this was the perfect setting for a relaxing pampered holiday. The tranquillity, visually pleasing landscapes, and temperate climate seemed to impart a special karma.

Once a hill station during British rule, the Cameron Highlands at more than four and a half thousand feet above sea level offered a pleasant break from the heat and humidity on the plane below, firstly for the British settlers but now was being discovered by international tourists as well as Malaysians themselves.

Robert, who was by now a respected foreigner with local residency status, was able to purchase a former grand residence and a modest home on the same parcel of land in the area of Tanah Rata, in Pahang only a mile from the thriving market at Brinchang.

The house was only a short walk from Moonlight Bungalow, made famous following the disappearance on March twenty six, nineteen sixty seven, of the American, Jim Thompson.

Jim Thompson had built the substantial Thai Silk Company business in Thailand and was on holiday in Cameron Highlands, visiting his Singaporean friends Dr. T.G. Ling and his wife Helen at the couple's secluded hilltop retreat. It is said that at around three o'clock on that day, Jim Thompson went off on a walk on his own into the nearby dense jungle. He was never seen or heard from again.

Robert and Annette were captivated by the landscape, the people and the climate. Daytime temperatures typically reach twenty five degrees centigrade and on some evenings it could drop to as low as eight or ten degrees. But this fertile land, now famous for its tea, was also becoming known for its fruit and its vegetables that grew well at this height and in this climate.

Robert and Annette began setting about recovering the grand residence and converting it into a swish hotel and spa. The black and white mock Tudor design was retained as were the many colonial features such as the plantation shutters at all windows, the open sala walkways, the high ceilings and the large lounges with their peaceful swirling fans.

But it was the open fireplaces with roaring log fires on the cool evenings that proved to be the most dramatic feature in this tropical climate!

The local community were to make the hotel the success it became. They brought charm character and the warmth of their personalities to the service that its wealthy clientele so admired.

The hotel was sold back to a Malaysian group to be run by the Malay's. But Robert and Annette now firmly established in their home alongside the hotel were welcome and frequent visitors to '*their*' hotel's restaurants.

Tanah Rata, in Pahang, Malaysia and a small apartment overlooking Cardiff Bay were to become home for Robert and Annette in semi-retirement. But retirement would probably be a long way off for these entrepreneurs of the hotel industry.

When Robert was in the UK, which was rare, he continued his search for his mother, always synthesising what he had learnt with what his sisters had managed to uncover.

~

In contrast to Charlotte and Robert, Maria was not to follow the direction her early career choices suggested. Having married, Maria went on to have two children with her husband, Neil. Never losing sight of her family and her roots, she called her first child Charlotte-Elizabeth and the second Ruth.

The two children, born two years apart were adored by their parents who gave them the loving, stable relationship Maria had never experienced. Though she never fully divulged the extent of her own childhood misery to her husband, he knew enough to know that her determination to be a good and caring mother was driven by what she felt she had lacked in her own upbringing.

Maria's successful career in finance seemed as though it would define her employment as she moved to increasingly more important and responsible roles. But Maria was inwardly convinced that her future lay in working with families, particularly those embarking upon adopting children or those whose children may need to be placed into foster care or adoption. She also felt strongly that much of what she experienced as a child with Charlotte and Robert should not be the fate of other children.

Maria and her husband Neil agreed that she should pursue her belief in herself that she would make a good social worker. She furthered her education at night school and went on to become a mature student at university, achieving a degree in social work in nineteen seventy five.

Maria and Neil sacrificed a great deal in her pursuit of this career, but the effort paid off.

Her family, who were very aware of Maria's commitment to the care of children, could not have had a better role model. They saw her driven by this urge to care and were also able to experience the love and care that she showed them.

To the friends of Charlotte-Elizabeth and Ruth, Maria was a 'super mummy', someone who had time for every child and someone who was fun to be with.

Family holidays were often taken with another child, and group holidays with their friends and their children were largely an opportunity for all the children to play and socialise together.

Maria became the mother others simply looked at in awe. Her fun personality, her energy and her room and time for children around her defined a woman who had many friends who simply adored her.

As Maria worked her way through the ranks of social work, she never directly pursued her dream of working solely with adoption. But happenstance played its part and placed her in the adoption unit at a large local authority where her calling became immediately apparent to those around her.

She began to see for herself that often physical abuse alone was not the reason why children were taken into the care of local authorities; it was simple and ugly neglect. Neglect of the human needs that all children crave, love, affection, protection and good role model parents who show care and support for their children.

Maria's own upbringing and time in a care home was only known to her closest work colleagues and then only as a result of the occasional unguarded comment. Hers was not a crusade to use her own experience as a child to define her work; indeed she increasingly put that to the back of her mind so that she was not overly influenced by it.

Her drive was that children should have a childhood, supported by families where that would work, or supported by foster or adoptive families where that was right for them.

Maria was a good social worker who only late into her career began to recognise that her own experiences were in part the reason she flourished in her role as head of adoption for her local authority.

Maria never used her privileged role to seek to find her mother, but she did use the knowledge she had gained to know how to trace her mother.

She wrote to the childrens home where she had been placed as a child only to find that their own records of the children in their care in the nineteen forties and early fifties had long since been destroyed. She wrote to the local authority to again be told the same that their records for that time were either lost or destroyed.

Robert and Maria had spent some time in the area of Eastbrook Farm where their father and Ruth had lived in the nineteen forties, asking locals what they knew of the family but they were always met with the same response that there was only a vague memory of the Carmichael family but no more than that.

CHAPTER TWENTY EIGHT

For Edward and Sarah, the children's rapid departure from the family home was met with some degree of personal satisfaction. They viewed the fact that the three of them had jobs and were independent as evidence that they had been successful parents and that they had been instrumental in the children's success.

At no time would they recognise any suggestion that they had been anything other than exemplary parents. Indeed, as time went by, the selective nature of their memory allowed them to boast about the children's successes as being entirely down to their upbringing.

Edward remained in the same job refusing any offer of promotion to move to other locations with the company unless those were in his beloved Lancashire. As he grew older, so he became more fixated about his roots in Lancashire.

Ultimately, he refused promotion and a move once too often and was confronted by his boss with the *offer* of early retirement, which he took.

This stubborn streak in Edward was also taking its toll on his relationship with Sarah. She tolerated his belligerent attitude to most situations with good grace, but she was also aware that Edward's uncompromising beliefs on most issues were placing distance between them and the very few friends they claimed to have.

Edward took early retirement at the age of fifty eight, in nineteen seventy eight and with little consultation with Sarah, he took the bold step of putting his pension and the proceeds of the sale of their family home into the purchase of a shop in Bowness-on-Windermere one of the Lake District's idyllic towns.

The shop sold tourist souvenirs and paintings but specialised in selling Lakeland slate items from stock with many pieces such as plinths often being made to order. Sadly, no one was worse suited to the retail sector than Edward. His rude, often brusque approach to customer service resulted in Sarah having to step in and separate Edward from his sometimes irate customers.

Sarah became the face of the business gently easing Edward into the back office or working with the clients who wanted to order bespoke items requiring precision drawings and measurements which played to Edward's strengths.

But for Sarah, living in a small apartment above the shop was a terrible come down from their middle class home in Lancaster. The accommodation had only two bedrooms, a small bathroom a modest size living room and a tiny kitchen.

Sarah found that the apartment was all too often cluttered with stock for the shop, particularly at the height of the summer season. To someone who was immensely house proud, she felt as though their once ordered and planned life was deteriorating before her eyes. This was made worse by her finding herself working very long hours in the shop and then having to manage their home.

The once strong relationship that Edward and Sarah were so proud of and which defined them as a couple was now constantly under strain as Edward's venture into the retail sector could hardly be described as a success. The business made a modest profit, but the toll it was having on their relationship was immeasurable.

Sarah remained quiet about the deterioration of her health, but even the less than observant Edward could see that after eight years they should accept defeat and sell up.

It took more than a year to find a buyer for the business, but the proceeds of the sale were sufficient to buy a modest bungalow which they retired to.

The couple spent much of their time in retirement in silent reflection on their lives. They rarely talked to each other and what words passed between them hardly passed as conversation.

Edward was bitter that the business had not gone well but never acknowledged that this was in no small part down to his peculiar brand of customer service. He simply would not accept advice from anyone which added to the hurt that Sarah felt.

They heard from Robert and Charlotte on an irregular basis, but when they were in the country, they dutifully visited their father and Sarah. Maria visited Edward and Sarah every few months, but Edward was hardly welcoming of her.

On one occasion, when Robert and his wife Annette were visiting from Malaysia, Sarah finally opened up to Annette when they were alone together.

She took Annette to one side and out of the earshot of Edward she offered help in finding Robert's mother.

"If Robert's father should die before I do, I will help you find Ruth the children's mother," she said, visibly wracked with regret and remorse. "It's gone on for too long, and the children have a right to know about their past and their mother. But I cannot help them while *he* is still alive, he simply would not allow it," she said, turning towards Edward to ensure he was not hearing what she was saying.

She drew Annette to her side and placing a hand on hers and in an extraordinarily unusual gesture of friendship she whispered; "We were very wrong when they were young but we were young too and we thought we were doing the right thing...but we weren't. Their mother abandoned the children.....she didn't die, and we were wrong to have said that."

That was the one and only time that such a conversation was to take place.

~

In the spring of nineteen eighty nine Sarah died. She had been losing weight for some time, but there was no evidence to suggest that she was so unwell that she might die. She was taken ill at home, taken to the local hospital and within days had passed away.

Edward was completely distraught. Like his father before him, his grief was a combination of intense sadness at the loss of someone he loved dearly and an acknowledgement that he was to face his own future alone, without a woman to care for him.

Edward and his father shared a belief that the women in their family had a *duty* to care for the men. In marriage, this was Sarah's duty, and now his darkest moments were spent wondering how he would cope with caring for himself.

Charlotte and Robert were informed of Sarah's death and without hesitation, they both flew back to England to be with their father and to attend Sarah's funeral. Despite the unconventional childhood they had experienced, they were conventional in their sense of duty towards their father. Despite never really having any relationship with him, they didn't hesitate to set aside their work and fly thousands of miles to be with him.

On arrival at the small bungalow that was his home, Robert was to find his father inconsolable. It was hard for Robert who never had a relationship with his father to know quite what to do. However, this was made easier for Robert, when Edward did as he had always done and simply pushed him away.

"There is nothing that *you* can do unless your wife is prepared to come and look after me," he snapped when asked by Robert if there was anything he could do. "A woman's place is with her husband," he cried; "why did she have to go first?" he asked, repeatedly.

Up until that point, Maria had tried to provide some comfort for her father, but his needs were practical.

"Who's going to wash my clothes and make my meals?" he asked. "Who the hell is going to clean the house now that *she* has gone?" he asked, knowing there was to be no answer.

All that Edward needed was for Charlotte to arrive which she did some twelve hours later.

Charlotte was met with the same questions, but now Edward was past the grief for the loss of his wife and was obsessed by dealing with his own needs.

"You had better get yourself back here to England as quickly as you can," he instructed Charlotte, "your place is here with your father not over there in Australia," he went on, failing to see the sheer selfishness of his proposition.

Charlotte was calm and said nothing, busying herself with Robert and Maria organising the funeral and dealing with the practical formalities of registering Sarah's death.

Because of the sudden nature of the death, it was to be a further two days before a certificate was issued allowing plans for Sarah's funeral to take place.

The official cause of death was congestive heart failure, caused by a pulmonary oedema. But Robert was convinced that Sarah had simply given up the will to live. He sensed that she could see that her life with Edward, had descended into the drudgery of being Edward's servant; the person who had to cope with his rudeness to neighbours; shop keepers, the doctor and anyone that didn't hold the same view as he did. He had become bitter and twisted.

This funeral, as with any funeral was a deeply sad and emotional occasion. What few members of the family who were still alive did make the effort to attend, but nonetheless, the numbers were depleted. They were depleted because Edward had either deliberately not invited people who would have wished to pay their respects or because they simply couldn't face being with the increasingly cantankerous, rude and obnoxious Edward.

Sarah's own small family attended, but a distance was placed between Edward and them. Sarah's sister and family who once tolerated Edward could hardly manage to be in his company...even on this day.

Sarah was cremated following a full Requiem Mass before her husband, the three children she had done her best to care for, and a handful of family and friends. Those that felt they could, or that under the circumstances felt they should return to Edward's house for tea and sandwiches after the funeral did so. But it was not long before they were all gone and the house had again fallen silent, with Edward and his three children simply not knowing what to say to each other.

Edward broke the silence in a now customary manner.

"So what's to be done?" he questioned, expecting and receiving the full attention of his children. "Are you going to stay to look after your father?" he asked, directing his question to Charlotte.

"No, I am not!" she replied, ensuring that he was absolutely clear about her intentions. "I have a husband and a business to look after, and well you know that. I will stay for a few days, but you are going to have to do what many other men have had to do before you; you're going to have to grieve, and get on with your life," she said, knowing fully that this was not what he wanted to hear.

"And what about you?" he asked, turning to Maria. "It's a daughter's duty to care for her father, and if Charlotte is *too* selfish and *too* busy with her husband and her business to do her duty, you will have to come and look after me."

Before Maria had a chance to respond Charlotte intervened.

"You don't seem to understand," she snapped, now becoming irritated with Edward's selfish and self-centred attitude. "You simply cannot click your fingers and expect any one of us to put our lives on hold because *you* have decided that we need to be here for you. I feel for you, and I feel your loss," she said, kneeling at the side of her father's chair.

"I will visit when I can, and you know that you can come and stay in Australia with me or in Malaysia with Robert for a holiday. I also know that Maria will come and see you when she can, but your expectations of any one of us are outrageous for someone who still has their health," she said, looking Edward directly in the eye.

Edward was apoplectic. He continued to argue that the women of the family had a duty to move to be near enough to his home to care for him. The suggestion that he might move to be nearer Maria resulted in Edward's well-rehearsed reasoning; "I'm a Northerner from Lancashire, and I'm staying in Lancashire."

~

A few days later, Robert, Maria, and Charlotte took time out to have lunch together before each of them would need to get back to their work and their lives.

In the intervening years, they had each continued to do whatever they could to try to find their mother, Ruth. Maria had managed to track down Mr. and Mrs. Oliver, the couple who had been foster parents to her and Charlotte in the nineteen forties.

She visited them at their home and was made extremely welcome by the now very elderly couple. They explained the circumstances leading up to the placement of Charlotte and Maria with them. However, their memory of the children being taken away to be placed in separate childrens homes was still raw with them.

Mrs. Oliver in particular, still believed, mistakenly that she should or could have done more. She explained that she and her husband simply were unable to cope with two energetic and lively young girls. But no matter what Maria said to Mrs. Oliver to assuage her sense of guilt, the memory of the two girls being taken to separate childrens homes was etched upon her memory and her conscience.

Mrs. Oliver did, however, let slip that she had offered to adopt one of the girls, that one being Charlotte. She explained that Edward had said no to them adopting Charlotte, but he had suggesting that she might take Maria instead.

Mrs. Oliver was candid and explained to the understanding Maria that she and Mr. Oliver had become very close to Charlotte, and as the older of the two girls they felt more able to cope with her.

Robert explained to his sisters that he had written to two organisations that specialise in tracing missing family members. Their extensive searches had so far found no trace of Ruth Carmichael, using her married name or Ruth O'Connor her maiden name. But they remained hopeful and optimistic that these agencies might ultimately be able to trace their mother.

At the end of a pleasant lunch Charlotte, Maria, and Robert said their goodbyes to each other and once again placed miles and distance between themselves. But not before they drove the short distance up the road to Glasson Dock.

When they arrived, they found that much had changed. The railway sidings had gone along with the wonderful old steam engines that had fired their imaginations so long ago.

There was no Tom Higginbotham, the security guard to chase them away; there was no friendly shop keeper and their local friends from all those years ago were gone too.

But their memories were as fresh today as if it were yesterday. They looked deep into the distance and into their own past and just for one moment....just for one precious moment, they could hear Charlotte calling from the footplate of their engine; "*Mummy, we're coming to find you, choo-choo... choo choo.*"

They felt again the wind blowing through her hair, and they felt again the drive to one day find Ruth, their mother.

CHAPTER TWENTY NINE

Charlotte returned to Australia and her vineyard; Robert flew back to Malaysia, and his beloved Cameron Highlands and Maria returned to her career in social work. But Edward had nowhere to go except to return to the bungalow he once shared with Sarah.

His bitterness that Sarah should die first was deep. He didn't grieve her passing; he raged at the injustice as he saw it that he didn't die first. He became increasingly difficult to be around and what few people he could now call friends were dwindling rapidly.

Neighbours, who had managed to see past Edward's bitterness and anger and were willing to provide some neighbourly support, were one by one dismissed by Edward when he thought they were attempting to pry into his life.

This came to a head when Edward became aware that there had been some local gossip that his children had been taken into care when they were very young. The neighbours had discovered that Sarah was Edward's second wife, and there was some speculation about why his first wife had abandoned their children.

Edward became aware of the gossip when a health worker who had made a routine call on him happened to ask after his children. In conversation and quite innocently she remarked about the photographs of the children displayed on a small table.

"I understand that they were in childrens homes when they were young," she said, pointing towards the photograph and genuinely trying to engage Edward. "That must have been a very difficult time for you Mr. Carmichael."

Edward shook with rage.

"How dare you probe into my past?" he shouted. "You bloody busybodies; don't you have anything better to do?" he shouted holding the front door open.

"Sling your hook," he roared at her.

She tried hard to pacify him but to no avail.

This kind of behaviour was to define the latter years of Edward's life. Despite the fortitude of the very best of Edward's neighbours, it was his unabashed rudeness that saw him increasingly isolated.

But it was people in authority who became the real target of Edward's anger; doctors, nurses, the local social welfare and the local Priest.

Maria visited her father rather more regularly than his behaviour justified. When she visited with her husband, she was confronted by a barrage of self-pity. Edward could not be persuaded from his fixated view that he should have predeceased Sarah. Because this didn't happen, he was obsessed by the view that the duty to care for him should pass "quite naturally," to his female children.

But the obdurate, irrational behaviour became a source of real concern when Robert visited his father with Maria.

He instantly saw that his father was ill. He was indeed irrational, but he was also having difficulty with his memory and with walking. He shuffled, and when he engaged in conversation, he was repetitive but also forgetful.

He regularly drove his car, much to the surprise of Robert, who viewed his driving as dangerous to both himself and other road users.

Edward would not entertain any suggestion that he should consider giving up driving and so, in sheer desperation, Robert spoke to his father's doctor.

Under considerable duress, Edward agreed to meet with his doctor, for what was sold to him as a 'health check,' where over the course of a few weeks he undertook a number of tests.

Each visit to a specialist was met with a barrage of abuse and rudeness. However, the experts were able quickly to diagnose that Edward had fairly advanced dementia, and they were increasingly concerned for his welfare and wellbeing. This concern was echoed by the local doctor, the health visitor and the social welfare department who were now engaged with Edward on a regular basis.

Over the same period, the emerging evidence that their father had lied about their mother having died was challenged by Maria and Robert. But, each attempt to invite Edward to open up about their mother was roundly dismissed by him. Despite his failing health and his self-evident short-term memory loss, he was still able to shut down an attempt at probing the past and his first wife, Ruth.

Questions were met by a well-rehearsed; "Let bygones be bygones," from a defensive and protective Edward. Pressing their father had no impact. He simply refused to allow his children to have access to the only information they so craved...an insight into their mother as a person and some knowledge of her whereabouts.

Over the course of an extended visit by Robert, decisions were taken that resulted in Edward moving into a private care home, with Edward's begrudging agreement. The decision was seen by Robert as being in his father's best interest and his safety.

As the dementia consumed their father's final few months, so Charlotte, Maria, and Robert abandoned further attempts to glean information from him, instead, simply ensuring that his final months would be comfortable and peaceful.

In dying, Edward took to his grave all insight and any direct account of his relationship with Ruth. He guarded his knowledge, even when others with his condition might have involuntarily let their guard down and revealed the shocking truth of their lives.

Charlotte, Maria, and Robert were now left with the unpalatable prospect that they may never access the truth about their mother.

CHAPTER THIRTY

As our story returns to the meeting in Brighton with Ruth's long term partner Clarissa, she turned to the Carmichael children in disbelief at what she had just heard.

Their's was a story of triumph over adversity. She saw disappointment but no resentment. She saw three very rounded, balanced people for whom there would have been every reason to act as victims of some heinous act of deceit. But instead, she saw three people who had simply pressed on with life, expecting no more than what they had put into that life and rejoicing at everything that came their way.

Charlotte rose from her chair and moved towards Clarissa.

"I hope that hearing something of our lives has given you some insight into why we must now complete our journey and know more about our mother's life and, importantly, we must also visit our mother's grave," she explained. "We hold no animosity towards her, no matter what is revealed in her small suitcase over there," continued Charlotte; "she lived her life, and we are living ours."

Clarissa had already decided that Charlotte, Maria, and Robert should take away the suitcase and its contents and particularly the manuscript from their mother and not be tempted to examine the contents in her company.

"I suggest that I give you Ruth's things now and that you examine them alone at your hotel. I will call by your hotel tomorrow morning for coffee when I will give you what I believe to be the final piece of the jigsaw....the letter your mother wrote just weeks before she died."

Charlotte and Maria gathered their coats while Robert took Ruth's case and placed it in the car. Clarissa warmly embraced each of them before they drove out of the driveway and returned to their hotel.

That night the Carmichael children read Ruth's account of her extraordinary life captured in her own words in her manuscript, the *children in my shadow*. They also quietly read the personal letter Ruth had penned to each of them.

Each letter had differences, capturing her tiny personal memories and giving each of them an insight into what they were like as babies. In the case of Maria and Charlotte, it revealed something of their lives during the precious time she had with them.

The letters were personal in nature but detailed and factual. There was no hint of regret, no explanation other than what they had read in her life story and there was no personal apology or explanation in the letters.

Charlotte, Maria, and Robert compared the contents of their letters having first scanned Ruth's explanation of her life in her manuscript.

What struck them all was the distance Ruth had placed between herself and the reality of what she had done. But once again the three of them saw no cause to judge Ruth; they charitably proffered the view that Ruth and her story was based in very different times.

Maria captured the mood of them all, quoting from Mother Teresa; *'If you judge people, you have no time to love them.'* And these children so wanted to love their mother. They so wanted not to think badly of her, but their innermost thoughts were indeed the same; why hadn't she tried harder to find them?

~

The following morning brought hope that the letter Clarissa had spoken of might fill in the final gaps. But there was to be one final twist.

The hotel manager rang Robert to say that there was an urgent note at the front desk for him. He collected the note and brought it to his sister's room.

It was a hand written note from Clarissa that read; *'I believe it might now be the time for you all to read the attached letter which was written by your mother. Passing this note to you completes the commitment that Mary gave to your mother and that I gave to Mary.*

I have enjoyed meeting with you and was deeply touched hearing your own very moving stories yesterday. But I see no merit in my calling at the hotel to see you again today as there is nothing more I can do or say that is not provided by your mother in her own writings.

I can, however, give you the address of Huw Evans, your brother who still lives in Bridgend. It must now be your decision if you wish to make contact with him or not. I wish you well with that decision and hope that you have found comfort in what you have read. Clarissa.'

The envelope contained Huw's address, the address of the cemetery where Ruth was laid to rest, and a separate envelope addressed to *Charlotte, Maria and 'Michael'*.

"It must be hard for you to come to terms with the knowledge that our mother personally christened you Michael and that Sarah insisted on taking that name from you," remarked Charlotte, who was clearly overcome by what she saw as a horrid act of spite.

Robert shrugged his shoulders, rather more consumed by what the letter might contain. Charlotte opened the hand written letter and read it to the others:

'I approach this final message to you with trepidation and a heavy heart. You will by now have read my account of my life and may well have reached the conclusion that you are pleased you never found me while I was alive, given what I have done to you.

Since coming to live here in Wales, I have lived in daily fear of being confronted by a stranger at the door. That stranger might have been you, but it equally might have been someone else from my awful past; someone who like you, would be able to connect me with the terrible thing I did in abandoning you all those years ago.

My fear was entirely selfish because I knew that at any time a stranger could shatter the illusion I had built with my family and friends here in Wales that I was a good mother, good neighbour, and good friend. If you had found me, I would have lost everything I had worked so hard to build.

But as I prepare to meet my maker and as I approach what I know will be the last few days of my life, I know that I have to do the right thing by you and tell you the whole truth. What you will have read in my own account of my life to date is broadly true. But I have deceived you in one important aspect of my life, and I need to put that right before I die.

You will have reached the conclusion from what you have read that having returned to Wales I never saw your father again. I have written in my manuscript that he came to Senghenydd in nineteen forty seven and threatened to take Huw from me if I ever attempted to make contact with him in the future. That was true, and it was also true that I was terrified that he meant every word of what he said. But there was a bond of love between us that was always going to be hard to break.....and while I feared his threats, I continued to hope that we could rediscover what we had in the past.

As I began to rebuild my life and settled down with Dai Evans, I began to put your father slowly out of my mind. He and his family had been cruel to me, and while I fully accept that the decision to leave you with your father was my own, it was made easier because of them and the way they treated me.

Hardly a day has passed without me thinking of the three of you, but I never once thought that I would see your father again, but I did. It was unexpected and initially frightening. It was March nineteen fifty three. I was in Bridgend shopping when I heard a voice behind me saying "I bet you didn't expect to see me here Ruth." I turned around to find your father with a broad smile on his face.

I didn't know whether to run or quite what to do. I took him into a cafe so that we should not be seen together. There we talked for an hour or so and once again I felt drawn to the man who was my first love.

You don't need to know the details, but you should know that we met on several occasions over the following months when he was visiting Wales on business. Every moment was stolen, every meeting putting at risk my relationship with Dai and my new family.

He wouldn't let me talk about you three but what he did say was that you were happy, settled and doing well. He told me that he and Sarah were married and that she was a good step-mother to you.

Every time we met he updated me on what you were doing, but to my absolute shame, my interest was only in your father, and yes, it developed into an affair.

Over the years, we would continue to see each other in clandestine rendezvous. I didn't know where he was living, and I never knew when I would next see him. It could be months and on a few occasions, it was a year or so between our meetings.

As the years passed by, our relationship became strong, and we took more risks. I began to travel to Blackpool once a year over several years, always in the hope that I might find out where you were living and just stand and watch you walking by. But my main reason was always to see your father.

I never did see you, but I also never pressed your father hard enough to make it possible to do so and I regret this.

As your father and I became older, the visits became less frequent and by nineteen, eighty two they ended altogether. He didn't make contact, and I didn't know how to get in touch with him.

I ask no forgiveness from you or God. I have done the most-wicked of things; the worst of all being to abandon you. And I know that even this last act....an act in which I attempt to salve my own conscience is a selfish act.

I have loved you all of these years, and I will take to my grave the knowledge that what I did was wrong. But I hope that this final act of contrition and honesty helps you to understand enough to know that I was not worth finding. My fondest love to you all. Your mother. Ruth

The letter stunned Charlotte, Maria, and Robert. The brutal honesty set alongside a real sense that throughout all the years she had remained attached to the children she abandoned puzzled and disturbed them.

There was little exchange between them as they drove from Brighton to Bridgend; a journey that retraced the one taken by Mary and Clarissa as they left Ruth's graveside on the day she was buried. Now her three abandoned children would stand in the same place and complete a journey they once felt would elude them.

EPILOGUE

the end of a journey

There can be few sadder sights than to see people gathered around a graveside consumed by grief and in tears.

The scene on this early October morning in the millennium year of two thousand, set beside a church on a hillside in South Wales was no different. Almost as though to complete the sad picture of mourners comforting each other, a fine misty drizzle fell, and a light breeze chilled the air.

This small piece of earth with its simple headstone and touching words written six years earlier was the final resting place of Ruth Dervla O'Connor.

It was also the end of a journey to find her for her three children who she had not seen since she abandoned them more than fifty years earlier.

~

As Charlotte, Maria and Robert touched the black granite headstone with its simple words encapsulating a life of great love and a parting that brought such sorrow to a family; they felt they touched again the mother they had never known.

What they had discovered along the way to this graveside rested heavy on their minds, as did the realisation that they would never look into the eyes of their mother or feel the comfort of her embrace.

Maria laid a small, simple wreath on the grave of their mother, stood back and without a word being said she put her arms around Robert and Charlotte. Their private thoughts were of what might have been had they found their mother earlier and been able to be a part of her life.

Quietly they turned and walked towards the cemetery gate where their car was parked, each deep in their own thoughts.

As they reached the exit, they passed three people walking towards them who seemed interested in their presence.

The eyes of the two groups briefly met... each momentarily believing they might know each other or....perhaps that they may have met before.

As Charlotte, Maria and Robert stepped into their car, they glanced back to the group they had passed to find them carefully examining the small wreath and card Maria had placed on their mother's grave.

As the group turned back, the Carmichael children had slipped away and were out of sight.

~

Robert drove the short distance from the cemetery to the address they had been given for Huw Evans, their brother. Their journey was again taken in silence, but as they drew up outside the house, Charlotte asked; "Are we sure we want to do this?"

Inside the house, Huw's wife had seen the car slowly approach and stop on the opposite side of the road and had noticed the three occupants looking inquisitively towards the house.

"Huw, there's a strange car stopped outside," she called, moving into the hallway to join him as he opened the door and stepped out onto the pavement.

Huw sensed a momentary connection as his eyes caught those of Robert, Charlotte, and Maria. But his encounter with his siblings was fleeting, as he watched their car slowly move away and out of sight.

Ruth's two very different families were to remain separated ...or at least for the time being!